Come Monday Mornin'

Come Monday Mornin'

by Chris Loken

M. EVANS & COMPANY, INC.
NEW YORK, NEW YORK

M. Evans and Company titles are distributed in
the United States by the J. B. Lippincott Company,
East Washington Square, Philadelphia, Pa. 19105;
and in Canada by McClelland & Stewart Ltd.,
25 Hollinger Road, Toronto M4B 3G2, Ontario.

Friday

H E COULD feel it coming on all week. His mouth was wet but his throat was dry no matter how much he swallowed. It was hard to get enough air an' ever once'n awhile he stopped doin' whatever he was doin' an' tried. Toward evening the dull hurt was there over his heart an' runnin' around down under his left armpit, just like he'd been worked over pretty good right there by a big lineman's forearm. The pressure was there too inside his head, pushin' away on the back side of his eyeballs, makin' them go right by what he was tryin' to look at, pressure hummin' away inside his ears so he couldn't hear very well what they was sayin' an' when he did he didn't even wanna.

Instead the crazy hot feelin' would come flarin' an' he wanted to smash somebody.

Anybody.

Maybe like Cathy. If she didn't get her ass home pretty soon an' cook the friggin' supper.

Maybe like the kid if he didn't stop that whinin' through his nose he called singin'.

Better watch himself tonight. Hang on. Play it cool. Get outta the house before somethin' happened.

Just stir the friggin' stew.

So what's the big deal about stirrin' stew? What the hell should he be standin' here squeezin' the spoon like it's somebody's neck for? Hell, he didn't mind cookin' all that much. Sometimes he even kinda liked it, particularly when she was there an' he didn't really have to an' they was laughin' an' jokin' around havin' just one drink or two an' he was whippin' up some number he learned from the cook when he had kitchen duty back on the County Farm an' he knew that night he could stop after just one drink or two.

Maybe even five or six. Maybe even get a little mellow an' send the kid up to bed early an' they'd eat when they got around to it an' for dessert he'd take her right there on the living room couch an' get up in the morning feeling good an' not guilty.

But today wasn't that kind of day. Today was that other kind of day. She claimin' she had to stay late for one'a those stupid teachers' meetin's so he had to stop tryin' to fix the tractor he broke tryin' like a horse's ass to buck through that big drift by the barn with the manure spreader on behind. He knew he'd loaded 'er too heavy too, sounded like the reduction gear in the right rear wheel, cost like a sum'bitch too, probably have to send to Albany for one if Tommie couldn't weld it. Still hadn't paid him for the work he did on the chopper last fall have to ask him though got to get that load'a shit off the spreader 'fore the whole damn works froze up tighter'n a nun's cunt—

"Cut that singin'!"

"I'm not singing, Papa."

"Well, cut that . . . whatever you're doin'."

"I'm humming."

Yeah, he'd have to watch himself tonight. He'd grabbed up the pot an' maybe he was going to smash the stove with it or maybe he wasn't but he had grabbed up the pot so now he set it back down on the burner again real careful like. The kid hadn't even noticed, he was still colorin' away makin' little hissin' sounds tryin' to whistle but he hadn't learned how yet.

Like a lotta things he hadn't learned how yet.

Russ laid down the spoon an' stood there watchin' him he couldn't see much of his face he was bent over too far just the top of his head his hair long an' curly like she liked it like a girl's for chrissake not like the way they kept his when he was a kid burred down tight the white showing through hell he couldn't even catch a football an' he didn't even care.

He was a good enough kid though. Even though he'd rather go to Mrs. Bartalotta's dance class an' now he was all hot about learnin' to play the guitar Cathy'd picked up second hand it didn't look like he'd ever learn to catch a pass no matter how many times Russ showed him how to hold his hands hell he couldn't even get that straight.

Man, he sure wouldn't wanna hurt him though. Go off half-cocked an' throw somethin' at him like he did that time he couldn't get him to hold his hands right an' he started beggin' to quit an' cryin' like a snotnose girl so he threw the football an' hit him didn't mean to though honest scared the hell outta him when he went down on the ground an' stayed there . . . quite a while too.

S'pose the kid still held it against him? It had been over a year now an' he still never seemed to wanna look Russ straight in the eye—'course maybe that was all just in his mind like Cathy said it was. Yeah, he was friendly enough an' all . . . but still . . . it didn't quite seem the same no more . . . Christ, he should never have gone an' done it .. . . what the hell gets into him sometimes anyway . . . ?

Like today. Standin' here bitin' his teeth like the dentist said he shouldn't belly sucked in against his backbone barely breathin' somethin' wild wild buildin' buildin' . . . just warming up a little stew.

Just warmin' up a little stew listenin' to the kid tryin' to whistle hell he didn't even have to cook it Cathy had done all that this morning before she left for work Christ knows it's easy enough an' she sure worked hard to help him out least he could do was give her a hand once'n awhile when she had to stay late for a meetin'. . . .

Sure seemed like she had enough meetin's lately though. Even when she didn't it seemed lately like she never got home on time—hell, it was only a ten-minute drive fifteen at the most an' she never got here before six—always claimin' she had those friggin' meetin's after school stickin' him with the cookin' like he ain't got nothin' to do runnin' the farm when she's probably down at Dobchek's right this minute suckin' up one'a her fancy drinks with that faggot English teacher—

"Thinks she's too good to cook!"

"Who, Papa?"

"Cathy. Now that's she's teachin' school . . . ah, nothin'."

"You really think so, Papa?"

"Think what?"

"Cathy thinks she's too good to cook now that—"

"Nah . . . !"

Hell, she couldn't even drink if she wanted to—two drinks an' she'd had it talkin' little-girl talk back cheerleadin' at Iola High singin' along with the jukebox *Those Were the Days, My Friend.*

When he was the one luggin' the ball ever' other play

she over there on the sidelines cheerin' for him between plays he'd glance over there just to make sure she was still there cheerin' for him.

She always was. Cheerin' like crazy jumpin' up an' down sis-boom-bah showin' her trim little ass under the short little skirt like all the girls wear nowdays even when they ain't cheerleadin' cartwheelin' right out there where ever'-body could see—

Dirty little show-off maybe she had stopped at Dobchek's! Maybe she's sittin' down there right this minute suckin' up drinks him stirrin' stew singin' along with the jukebox listenin' to the kid tryin' to whistle *Those Were the Days, My Friend* with the faggot—

Nah! She wouldn't do that. Not Cathy. Leastways, not without callin' him first—

"When's Cathy comin' home?"

"Pretty soon now."

"When?"

"Pretty soon."

"But when . . . ?"

"How should I know?!"

"You're the Papa, aren't you?"

"Yeah, s'posed to be."

"Well . . . ?"

"What'a ya want her for?"

"I need something."

"I'm here, ain't I?"

"You're not supposed to say 'ain't'."

Hell, she is down at Dobcheks! It's Last Friday, pay-day she an' the girls always stopped to cash their checks they had to the bank was closed by the time school let out.

Last Friday. Payday. Now he'd have to go into town to-night whether he wanted to or not pay up some bills . . . 'course just to pay up some bills.

The crazy wild somethin' came again this time different

this time that sweet little ache starting down deep an' low tinglin' through his balls spreadin' warm through his belly sockin' away inside his chest chokin' his throat his face blushin' for chrissakes blushin' the little prickles goin' up his neck runnin' around all over his head.

Nah, he better not.

'Course he still had to go into town he'd promised Wiff he'd be in next Last Friday to pay some on the feed bill better do it too Ole Man Wiff could barely look him in the eye last time that means he was just about ready to cut him off.

He should see about the tractor too. Maybe even pay Tommie a little on his bill. Kinda hard to get him to do it on a weekend though he'd be out boozin' it up too . . . no he wouldn't but Tommie probably would be he did damn near every weekend how the hell could he get away with it he must be makin' plenty 'course he ain't farmin' neither.

Maybe if he covered the shit with straw threw the big tarp over the whole spreader she could sit to Monday . . . 'course he'd have to go ask Tommie first thing come Monday mornin'.

Maybe he'd even run into Tommie over the weekend— 'course that wasn't likely an' even if he did Tommie wasn't the kind to call for a bill when he met a guy out drinkin' more likely to slap 'im on the back an' offer to buy one— still just in case he'd have a little somethin' in his pocket yeah it'd be all right so long's he had a little somethin' in his pocket.

Shit, things weren't all that bad.

Maybe he could sneak a couple.

He tried whistlin' a little too. The kid looked up kinda funny like.

"Hey, when'd you learn to whistle?"

" 'Bout twenty years 'ago."

Russ swung into *Those Were the Days* hittin' it hard an' fast throwin' in a few fancy licks here'n there just to show the kid what whistlin' was all about.

"Hey, that's neat . . . !"

Russ built the ending up an' then snapped it off at the top just like the jukebox did. The kid was lookin' up at him like he hadn't since he hit 'im with the football.

"Man, you're sure some whistler . . . !"

Russ felt like reachin' out an' rubbin' him on the head but he didn't just turned an' started dishin' him up a bowl'a stew.

"Boy, you jus' better believe it . . . you jus' better believe it."

Usually she was home by this time though. Maybe they were havin' one.

He finished dishin' up the bowl'a stew an' slid it over under the kid's nose. He was back to colorin' now so he just grunted didn't even miss a stroke.

Man, that was another thing—that kid never had been taught to snap-to like he had to back on the Farm. 'Course you couldn't really blame the kid he'd never had a hand laid on 'im 'cept for those couple'a times his jumped out there 'fore he could call it back barely nicked 'im but listen to her scream you'd think he'd tore half his head off that's what comes'a followin' along after that Doctor Speck even her own mother said so only time she ever agreed with him.

Funny thing ever' once'n awhile he even caught himself wonderin' if he much cared for the kid—'course he had to hell he was the father wasn't he? Who ever heard of a father didn't even like his own kid?

Shit yeah he liked him all right.

"Eat your stew."

"When's Cathy getting home?"

"Should be any minute now."

"How come she's always late, Papa?"

"She ain't—isn't . . . always late."

"That's what you say—"

"Eat your soup."

"It's stew."

The kid laid down his color an' took a couple'a picks at it his face screwin' up when he tasted it like Russ had just forked his plate full off the spreader.

"S'pose that ain't good enough for you."

"There's that 'ain't' again, Papa."

He said it in that laughin' way Cathy used when she corrected him. Man if he ever blew 'an laid it on him it'd make the football deal seem like a pat on the back.

"She must be late. You know how I can tell?"

"Eat."

"Your face is getting red, that's ho—"

"Shut up!!!"

The kid's face dropped when the word slapped him his lower lip workin' pretty good a clump of hair danglin' in the stew. Russ couldn't figger out whether to beat 'im or give 'im a hand. Finally he took the dishrag an' wiped out the gravy lettin' his hand stay on the kid's head a little longer'n he really had to 'cept he kinda not really but almost shrugged it off.

Russ moved away settin' down in the chair by the stove lookin' out the kitchen window at the side of the old shed. Funny thing—he felt like cryin'.

"What was so bad about that, Papa?"

"Nothin', baby . . . nothin'."

Maybe he better have hisself a little shot now before he ended up doin' somethin' goofy. Just one to ease him down a little. Sure be a helluva lot better'n the way he was. There wasn't nothin' in the house she'd made sure'a that after the last one but he had his just-in-case bottle under the truck seat . . . 'course she could always smell it the minute she walked in christ she had a nose like Simmy's beagle then she'd sneak that quick little look at his eyes where she claimed it always showed.

Hell, how could one quick one show—?

Maybe not today though! Maybe not today if she's havin' one herself maybe even two they say if two people are drinkin' one can't smell the other must be true too he never smelled the ones around him down at Dobchek's.

Hell yes she must be havin' plenty! No way she shouldn't be here by now—

Then he thought'a somethin' else. This one hit him so hard right under where the dull hurt was for a second there he thought he was maybe havin' a heart attack so he sat back down on the chair there by the stove an' went to lookin' out the window at the side'a the old shed again waitin' for his grip to come back.

What is she was dead?

He glanced around to see if the kid looked any different . . . he had given up on the stew again an' was just sittin' there colorin' an' singin'. . . .

". . . those were the days my friend we thought they'd never end we'd sing an' dance forever an' a day those were the days my friend we thought they'd never end we'd sing an' dance forever an' a day those were the days—"

"Baby, please . . . please don't sing anymore."

"What's the matter, Papa?"

"Nothin'. Just . . . eat your soup."

This time the kid just went ahead an' did it laid down his color started eatin' chewin' with his mouth open with that little smuttin' sound he made when he wasn't thinkin' to keep his mouth shut or Cathy wasn't around to tell him.

What if she never would be? What if she had stopped with the girls to cash her check had a whiskey sour or two strong as they make 'em at Dobchek's an' she can't handle 'em anyway an' she got in her car an' started out an' was turnin' out on 9H an' forgot to look both ways an' one'a those big Grand Union semis came roarin' down over the hill an' totaled her—?

"Want me to rub the back of your neck, Papa?"

"What . . . ?"

"Want me to rub the back of your neck, Papa?"

"It's all right, baby."

He hadn't noticed the kid get up an' come over to stand alongside his chair an' now when Russ lifted his head an' opened his eyes to see him he took that for the invite an' wormed his body up under Russ's arms an' up on his lap an' laid his head back against Russ's chest an' shut his eyes an' started that little rockin' motion with his body first time since the football deal.

"Want me to sing you a sad song, Papa? You know, the kind you like?"

"Ah . . . yeah. Yeah, sure."

"You start rocking first."

Russ started rockin' his body like he always did makin' like they was in a rockin' chair the kid started singin' the soft slow sad way he always did when they was doin' this together makin' up the words as he went along not doin' bad either for a ten-year-old somethin' about little boys walkin' along under sad skies hopin' to see a rainbow the same words over'n over Russ squeezin' him a little tighter not too tight Russ all the while listenin' to the other one singin' in his head. . . .

". . . those were the days my friend we thought they'd never end we'd sing an' dance forever an' a day—"

What if she was? What would happen to him? Probably lose the farm. If he had to be honest . . . hadn't been for her goin' out an' gettin' the job . . . probably would'a lost it long time ago. 'Course maybe he would'a done things different then . . . nah! That's why she had ta take the job in the first place. Still . . . things didn't seem so

bad then—sure they was bad but . . . different bad! Jus'
. . . money bad—hell, what difference had it made they
never seemed to have nothin' neither way . . . 'course lotta
that was his fault.

Yeah, he wasn't stoppin' tonight. No way he was stoppin'
tonight. That ole red truck was gonna roll right by an'
wasn't stoppin' till it hit the loadin' platform at the feed
mill.

Maybe he wouldn't be goin' anywhere though if . . .
somethin' had happened to her. 'Cept maybe down to the
morgue to say it was really her like you see on TV—'course
he really wouldn't have to do that around here ever'-
body'd know it was her they could tell by the car . . .
what would a man have to do around here?

Would he get hung up with another woman? One'a
those big-tit young ones just gettin' outta high school
startin' to hang around Dobchek's more'n more nowdays
Andy says they'd put out "if any'a you married guys had
guts enough to take 'em."

More likely he'd end up with somethin' like Carol Gore
least she knew enough to keep her mouth shut didn't play
any'a those greasy kid games all you had to do with her
was point at the door she'd be waitin' out in the truck—

'Course he wouldn't even have to do that if there was
no Cathy. If there was no Cathy Carol or any of 'em
could sit right there at the bar with him big as you please
boozin' it up together pressin' their legs against each other
holdin' hands like he an' Cathy used to—

He jumped up off the chair so fast the kid almost fell
off on the floor he'd forgotten all about the kid sittin' there
on his lap singin his sad song all the while.

"Hey, Papa . . . my song's not over yet!"

"Be right back—I gotta make a phone call."

Man, he didn't want to be sittin' at the bar right out
there in the open doin' those things to Carol or any of

'em. He'd rather be doin' them to Cathy . . . what if she was dead?!

For the first time he was almost startin' to believe it Christ she was always here by now half-past six she'd never been this late for a minute there he couldn't even remember the number an' when he could his fingers were actin' so goofy he couldn't dial straight an' had to do it again.

Christ weren't they ever going to answer maybe the place was burnin' ever'body trapped inside—

"Dobchek's. You open?!"

He had jumped right in on top the voice comin' from the other end now he waited to hear what the other guy sounded like Andy was sayin' ". . . open, it ain't Tuesday, is it?"

"Andy, this is Russ—Russ Simpson, Jr."

"How you doin,' Russ?"

"Good—say, Andy, is my wife Cathy there?"

"No, neither is none'a the others."

"What? Oh. Say, Andy . . . did she stop in—to cash her check?"

"What's the matter—can't you wait till she gets home to get your hands on it—?"

"Andy, this is serious—I mean, it might be . . . see, she ain't home yet . . . !"

"Should be—she left here quite a while ago."

"Ah . . . how long, Andy?"

"Fifteen, twenty—maybe even a half hour—"

"You . . . sure, Andy . . . ?"

"Yeah . . . say, let me check. . . ."

He was gone from the phone quite a while Russ could hear laughin' an' talk comin' through sounded like *Release Me* playin' on the jukebox where the hell could she be—

"Yeah, it's been at least a half hour, Russ. Russ . . . Russ, something wrong, Russ?"

"She should be home by now, Andy."

Russ hung up the phone an' walked to the living room windows stood lookin' down 9H but he couldn't see her little blue Volkswagen comin' nowhere. Man if she lived through this one he was goin' to go out an' get her the biggest toughest sturdiest car in Columbia County he didn't give a shit what it cost nothin' like the one she's drivin' now hell one'a those big Grand Union semis'd squash that like'a eggshell yessir a Lincoln or somethin' first thing come Monday mornin'.

If she was still here come Monday mornin'.

Christ he'd never be able to live without her hell she'd been his girl since the first day they were freshmen she was standing there waitin' to get her books too she looked over at him pretty as you please he hardly dared look back 'fraid she'd notice his Levi's ever'body else was wearin' dress pants.

The kid'd been callin' quite a few times now so Russ walked back in the kitchen Christ how would they ever make out alone man she had to be all right how could he ever tell the kid she was the only one he really cared about he wouldn't give a damn if it was Russ. . . .

He picked up the cuttin' back of a four-cylinder engine slowin' down for the turn even before he heard the crunchin' of the tires on the frozen snow when she turned in the driveway. Man ain't it funny goin' on eleven years now every time he heard her comin' there'd be that little clutch in his stomach seemed like he'd miss a breath his heart would pound a couple'a times real hard an' fast like today even more than most today quite a bit more than most today—

"There's Cathy!"

The kid had heard the car door slam the minute it did he slammed away from the table dumpin' his stew he should'a ate already over on his colorin' book. The crazy hot feelin' come slammin' through Russ.

"Damn you anyway! What the hell's the matter with you?! Actin' like a big sissy sucktittie ever'time she drives in the yard!"

Before either of 'em could make a move the door popped open an' she come popping through just like she was back leadin' cheers at old Iola High sis-boom-bah her whole body sockin' out her love for them.

"Cathy, Cathy!"

The kid broke the point he'd been holdin' an' skidded across the kitchen floor to her still standin' there in the open doorway kinda strikin' a pose her hands out toward them waitin' now for them to come to her Russ couldn't help but think of the Junior Class play they did *I Am A Camera* she was Sally Bowles comin' through the door like that he didn't have no part he couldn't say shit with a mouthful up on no stage.

Now the kid was huggin' her around the waist his face buried in the folds of her coat from the back Russ could only see his hair sure's hell looked like a girl's.

"Cathy, Cathy . . . I love you, Cathy!"

The whole thing was kinda sickenin'. It always made him gag a little to hear the kid say the word right out loud like that.

"I love you too, baby."

Funny the way the kid always called her by her first name 'ceptin' maybe when he was hurt or sick or tired or somethin' like they was just big buddies or somethin' instead'a her bein' his mother maybe they got that from that Doctor Speck too 'course he always called Russ Papa.

"Hi Sweetie."

That was for him. So was the big smile an' flashin' eyes over the top'a the kid's head.

Yeah, he loved her too all right an' he wanted to say so too man he was glad to see her home alive an' he wanted to say that too but instead he just stood there watchin' them hangin' on to each other somethin' dead startin' to rise up in his throat he didn't say neither one.

"Shut the door—you're lettin' all the heat out."

He saw it strike home the hurt flicked in her eyes but she tossed her head and it away.

"It's Last Friday."

She moved toward him, hard to walk because the kid was still huggin' her tight around the waist, holdin' out the brown envelope to him all the way that happy proud smilin' look on her face like she was comin' toward him from the sidelines when he come trottin' off after scorin' the one that counted only now it was her doin' the scorin'.

"It's all there, Sweetie—all except my one 'cashin'' drink."

"I figgered you was out havin' yourself a time."

"Time . . . !"

Her bubbly little laugh was to tell him there was no point in him tryin' to pick an argument it was Last Friday she'd had one drink she felt too good.

"Sure, if you call one Bacardi and twenty minutes a time."

Russ let his face put on its mean who you tryin' to kid look the one he didn't even like himself then made a big show'a lookin' at the clock on top'a the refrigerator it said 6:35 all the while he was doin' it knowin' she'd have the answer an' she did.

"The groceries are in the car. I ran over to Safeway to pick up the Friday specials before they closed."

The way she said the next he couldn't tell for sure if she was just proud of herself or tryin' to turn the knife in him a little.

"I had enough left over from last month's food budget."

Russ almost shrugged so what who cares but he caught himself in time jus' went ahead took the fairly thick sheaf of crisp new twenties looked like they just made up a fresh batch counted 'em even though he knew they'd all be there just like she said hell they always were then folded the whole works over once started to put them in his Levi's side pocket real casual-like—

"Russ, you really shouldn't carry it all on you—I mean, just loose like that in your pocket . . . ah, doing chores and all. . . ."

"Why not?"

"Why, you might bend over—lose it in the hay—"

"Never did before, did I?"

". . . No."

"Cathy, come see what I made in school today—bet you can't guess what it is."

"Something for me?"

"Geeee, how can you always guess . . . ?"

"My little fairy tells me."

Pretty soon they was laughin' an' gigglin' together jumpin' up an' down over the little nothin' the kid had made for her at school all of a sudden jus' like that outta the blue came that hard hot jolt in his throat so hard it like to cut his wind off right now he couldn't stand the sight of 'em much less the sound of their voices.

"What's the matter—don't you trust me?!"

"What?"

"If you two'd quit actin' like two-year-olds maybe you could hear yourself think around here!"

He was up jerkin' the door open before he even knew it himself. Least it made them stop their grab-assin' an' look over his way.

"Where you going, Russ?"

"Where you think I'm goin'?!"

"I . . . don't know."

He hesitated there in the open door, not really wanting to go, not really havin' anyplace to go . . . 'course now he had to go someplace.

"Barn. Do the feedin'."

Now it was her turn to glance over at the clock on top

the refrigerator an' he knew she knew he'd always done
the feedin' by now.

"Milk then! . . ."

"Aren't you going to have supper with us first?" She wasn't
smilin' so good anymore now but she tried to bring it
back. "Say, I forgot to thank you for putting on supper—"

"I ain't hungry."

He was halfway across the porch when her voice stopped
him. He stood for a while, stubborn, looking out toward the
barn, but finally he turned to look at her. She was framed
there in the open door the light from the kitchen settin'
off her body good.

"Russ, you planning on . . . going into town tonight?"

He hesitated a little longer then he meant to hatin' himself for doin' so fightin' to keep his head up his eyes meetin'
hers but they finally dropped a little just for a second a
dead giveaway an' he hated himself even more.

"Yeah. Yeah, I got to go around . . . pay bills."

"Maybe we could ride in with you . . . ?"

When he couldn't think'a nothin' to say hell he couldn't
just come out an' say he didn't want them couldn't start
out tryin' to tell her how a man felt headin' down the road
all alone the truck growlin' along under him a little somethin' in his pocket christ knows what might happen—when
he couldn't think'a nothin' to say she did you can always
count on a woman for that.

"Say, I have an idea: we'll all hurry up and eat, come
out and give you a hand with the milking, throw on some
clean clothes, whip around and pay the bills and still have
plenty of time to catch the second show at the Rosa—"

"Cathy—"

The kid had been hangin' tight behind her all the while
an' now he started jumpin' up an' down yippin' an' yap-
pin' away in his squeaky little babytalk voice jerkin' like
a bastard at the tail of her coat.

"Yea, yea, a movie yea yea a movie—"

When Russ didn't say no right away she thought she had a chance so she came on talkin' fast puttin' the pressure on who knows if she'd'a quit while she was ahead known enough to shut her mouth the kid too who knows he might'a gone along with the deal.

"Russ, *Romeo and Juliet's* playing, it would be so good for Russell to see, we haven't done something like this all together for such a long while—"

"Yea yea a movie yea yea a movie—"

"I . . . I got to take the truck—"

"We can all fit in the truck, three can fit in the cab easy, we've done it a thousand times—"

"But . . . I gotta grind feed—yeah, I gotta grind feed, take a load'a corn an' oats to the gristmill—"

"So—half our going out's been done in that truck with a load of feed on—"

"Yeah yea a movie yea yea a mov—"

"Nah! ! !"

It came out even meaner then he knew jumpin' all the way from his burnin' guts in one fast shot slashin' out at them their heads snappin' back now the happy eager look dyin' slow on their faces the hope dyin' dead in their eyes even the dog laid down flat on his belly.

It was so still there on the porch you could hear a semi shiftin' up the grade the other side'a Dobchek's. They all stood real still an' listened to it awhile like it was somethin' important they had to do. The dog whined low down deep in his throat lookin' up at Russ his eyes pleadin' Russ to give him the word but Russ couldn't so he stayed right where he was an' so did the others . . . the semi crestin' the hill now double-clutchin' into high roarin' down the highway toward them comin' closer closer right out in front hammerin' by . . . fadin' away . . . away . . . gone.

It was the kid who finally said the words.

"Papa, don't go to Dobchek's—every time you go down there you get that funny look on your face—"

"Go inside, Sweetie—Papa and I would like to discuss something."

She always used proper English like that, particularly when she had something to chew on him about, an' that's when it bugged him the most—just like he couldn't use it too anytime he felt like it.

She waited until the kid was inside and shut the door.

"Russ, you don't have to go to Dobchek's—we can put Russell to bed and have a few drinks right here. I'll cook you a nice supper if you don't want the stew—"

He waved her off with his hand.

"It ain't the stew."

"I know it isn't, Russ. Don't eat anything if you don't want, just have . . . a few—and then when you get good and . . . relaxed we can go up to bed . . . like we used to. . . ."

She had hold of his arm by now lookin' up at him startin' to press against him he knew she was really horny not just puttin' on a show like some women would at a time like this. He could feel it comin' too but he or somethin' else stopped it an' he pushed her away not hard but enough to hurt.

"Look . . . I gotta get those cows milked . . ."

There was hurt in her eyes now somethin' else started to show there too. Her nostrils flared an' started to quiver but when she spoke her voice didn't. She held out her hand palm up an' hit him back where she knew it hurt the most.

"Give me back my money then."

"Your money . . . ?!"

"Well . . . our money then."

"I knew you'd get around to sayin' it sooner or later."

"I'm sorry, Russ . . . but . . . somebody has to pay the bills."

"You tryin' to say I ain't man enough to handle the money in this here family . . . ?!"

"Russ, you know what happened the Last Friday—"

"You sayin' you don't believe I ain't headin' straight for town to pay the bills first—?"

"I'm not saying anything, Russ—"

"Just because you teach school don't mean I can't add two an' two an' get four."

"So can I, Russ. More than four."

"You think you're really somethin', don't you?"

"No, but I can add up all the Last Fridays and the binges and all the money you've thrown away."

"Well then why don't you just go ahead an' tack this one on too? Go ahead—before I even go! Shhhitt, you know you can count on me—I won't do nothin' to fuck up your nice tidy little list!"

"Don't swear at me, Russ . . . please."

"I swear at anybody . . . I goddam . . . please."

She gave him a little more time to get ahold'a himself. When it looked like he had she reached out an' touched him once just once on his cheek almost like she didn't even know she was doin' it just kinda had to then stepped back an' stood there waitin'. She had him goin' her way now, his head startin' to drop he had the funny feelin' she was taller'n he was he was 6'2" an' 190 she went about 5'7", 114 in her stockin' feet.

"So it's all my fault, huh?"

"I've been trying to think how it might be mine, Russ."

He dug out the roll peeled off somewhere near almost half laid it in her hand without lookin' at it or her.

"You have your milk check too, don't you, Russ?"

"Nah, that went on the mortgage."

"All of it . . . ?!"

"It . . . weren't much.'

The words came out fast from back there where she kept them stored. "Russ, why don't you sell out—take that job at the school—"

"I ain't no janitor."

"It's not being janitor—it's the engineer job—"

"It's janitor to me."

He was halfway to the barn when she called to him.

"Now you come in and change before you go down there."

"Who said I was stoppin'?"

"Just in case you decide to. I don't want you sleeping at the bar in your barn clothes like you did the last time."

"Man, you sure gotta lotta faith in me."

She just turned and went back in the house. When she opened the door the yellow light came spillin' out. He stood there in the snow surrounded by the dark he felt kinda lonely wishin' maybe he was back inside there in the yellow light eatin' a plate'a stew with them.

Then the door closed.

He felt better when he got inside the barn. There's somethin' about bein' inside a barn full'a his own cows makes a man feel better. Maybe just listenin' to 'em chew their cuds, knowin' it was him who broke his back puttin' up the hay for 'em last summer. Smellin' the silage an' the ground feed —man he'd had his hand in everything they ate. An' then again after they ate it.

He stopped an' leaned against the empty horse manger watched the cows chew a little. Man it was really somethin' the way they could eat it down once then one'a their bellies'd wrap it up in neat little balls then when they was layin' around with nothin' better to do their throat'd give a little jerk an' up it'd come again then they'd lay there an' chew real slow an' easy like really enjoyin' it gettin' all the taste outta it then swallowin' it back down in their big belly.

Funny thing there was times when he wouldn't even mind bein' a cow. Well maybe not a cow they was too

much on the woman side havin' calves an' milkin' an' all
—more like a horse. A stallion. Nothin' to do but stand
around an' eat an' sleep an' jump mares—hell, they even
brought the mares to 'im if he was a good one leadin'
them in one after the other mares all juicy barely able to
wait hell he remembered seein' 'em when he was a kid on
the Farm so horned up they'd try to mount the stallion
when they was turned in with him 'course that's no different'n women catch them at just the right time.

Particularly Carol Gore. Nothin' she liked better'n to
give him a good tough ride jockey style her feet short-
stirruped knees ridin' up right under her chin drivin' for
the finish line hell she'd probably whip 'im too if she ever
thought to bring along a quirt.

'Course this wasn't gettin' his milkin' done. All he was
gettin' was a hard-on an' Levi's ain't made for them. Besides he wasn't stoppin' down there tonight anyway the
damn thing might just as well lay down an' play dead.

"All right, let's go—on your feet! Up an' at it! You can't
gimme no milk layin' down—c'mon Crooked Horn you
lazy ole bastard on your feet. Let's go Backward Seven—
let's get those few drops'a yours."

They came to their feet one by one their hindlegs first
pitchin' their weight against the stanchions shakin' their
heads bothered at bein' bothered some of 'em bellerin' low
in their throats but all of them comin' to their feet now
settlin' down standin' still waitin' milk already leakin'
from some of the fresh one's teats.

"Get over there, Tiny, let's get some'a that before it all
runs in the gutter."

He put the milker on Tiny first she always gave down
her milk too easy when she first come in while he was doin'
it he sang *Those Were the Days My Friend* he never could
carry a tune in a bucket but he always liked to listen to
them that could particularly if they was singin' Country

an' Western shit he didn't know nothin' about the others didn't like what he did.

He was feelin' mighty good now. Not jumpy an' jerky like he did in the house. One thing he'd say about cows they knew enough to keep their mouths shut.

He finished puttin' the rubber tit-cups on Tiny stroked her bag nice'n' gentle helpin' her to let her milk down her nice soft warm skin full almost to burstin' with the milk hearin' the slurping sounds as the suction sucked the milk through the rubber cups.

He straightened up and leaned against Tiny's side rubbin' her on the back the way she liked it.

"You know somethin', Tiny, you remind me of Carol Gore."

The way he laughed anybody'd walked in they'd'a thought he was crazy.

He had to walk through the kitchen to get to the stairway. They was bent over the table playing Monopoly. They didn't look up he stopped a second makin' like he had to do something finally took off his barn cap said JOHN DEERE SALES AND SERVICE across the front hung it up on the nail by the stairway door they still didn't look up the kid threw the dice gave a little-girl shriek landed on Go Directly to Jail Do Not Collect Two Hundred Dollars When You Pass Go they still didn't look up.

He went up the stairway an' changed clothes.

He didn't stop even a second on his way out seemed like her head came up just when he hit the door but if she said something he didn't catch it.

He slowed way down as he pulled by the house. He could see them through the kitchen window they were still bent over the table he lifted his hand to wave but they still didn't look up so he gave the horn a toot just to let them know he was on his way.

His old red Ford truck was piston-slappin 'a little as he pulled out the driveway onto 9H so he shifted back down into low an' eased up on the gas. Man all he'd need now would be for her to blow—maybe he shouldn't'a loaded her so heavy she was goin' on fourteen he'd put some mightly rough miles on 'er since he picked 'er up an' she was already third-hand then.

Funny thing how a man can get so tied up with an old piece'a junk like this. Nothin' but steel an' rubber an' a little grease'n oil in between. A tank'a gas to make 'er go. Bright red paint to let people know she's comin'. ELM-GROVE FARM SIMPSON & SON in big black letters on the driver's-side door the head of a Holstein cow painted in between he'd painted 'em there the year the kid was born shit don't look now like he'd ever grow up to be a farmer.

The engine groaned carbon-clattering a little when he dropped 'er into high maybe he ought'a throw a little high-test into her the next time burn 'er out a little.

Still a pretty damn good old buggy though. Started right off the coldest day'a winter hell many's the mornin' he'd end up pullin' Cathy's car an' it was just barely four years old got it secondhand the fall she started teachin' christ had it been two years already goin' on three when she took the job it was only s'posed to be for the year till he cleared up a few'a his bills only they never did get cleared up just grew bigger man he better not stop tonight.

Never would forget the day he bought the truck. Few days after they moved on the farm went over to Honest Al's picked 'er up for two hundred bucks cash on the barrelhead got in an' drove 'er away bet none'a them knew he'd waited all his life to do just that.

Man did he feel like somethin' drivin' home. Home! To his own farm. His own wife waitin' there for him his own kid inside her belly. Drivin' home in his own truck sittin' up there high in the cab feelin' all that power underneath him power he could feel right through the seat'a his pants up through his body runnin' out his arms fingers grippin' the wheel a little tighter'n he had to turnin' the wheel a little even when he didn't need to wavin' at every other truck he met it didn't make no difference if he knew the driver or not givin' 'em that little one finger up off the wheel wave he'd seen the big truckers give like they didn't dare risk takin' a hand all the way up off the wheel watchin' the cars come up behind him in the big load-extension mirror givin' them the "all-clear" when it was OK to pass . . . then swinging in his own driveway turn signals flashin' red she was standin' out there in the yard waitin' for him he could see her belly already showin' round. . . .

Man he'd felt big that day.

He could see the lights from Dobchek's when he was still half a mile away. They was showin' there when he swung the wide sweepin' curve by Johnson the veterinarian just like he knew they would. It was one'a those clear cold winter nights, the light hangin' blue an' sparkly out away from the neon jumpin' right out at him the nearer he got.

He better stop for the crossroad—good thing he did one'a those young beerheads come roarin' through even though he had the right-a-way that didn't mean shit to them they get behind the wheel'a one those souped-up Mach 2s drivin' one hand fancy their girl sittin' so close you can't tell for sure which one's drivin'. . . .

Looked like quite a crowd tonight—cars everywhere main parkin' lot full spillin' over into the Shell station even across 9H into the overflow lot.

Must be a banquet or a weddin' or somethin'—sure, a weddin' he had read about it in the *Register-Star* just yesterday Franz Diestel an' that little Olson girl from Rosholt havin' their reception there funny he'd forgotten about it when he read it he'd thought to himself maybe he'd mention it to Cathy maybe she'd like to go.

Carol would be there. Carol was a good friend of the Olson girl. Might even be in the wedding party bridesmaid or somethin' probably wouldn't wanna do it on the truck seat if she was might be a little rough on one'a those long gowns they never looked to him like they was made too sturdy 'course if he got the cab good'n warm—

What the hell was gettin' into him?! He wasn't havin' nothin' to do with that old pig even if he did stop—an' who said he was gonna?

Hell he better do somethin' pretty soon though cars were startin' to pile up behind him on 9H some startin' to honk their horns—

He jerked the wheel like he was mad at it an' the old red truck followed along off 9H into the overflow parking lot. Leastways it'd give him a chance to do a little thinkin' without every bastard in Columbia County blowin' his horn at him.

'Course it wouldn't hurt to stop'n say hello. Least he could do was give the couple his regards maybe even buy 'em one drink hell he had practically grown up with Franz an' the Olson girl was some kinda shirttail relation'a Cathy's—

Funny they weren't invited to the reception. . . . Maybe they was but Cathy didn't let on. Seemed lately like she didn't much care about goin' out with him where there was drinkin' goin' on . . . acted sometimes like she was kinda . . . ashamed of him. . . .

He reached under the seat for his bottle couldn't put his hand on it right off the bat it must'a slid further back. He leaned way forward feelin' his hand around as far as he could funny thing he hadn't felt the big thirst once he knew he'd be goin' but right now he did.

He still couldn't feel it. For a second there he thought he

did but it was only the stock of his .270 Winchester he kept under there smooth an' slick an' shaped like a pint hell he never knew when he might run across a nice big buck the price'a meat bein' what it was nowdays.

Where the hell had it gone to?

He laid down on his belly on the floorboards pokin' around with both hands finally pullin' ever'thing in there out the deer-rifle jack pliers binder-twine grease-rags . . . no jug!

She'd got it! The dirty little sneak! He laid the .270 back down he'd been squeezin' it like it was her neck hell she'd only been doin' it for his own good least that's what she'd go 'round tellin' herself . . . still she had no call to go messin' 'round with that little bitty pint in his own truck shit a man's gotta have some place a woman don't touch.

Funny thing . . . she'd never done nothin' like that before. Maybe she was tryin' to tell him somethin' . . . ?

Ain't no woman tells Russ Simpson, Jr. nothin'!

He slammed the .270 back under the seat pushin' 'er way back under pushin' the other stuff in front so the game warden wouldn't see 'er if he should just happen to glance under like he did that time last fall when he stopped Russ for shinin' deer the other side'a Brainard's bridge man he was lucky that time.

Worst thing she could'a done. Hell if she hadn't'a sneaked that pint on him hell he would'a just taken one little snort here in the truck pulled right on in to the mill wouldn't even'a set foot in Dobchek's wasn't even plannin' on it just goes to show how a woman can outsmart herself sometimes.

First thing though he better park the truck over in back'a the overflow lot it'd be outta the way just in case he should get hung up a little or somethin' people wouldn't be so likely to notice Carol gettin' in . . . shit what the hell was he thinkin' about he'd never be here that long the unload-

ing dock at the mill closed at nine he'd promised Wiff
he'd get in before closing pay him a little on the bill yeah
he'd just have a couple now whip into town grind feed
pay on the bills stop on the way back things wouldn't
start swingin' till after 'leven anyway.

He parked 'er good way back outta the light—light
dancin' across 9H from the big neon sign DOBCHEK'S
underneath in smaller letters STOP! GIVE YOURSELF A
BREAK light spillin' out from the big plate glass windows
light shimmerin' down from the floodlights atop the roof
funny thing he felt better'n better the closer he got to the
light the light kinda reachin' out to him makin' it easy to
walk like them astronauts when they was in space his
mouth wet salvin' down his throat walkin' easy gettin'
plenty'a air the dull hurt gone from over his heart walkin'
easy the pressure easin' inside his head walkin' easy eyeballs seein' what they was lookin' at walkin' easy ears
hearin' everything they wanted to.

Now he was in the light. Lookin' down at hisself likin'
what he saw. Black calf boots zipper pocket over the right
ankle round gold ring hangin' down he kept his Camels
in there. Brown cavalry pants slim legs tucked inside the
boot tops he stopped an' tucked one inside a little more'n
the other kinda like they just happened that way. Tan deerskin jacket he'd had made up from the buck he got the
night before season opened he remembered just in time an'
put on the deerskin gloves too.

He could see the place was pretty well packed while he
was still crossin' the road. All the tables along the big side
windows were filled with them who could afford to eat
out—funny how he always seemed to see the same faces
lawyers doctors dentists contractors construction men
plumbers the big fruit growers from down around Linlithgo
maybe one'a these nights maybe next Last Friday he'd
surprise Cathy get Flo down the road to stay with the kid

an' take her out to eat call in ahead get a reservation an' ever'thin' hell it didn't cost all that much they could just order somethin' down there near the bottom steamed clams or spaghetti or somethin'.

Hell they used to be able to do that ever once'n awhile before things went bad an' he got hisself so far in the hole. Hell back when they first got married they used to get out to eat or a holdin' hands movie least once a week—back before they had the kid an' she had to get out an' take the teachin' job. Funny thing seemed like they'd had more money to spend back in those days when all they had was comin' in on the farm an' she was there workin' alongside. Them days they figgered all they had to do was pull hard together an' it was bound to turn out. Seemed like nowadays . . . it wasn't . . . just the same . . . no more—

"Hi Russ, long time, no see."

"Not since last month, Buddy."

Funny thing he didn't even remember comin' in here he was standin' at his usual spot down by the service bar. The bar was almost empty just Phooie and Bloodclot holdin' down their spots the other side the liquor island looked like they was already about three sheets to the wind must'a put the bib on mighty early.

"What you been up to?"

"Nothin'. Stay outta trouble that way. Gimme a drink —shot'n a beer."

He could hear a dance band swing into a polka sounded like it was comin' from the new banquet hall the reception must be goin' on back there.

"Ah, Russ . . . Cathy was in this afternoon—to cash her check."

"I know it."

"She . . . looked great."

"Still looks the same I guess."

"Yeah, she sure don't show her age much."

"Hell, she's only twenty-nine."

"Still, a lotta women younger'n her don't carry it near so good as she does."

"Lotta women don't have what she had to start with."

"Man, you kin say that again."

"Or get what she got."

"What'd she get . . . ?"

"Me, you dolt . . . !"

"Yeah, hehheh, yeah, that's one box'a Cracker Jacks she never should'a opened!"

Buddy started off laughin' like he'd just pulled off the biggest deal since sliced bread. Russ didn't think it was nowhere near so funny.

"What'a'ya—some kinda goddam hyena? How about that drink—I gotta get into the mill an' unload before he closes."

Buddy stopped laughing real sudden-like seemed like he remembered just then he had to wipe off the bar 'cause he grabbed up the bar-rag an' started scrubbin' away Russ couldn't see nothin' there to wipe.

"Just . . . havin' one on your way in, Russ . . . ?"

"Maybe."

Buddy just kept wipin' the same spot then he took a deep breath an' started talkin' never once lookin' at Russ.

"Russ, maybe I shouldn't even mention this but—you know, after last Las' Friday when you come in here an' got all snockered outta shape . . . well, Nick an' Andy they had a little meetin'. . . ."

"What'a'ya gettin' at . . . ?!"

"Hell, it ain't me, Russ, I jus' work here, you know that. Sure, I always figgered you were a little on the wild side when you get a noseful—"

"Buddy—"

"Nick an' Andy they thought maybe we oughta try'n hold you down a little. . . ."

"What the hell you talkin' about, Buddy?"

"Don't get mad at me now, Russ, I always figgered you'n me was pretty good friends from way back I jus' work here—"

"Gimme my drink."

"Sure, Russ."

Buddy looked both ways before he did like a kid waitin' to cross a road must be he didn't see no car comin' 'cause he set a shot glass in front'a Russ an' poured it full'a V.O. then reached over an' drew a glass'a beer an' set that in front'a Russ too.

It went down just like Russ remembered. Now all he had to do was wait for it to work down his legs. When it did that an' he could feel it there he'd know he was really here.

"Gimme another—hold the wash."

"Russ, Cathy's thinkin'a havin' you posted."

Buddy blurted it out just like that Russ could see he was sorry.

Russ waited till he had swallowed the mouthful it got hung up in his throat a little an' took quite awhile goin' down but he still couldn't think'a nothin' much to say.

"Posted . . . ?"

"Yeah, I wasn't goin' to tell you, I didn't wanna hurt your feelin's or nothin', but that's what she was in here today talkin' to Nick an' Andy about."

Buddy found another spot on the bar he had to give a lotta attention to with his bar-rag.

"They said it was up to her but they was thinkin' a doin' it themselves enaway. . . ."

Buddy kept rubbin' away like he was gonna work his way right through to the cellar.

" 'Course you know who always ends up havin' to do their dirty work—"

"Posted. Well, if that ain't the cat's ass . . . ! Russ Simpson, Jr., posted!"

Andy sidled up alongside Buddy from where he'd been hidin' the other side the liquor island.

"Keep it down, Russ."

"So this place's gettin' too fancy for a farmer to do his drinkin' in, eh Andy . . . ?"

"You know it ain't that, Russ."

"You'n Nick don't like the smell'a cowshit in here no more—"

"Cut it out—we're doin' it for your own good an' you know it."

"Now that's a switch. I don't remember you ever doin' nothin' for nobody but Andy Dobchek."

"Just say I'm doin' it for Cathy an' your kid then—"

"You shut up about them, Andy Dobchek . . . !"

"Don't you go pointin' your finger at me, Russ Simpson . . ."

"I'll point my finger at you any damn time I feel like it, Andy Dobchek!"

"Buddy, go get Nick outta the kitchen."

Buddy went.

"What'a'ya gonna do—get up a small army an' throw me out?"

"Russ, cut it out. Look, Russ, you an' me an' Nick, we been friends for a long time—hell, we played on the same team together."

"Not exactly the same team, Andy."

"So I sat on the bench an' you was the big honcho—we was still friends, wasn't we?"

"Yeah, we were."

"Man, we still are. Russ, me'n Nick . . . we're worried about you—we all are, Cathy, Buddy, hell, I even hear talk up an' down the bar—"

"Quit slobberin', Andy. Don't nobody have to do no worryin' for Russ Simpson, Jr. Besides, that ain't what the whole thing's about nohow . . . nah . . . it's about that white shirt an' black bow tie you're wearin'—this big fancy bar you just got through remodelin', them doctors an' lawyers you got sittin' over there along them plate glass windows . . . nah, it ain't me you're worryin' about, Andy, what you're worryin' about is me gettin' drunk an' sayin' a few shits an' fucks, maybe even slippin' my hand up one'a your doctor's wife's snatch after she's asked me two-three times—what you lookin' around for, Andy, ain't nobody that counts kin hear me . . . hey, Andy, remember before you remodeled, when the liquor room was downstairs right across from the ladies' can—how we use'ta take turns waitin' for Mary C. to go to the can so we could pull 'er in an' pound 'er right there on a pile'a empties ha ha her husband old Doc C. sent her to the clinic to have her bladder tested she had to go so often—"

"For chrissakes, Russ, hold it down—"

"See . . . ? See what I mean, Andy? All of a sudden this place is gettin' 'too good for me."

Nick came lurchin' through the swingin' kitchen door all 240 an' crooked grin the veins poppin' across his nose an' up along his cheekbones hell Russ couldn't help but like that big shufflin' bear nobody else could neither.

Nick stopped across the bar from Russ wipin' his hands on his bloody greasy apron looked like he'd been in the middle'a cuttin' meat the big stupid grin plastered on his face teeterin' back an' forth just a hair his blue eyes watery somethin' kinda painful like showin' there Russ could see he'd been hittin' the sauce pretty hard today.

"You think this place's too good for me too, Nick?"

"Shit, yeah. For me too. Hell, nowdays I gotta get a written pass from Andy here to come out front."

"Nick, all I asked you to do was put on one'a those clean chef's outfits—I mean, what's the point'a orderin' 'em if you're not goin' to bother—"

Nick cut his little brother off with a wave'a his big paw.

"Pour me one, Andy."

Andy poured a couple'a inches in the frosted cocktail shaker Nick drank outta so nobody's s'posed to know he's drinkin' but everybody in the place does.

"Don't forget the booze this time—I got better dishwater back there'n the last one you sent out."

Andy shrugged kinda helpless-like an' set the bottle'a V.O. back down on the bar gutter.

"Nick, whyn't you just take the whole goddam works back there with you—?"

"Oh no, can't do that, Andy, remember the new rules . . . !"

Nick turned back to Russ. "Andy's wife the bookkeeper's got us on the perpetual inventory now you know—she's afraid I was drinkin' up too much'a their cut—"

"That's not the reason an' you know it, Nick. Christ, it's about time we got a little system around here—I mean, shit, we gotta pay for all this . . . !"

Nick took the top two inches off his drink with one gulp an' wiped his mouth with the bottom'a his greasy bloody apron.

"Remodelin' wasn't my idea."

"Whose was it then?"

"I dunno—maybe you better check with your wife, Andy."

"Why don't I just check with yours instead . . . ?"

Andy moved down the bar kinda huffy-like but not so far he couldn't hear what was goin' on just in case he wanted to get his oar back in. He wasn't really mad they always carried on like that hell an outsider'd listen to them two when they really got goin' he'd think they hated each other's guts their wives too 'course they probably did at least the wives did each other's Russ knew that much for a fact this time though more'n likely they was puttin' on their little show for Russ's benefit a little somethin' to take the heat off im soften him down a little hell these two boys ain't

dumb even if they was Polocks don't ever get to thinkin'
they are just because they ain't had much schoolhousin'
when it comes to makin' money those two brothers'd get
closer together'n those teen-agers Russ'd seen comin' through
the crossroad in the front seat of that Mach 2.

Nick took another two-inch slug went through the
mouth-wipin' routine all the while waitin' for Russ to say
somethin' so he finally did hell he might just as well looked
to him like they'd already made up their minds.

"You got it all legal-like, Nick . . . all written up down
there at the town hall?"

"Don't need it, Russ. We got the right to refuse anybody
we want—says so on that sign right over there by the
license."

"In a pig's ass you have."

"In a pig's ass we don't."

There wasn't much more Russ could say to that.

"You're a helluva one to be postin' me."

Nick's lopsided grin hung right where it had been all
along wrestlin' the words out through it with the help'a
his talkin' hands stabbin' his big scores in with a pointed
trigger finger that made a few shaky loops before it finally
zeroed in a few inches from the end'a Russ's nose.

"That's just it, Russ, that's the whole ball'a wax. . . .
Sure, I had my quart today—ever' day. But take a look at
me . . . go ahead. . . ."

"Aw, for chrissake—"

"Go ahead—take a good look!"

"All right, I'm lookin' . . . !"

"Well, what'a'ya see?"

"You ain't exactly no ravin' beauty, Nick—"

"I mean what do you really see?"

"A drunk."

"What'a'ya mean, a drunk?"

"Just what I said—a drunk."

"Aw right, so I'm a drunk—is that all you see?"

"Well . . . a drunk cook in a dirty apron—"

"No, no, you don't get it, Russ . . . how am I actin'?"

"Pretty goddam goofy, I'd say. . . ."

Now his trigger finger came punchin' at Russ's nose like he was about to score some big deal point.

"But am I actin 'normal . . . ?"

"Yeah, for you."

"Do I change color ever' drink I take?"

"No, you stay nice'n even red."

"Do I light up like one'a those moon shots an' go off in some half-cocked crazy orbit every payday weekend?"

"No, you just pass out an' puke all over yourself on your Tuesday nights off."

They wasn't just exactly the answers Nick was lookin' for so he picked up his frosted cocktail shaker to demonstrate a little.

"Now watch me close—what am I doin' now?"

"Oh, I'd guess you was mixin' yourself another drink—"

"Russ, let's just . . . say I'm buyin' myself this drink—I mean, like I'm a customer . . . like you, OK? As a point'a fact, let's just say I'm a customer quite a bit like you, Russ."

"Yeah, mighty goddam thirsty."

Nick made like he didn't hear Russ took a nice slow pull'a his new drink set it back down on the bar the same way.

"Now how'd I drink that?"

"Like it tasted pretty good."

"Did I drink it straight down with one hand an' hammer the bar for another with the other hand?"

"You don't do that in here, Nick, you just do that when you're in somebody else's place."

Nick's grin was startin' to slip a little by now his finger just barely missed Russ's nose.

"This ain't got nothin' to do with me, Russ Simpson— this has got to do with you."

"Don't you think I know it? I mean, I'm no goddam dummy—go ahead an' say it!"

"All right, big shot, you asked for it!" Nick reached under his greasy bloody apron and pulled out a roll big enough to choke a cow slammed it down on the bar in front'a Russ. "Do I come in here or anyplace else playin' the big shot slammin' down ever' dime I got an' a few besides? Buyin' rounds'a drinks for the house like a man with a paper asshole, throwin' away food outta my baby's mouth—"

"Watch it, Nick . . . watch it . . . ! That little boy'a mine . . . he ain't never gone hungry—"

"He woulda."

"What'a'ya tryin' to say, Nick?"

The grin never moved but his finger did. Russ almost started to slap it outta his face but he could still think well enough to know he did that he'd better be ready to go the route.

"He woulda."

Andy an' Buddy moved in between 'em Andy worried lookin' over his shoulder at his lawyers an' doctors some of 'em cranin' their heads around to see where the noise was comin' from.

"For chrissakes you two, hold it down—can't you ever discuss nothin' like normal human bein's, I mean, this ain't no goddam boiler factory!"

Russ an' Nick hadn't moved Nick still holdin' his finger in Russ's nose Russ pressin' his chest over the bar fingers grippin' the bar ridge both tryin' their damnedest to keep from bein' the first one to blink an eye.

"Thanks boys. Thanks a lot. Throwin' it up to me 'cause my wife had to get out'n work."

"I never said nothin' 'bout Cathy workin'—"

"Yeah, you did, Nick . . . yeah, you did."

Now the other half'a the relay team figgered maybe it was time to grab the stick. Nick backed off taking his finger with him. Russ sat back down on his stool. Neither one of 'em had blinked yet it was a tie.

"Hell, Russ, both our wives work too—"

"For you. In your own place, Andy."

"What difference does that make?"

"It makes a lotta difference."

Buddy threw in his two cents' worth over his boss's shoulder. "Hell, Russ, ever'body's wife works somewhere —mine's been down to the egg plant goin' on eight years now, just got promoted from packin' to candlin' last week—"

"Buddy, go wait on the customers."

"There ain't any, Andy."

"Find some."

Andy waited until Buddy moved to the other side of the liquor island.

"Russ, it ain't 'just got to do with your money when you're in here on a spree, it's got to do with ours too. Hell man, when you get to cursin' broads an' slappin' guys off stools if they so much as look crosswise at you—shit, you can clear a bar'a decent people faster'n fire rollin' outta the kitchen."

"Oh, so I ain't one'a them 'decent people,' huh, Andy?"

"Not when you're actin' like you been lately, you ain't. I mean, how'd you like it if I come up to your place an' went runnin' through your barn kickin' your cows in the bag just when you was gettin' set to milk 'em . . . ?"

Andy had a pretty good point there.

"I . . . I wouldn't like that . . . much, Andy."

"You bet your sweet ass, you wouldn't. I mean, what the hell makes guys like you think makin' money in a saloon's any different'n anyplace else? That you kin act different in here than any other business? Hell, you wouldn't go into the grocery store'n rip open the bread an' knock somebody down ahead'a you in line an' curse out the grocer if he didn't give you free ever' third can'a soup —then puke on the floor on the way out!"

Andy picked up the bar-rag Buddy'd left layin' there on the bar looked at it a second then flung it under the bar in one'a the rinse tanks.

"I mean, some'a you guys act like your doin' us some special kinda favor by drinkin'—goin' around sayin' to yourself, 'Course I don't really have to have a drink, I mean, it's not like meat'n potatoes—I'll just stop in an' have a couple give the Dobchek boys a break' . . . then expectin' with every shot'a booze you get a side dish'a the bar owner's ass. . . ."

Nick reached over an' laid his big paw on his baby brother's shoulder.

"Andy boy, you're gettin' bitter."

"Better'n stayin' drunk!"

Nick took his hand off Andy's shoulder an' reached in the ice tank for a couple'a cubes.

"Maybe."

Andy just sniffed an' moved down the bar by Buddy. Man, the boys were puttin' on a good show tonight Russ was almost startin' to feel sorrier for them then he was for himself but not quite.

Nick picked up the bottle'a V.O. an' give the two ice cubes a few inches to float in this was the size he usually made to hold him awhile back in the kitchen Russ knew he'd better get some talkin' in while he had the chance most people wouldn't believe it to look at them but Nick was a helluva lot softer'n Andy.

"What about me, Nick?"

Nick just took a drink not even lookin' at Russ or actin' like he heard but when he set his shaker down he turned to look at Russ real close-like his eyes runnin' over Russ's face like he hadn't seen it for a good long while an' wasn't even sure he remembered.

"What the hell ever happened to you, Russ? What's got into you these last few years? Remember back when . . . when. . . ."

Nick was just standin' there now kinda lookin' over Russ's shoulder. That last drink must'a been awful strong seemed like his eyes was even watery'r than usual. Russ could think'a somethin' to ask him too hell he was no dummy neither but he figgered right now he better not it looked like he might be gettin' ahead so he just asked the other thing instead.

"What about ole Russ Simpson Jr., Nick . . . ?"

That seemed to kinda bring Nick to. He looked down in Russ's face again then his hand reached down an' brought back up the V.O. jug just went ahead an' poured an inch or so in Russ's glass funny thing a simple little thing like that Nick pourin' him that inch'r so'a booze . . . hell Russ felt like kissin' that big bear!

"Have one on me, ole buddy."

"Don't . . . mind if I do, Nick."

Andy had been keepin' his eye peeled from behind the Old Grand-Dad when he saw Nick make his move he stepped in fast right on cue.

"You sure you know what you're doin', Nick?"

"Yeah, I know what I'm doin', Andy."

"I hope I don't have to say I told you so."

"I sure do too, Andy."

The bar was startin' to fill from the tables now the doctors lawyers contractors startin' to holler for Drambuies Andy just shook his head moved down the bar to serve 'em shakin' his head all the way like things weren't goin' just the way they'd planned them.

Nick leaned in close across the bar so the high-rent district couldn't hear what he had to say to Russ.

"Tell you what I'm gonna do, Russ . . . I'm gonna give you one more try in here, see how you act this weekend."

All of a sudden Russ felt like tellin' him to stick this place but he didn't so Nick kept on talkin' low.

"I just got one small favor to ask—let me hold Cathy's money in the safe over the weekend. You can drink free for all I care, so long as you don't go crazy makin' stupid bets an' buyin' drinks for the house—"

"I hold my . . . own money."

Nick stood starin' at Russ a second then he nodded his head up an' down like he understood.

"Suit yourself."

Now the finger in Russ's nose again.

"But one more drunk in here like the last one, ole buddy, it's all over . . . all over!"

Nick picked up his shaker an' turned to go but Russ stopped him.

"Say, Nick . . . ah, Cathy—did Cathy ask you to do it?"

"You mean about the money?"

"Yeah, that . . . all of it?"

Nick's grin widened up a little.

"Nah, me'n Andy thought it up all by our little lonesomes."

Andy looked over their way Nick jerked his head at him they both walked from behind the bar through the door marked OFFICE (*Private*) to talk about Russ some more.

Russ just sat there starin' at the door. He didn't know whether to believe Nick or not.

But he just kept sittin' there anyway. Sittin' there starin' at the door marked OFFICE (*Private*) then when he got tired'a that sittin' there lookin' at what he could see of his face showin' up there on the shiny brass back side'a the Schaefer tap till he couldn't take that no more so he tried watchin' Buddy pourin' the next wave'a doctors an' plumbers their Drambuies their wives havin' green creme de menthe over cracked ice the fattest ones had Grasshoppers an' talked the most.

Nobody was lookin' so Russ reached out shined up the brass a little with the left sleeve of his deerskin jacket he still didn't look too sharp seemed like his face was gettin' awful pointy nowdays a lotta big hollows sharp hills rivers runnin' ever' which way two lights burnin' way back in a couple'a caves just waitin' to come jumpin' out.

Why'n hell didn't he just up an' go? Shit right now he didn't even wanna be here . . . ! Kinda felt . . . funny. Like maybe . . . outta place. Yeah, for the first time in his life he kinda felt out of place here . . . like maybe he had no right to be here. . . .

Like if he wasn't grippin' so hard on the bar ridge with both hands he might'a just jumped up an' run right outta this friggin' place never come back—

"Give me another drink, Buddy."

Russ knew who it was the minute he felt the hot clammy hand on his shoulder before he even turned his head he could smell him no workin' man ever doused himself up with perfume like that.

"Well, Russ, what a pleasant surprise. . . ."

" 'Lo, Duane."

"Say, can I buy you a little drink . . . ?"

"That's what I come here for."

"Good . . . good! Say, by the way, Russ, now that it just happened to cross my mind—of course, I don't like to mix business with pleasure but you know I feel it my responsibility to remind you that you only have ten more grace days left on your mortgage-life policy."

"Say, that is good news, Duane."

"Yes—that is . . . what are you planning to do about it?"

"Beats me, Duane."

"Yes, well I . . . of course you know it's up to you, Russ, surely I'm not going to try to tell you what to do, but you do have over ten years paid in on it already—sure be a shame if you were to let it lapse now."

"Yeah, go ahead an' cash it in for me, Duane."

"Cash it in . . . ? Russ, surely you must remember my telling you this particular policy has no surrender value —this is straight mortgage-life."

"Funny thing, Duane, I don't remember you tellin' me that . . . 'course if you say so I'm sure you must'a."

"Of course, I did, Russ—you must be thinking of one of the other policies I offered you."

" 'Course."

"Not that this isn't a good policy, Russ—you get more protection here for less money than you can anywhere else in the business—you get your mortgage paid up plus twenty thousand life for less than four hundred a year with deescalatory premiums contingent on the face of the mortgage . . . now how can you beat that?"

"Don't believe I can, Duane. Don't believe I can."

"Of course you can't!"

" 'Course not!"

Duane was startin' to sweat a little now looked like he couldn't wait to get in the men's room douse up a little more.

"Russ, now I don't want to get into the fact that you owe this protection to your family—"

"Don't.

"It's my duty! Now of course I don't know your particular situation—you may have ample reserves set aside to meet any such emergency but it has been my sad experience—"

"Duane, cut the shit. I ain't got a pot to piss in or a window to throw it out an' you know it."

"See . . . see! Isn't that exactly what I've been trying to tell you—you owe this protection to your family, you more than most—"

"Duane—"

"Russ, where would they be if something happened to you?!"

"I dunno—probably with that faggot English teacher."

"What . . . ?"

"Nothin'. Say, Duane, I got an idea—you lend me the four hundred bucks an' I'll pay up that premium first thing come Monday mornin'."

"Lend you . . . four hundred . . . ? Oh, well, I . . . I couldn't do that . . . !"

"Why not? I'll give you my policy to hold for security."

"Russ, I . . . I'm sorry, but I'm afraid . . . that wouldn't be quite . . . ethical—no, I'm afraid that wouldn't be quite ethical at all. Yes, well. . . ."

Duane clapped Russ on the shoulder seemed like he was in quite a hurry to get going he was walkin' before he even got through talkin'.

". . . I'm afraid I must be getting along—remember, you're in good hands with Allstate."

Russ said it loud enough but Duane acted like he didn't hear 'im kept on walkin' fast.

"Cheap bastard—never did order the drink."

Why'n hell didn't he just up an' go?! Shit here it was almost nine if he didn't go right this second right this goddam friggin' second he'd never make it to the mill on time hell it was a little better'n five miles no matter how you cut it take a minute or so to pick up an' get outta here another minute gettin' out to the truck another gettin' her started an' outta the lot up on the highway eight-ten minutes gettin' over there what with all the crooks an' turns the truck loaded heavy as she was . . . one an' one an' one an' eight or ten makes eleven or thirteen—shit!

Here it was already ten-to . . . ! Here he'd gone an' let hisself get hung up listenin' to their bullshit an' now he couldn't even make it to the mill on time no way he could make it there on time Wiff was mighty strict about that too if the tailgate'a that truck wasn't touchin' that unloadin' dock when that big hand touched twelve he might just as well have that load the other side the county.

"Gimme one, Buddy."

"Say, aren't you Russ Simpson?"

"Yeah . . . that's right. Don't seem like I . . . know you."

"Good thing you don't! har har har. . . ."

The big Drambuie-faced man in the two-hundred-dollar suit stuck out his hand. When Russ took it the big man clamped down so hard Russ thought for a second there he wanted to play a little down-on-your-knees.

"I'm Joe Hogan, District Attorney—this here's the War Department."

The War Department had on a red knit dress with a chain'a minks hooked ass to mouth around her neck she was one of the Grasshopper fats. She stuck out her hand with the drink still in it three four rings on her wedding finger one of 'em had a rock big's a horse turd. Russ shook her hooked out little finger they all thought that was pretty funny.

The D.A. gave Russ a big clap on the shoulder left his hand there like they was ole buddies.

"Look here, boys—remember '59, what we did to Hudson back in good old '59 . . . ?"

The tall skinny drunk with the blinky eyes an' the twitch in his left cheek picked up the ball—Russ remembered him now he was the doctor used to give the team the yearly examination ever'body hated his breath Russ never smelled nothin' like it outside the bear cage over to Little Falls 'round the Fourth'a July shit that time Russ got the wind kicked outta him couldn't get his breath they called ole Greenteeth down outta the stands hell he didn't even have to bother bringin' along the ammonia stick he started bendin' over Russ got his breath back right fast shit he had to looked like old Maggot Mouth was gonna give him mouth to mouth resuspiration.

"By God, it's Russ Simpson, isn't it?"

He leaned in close to make sure yeah it'd still gag a maggot off a gut truck.

The D.A. didn't seem to like nobody else doin' no talkin'.

"It sure as hell is—just the guy who was the goddamedest tailback we ever had . . . ! Just the guy who personally kicked the livin' shit outta Hudson—54 to 14!"

One'a the War Department's creases slit a little in one corner.

"Joseph—your language."

The D.A. had the score a little wrong so Russ corrected him.

"34 to 21—"

But he rode right through both of 'em. "Yessir, 54 to 14! Harharhar—hey boy, give my ole buddy Russ here a drink —give us all one!"

Buddy came shufflin' over his eyes kinda beggin' from side to side like he was lookin' to see if Nick or Andy was around to help him out but Nick was in the kitchen an' Andy was workin' his usual shirkin' spot behind the liquor island so he had no choice but to do what the D.A. told him he poured the drink but Russ could tell he wasn't too happy about the way things was startin' to go.

"How many yards you go for that day, Russ ole buddy?"

"Two-hundred forty-six. Four touchdowns. Four points after. Two field goals."

The D.A. musta thought that was pretty funny he laughed like crazy kept poundin' Russ's back all the while the drink he was holdin' in his other hand tricklin' down the front'a his two-hundred-dollar suit.

"Joseph—your suit."

"Two-hundred forty-six! Four touchdowns! Four extra

points harhar two field goals! Harhar—you hear that boys —he scored every . . . harharhar . . . motherhumpin' point!!"

"Joseph. Watch your filthy mouth."

The D.A. was laughin' so hard now ever'body in the place was lookin' ever'time his laugh boomed out his whole body shook an' the drink kept sloppin' over on his chest now it was wettin' right through his white shirt the hand-painted horse startin' to gallop off his tie.

Now the hand came down on Russ's shoulder again the squeeze was so hard Russ had to work a little just to keep from sayin' ouch.

"Yessir, boys, they don't make ballplayers like Russ Simpson no more—them long-haired faggots nowdays don't come bustin' outta the backfield luggin' that ole pigskin like this boy use' to. Hell, all he had in front'a'him was the old single wing, ever'body knew he was comin', the only play ole Clyde ever had was give it to ole Russ Simpson an' watch the shit hit the fan—Whatever happened to the single wing, Russ?"

"Dunno—guess it's . . . still around."

The bar was fillin' up pretty good now the Friday night drinkin crowd was wanderin' in the younger ones who couldn't afford to come to eat the mill hands the machinist helpers the carpenter's apprentices the dental techs the telephone operators the little girls barely outta high school clerked downtown Hudson the ones with the big tits checked out at the A&P all standin' around three-four deep at the bar hollerin' out their drinks over the stool-sitters' heads at the hustlin' bartenders back behind.

"So what you intah nowdays, Russ ole buddy?"

"Ah, farmin'. Got me a nice little spread up 9H a ways."

"Farmin'—thought I heard someplace you got a scholarship to play ball some big college down south?"

"Yeah. Arizona State."

"Good boy."

The D.A. set his glass down real careful-like asked the question fast swingin' his big head 'round so he could look Russ square in the eye one'a those little courtroom tricks he'd probably picked up watchin' Perry Mason.

"How'd it go?"

"Good."

The D.A. just kept starin' into Russ's eyes so Russ just kept starin' back in his.

"Fine. That's just fine."

"Yeah."

The D.A. finally turned back to the front an' picked up his glass again but he didn't take a drink right away just kept starin' at his glass maybe a fly had took a shit in it.

"Always kinda figgered you'd make it to the pro's . . ."

"Bad wheels. 'Course Green Bay drafted me anyway . . . but, what the shit, I decided to hang 'em up—no point in endin' up crippled for life."

"No, no point in that."

The D.A. finally took that drink started liftin' hisself up off the stool.

"Course, there's nothin' wrong with farmin' neither—best place in the world to bring up children I always say."

The D.A. picked up his change an' cigarettes started movin' over to where the bad-breath Doc was tellin' a dirty joke to the rest'a his crowd.

"Hey, where you goin'—I was just goin' to buy one . . . !"

Must be the D.A. didn't hear him he just kept on goin' his shoulder low bullin' his way through the crowd. The D.A.'s wife musta heard 'im though—the crease that was painted red opened for just a second there.

"Grasshopper."

"Hey, Buddy, set the table here."

The stool the D.A.'d been sittin' on didn't even get a chance to cool off before a chunky little fella in a white turtleneck an' a blue blazer the kind the college kids use'ta wear before they gave up clothes 'course Jimmy never did get to college so he still dressed like he did didn't look too bad on him neither even if he was forty if he was a day still plenty'a hair slicked back on the sides a little curl just happenin' to be fallin' down on his forehead slipped in an' sat down between Russ an' the D.A.'s wife Russ recognized him right away Jimmy LaForce ran a little beer joint over by the thruway bullshit artist from the word go.

". . . give me one, Mrs. Hogan there'll have a Grass-hopper, ah, might as well catch Jimmy here too, he ain't no orphan."

"Thanks, Russ. Chivas an' Coke, Buddy."

Jimmy talked in a low gravelly voice he was a great hand for goin' to the gangster movies at the Sunset Drive-in wore them built-up shoes too.

Buddy mumbled somethin' Russ couldn't quite hear an' went ahead an' fixed the drinks.

"How you hittin' 'em, Russ?"

"Can't complain."

"Haven't seen you over my way in quite a while."

"Too busy. Expandin' a little, you know."

"Yeah . . . ? Me too."

"Plannin' on buildin' on—like the boys here did?"

"Yeah, maybe, two-three rooms—'course I got me more business'n I know what to do with right now."

"Things really boomin', huh?"

"Terrific."

"Yeah, me too."

Jimmy's beady little eyes cased the bar he kinda re-minded Russ of a fox eyein' up a full chicken coop.

"Got me two-three times as many—got so bad I had to get out for a little breather, been jumpin' since nine o'clock this mornin'."

"Who you got tendin' while you're gone?"

"Oh, three-four guys—I forget half their names."

The fox checked over the chickens again Russ figgered things were probably so slow over to his place he'd stuck his wife behind the bar went out cruisin' to see where they was all at pretty hard to go up against the Dobchek boys particularly since they remodeled made their place so fancy an' all.

"Russ, you wouldn't believe the broads I got hangin' out in my place these days—man, where they all come from?"

"Beats me."

"Must be that postwar baby boom—Christ, it's almost scary, Russ, I get me three-four screws, two-three blows a day—I mean, I ain't got too much left for Bernice come closing time."

"Those broads hang out at your place'r a little young, ain't they?"

"What'a'ya kiddin', Russ—I mean, if they're old enough to bleed they're old enough to butcher."

"Yeah, I guess that's about it, Jimmy."

"Russ, listen to me, I'm tryin' to tell you, it's downright scary—what the hell's gettin' into these kids nowdays? I mean, they don't think anymore'a pullin' their pants down or coppin' a joint then they do eatin' a hot dog. An' my two girls ain't a damn bit better—hell, Bernice caught one of 'em out in a car back'a my place with that goddam Shesder looked to her like she was goin' down on him good god Timmy's damn near as old as I am!"

"Yeah, he's five-six years older'n I am—"

"Ahhh, what'a'ya gonna do?! Buddy, give us another round here. Guess it's just like that head-doctor we took the other one to said—we gave 'er too much'a everything, made things too easy for 'er, the big cars an' the fancy clothes an' all . . . shit, Russ, how the hell's a daughter'a mine s'posed to go—I mean, I ain't gonna send 'er out in rags on a bicycle . . . ! I mean, how the hell would that look?"

"Not too good, I gu—"

"You know what that damn fool said?"

"No."

"Said I oughtta think about gettin' outta the saloon business—for their sake! Now what kinda talk is that—one businessman tellin' another to go outta business! I sez where do you think I get the money to buy the big cars an' the fancy clothes—he sez see that's just what I mean—so I sez where do I get the twenty-five bucks a crack to pay you then—he sez sorry the hour's over we'll talk about that next time. . . ."

"Yeah, it's a funny world, all—"

"But that ain't the topper, Russ—guess who I found hidin' in the ladies' crapper after closin' last Tuesday night? Who was down gobblin' my gook three seconds after we heard Bernice slam the back door? Who drove away smart as you please in her old man's Continental five o'clock the next mornin'? Four blows an' three screws later? Russ, now who do you think that was?"

"Jimmy—"

"Go ahead, take a guess—who do you think that nineteen-year-old college freshman was?"

"Your other daughter."

"No jokin', Russ, just who do you think laid there on my back booth bare-ass naked cryin', beggin' me to let her hide out in the ladies' crapper again the next—"

"The head-doctor's daughter."

"Damn right!"

"Jimmy, I mean to tell you, sounds like some pretty fantastic things'r goin' on over to that place'a yours."

"Hell, you know what it is, don't you?"

"No, Jimmy, don't believe—"

"It's that goddam marijuana! Hell, they're all puffin' on

that shit eight-ten hours'a day—I mean, I got more of
'em hangin' out in the crappers than I got at the bar. Let
me tell you, Russ, things don't start straightenin' out I'm
gonna close off the dance hall an' start takin' tickets in
the crappers—I mean, why pay good money to get your
eardrums ruptured when all they wanna do is sit around
in a daze? Hell, I'd be better off to throw out the dance
band, that dancin' thing's over the hill now anyway, hire
a couple'a those harp players from the Catholic Church
over to Big Falls an' pipe it intah the crappers . . . yeah,
spread a few mattresses around, put in those dinky red
light bulbs, a secret passage connectin' the boys' crapper
with the girls'—yeah, listen to me now, Russ, that'd be big,
they could play their little games with peek holes an'
secret passwords, that kinda shit goes over big nowdays
. . . yeah, should be able to knock down eight-ten bucks
a head for that kinda setup . . . eight-ten big ones a night
on the gate alone, nine-ten thou a week countin' everything, should gross a half a mill a year easy—"

"Jimmy, ah, hold my stool for me, will ya—I gotta go to
the cra . . . men's room."

Russ wasn't sure Jimmy heard him or not he had that
glazed look on his face he got when he started money-
talkin' must be somewhere in the billions by now funny
thing of it was the silly sonuvabitch always seemed to end
up makin' plenty least a helluva lot more than Russ did.

Russ could feel his size as he worked his way through
the pushin' drinkin' laughin' talkin' crowd to the men's
room. Funny thing he didn't feel how big he was much
any more but right now he could so he straightened
up pulled his shoulders back felt even bigger seemed like
nobody in the crowd was nowhere near so big as him hell
none of 'em were—6'2" is a pretty damn fair-sized man.

There was no one else in the men's room so he leaned

against the white tile with both hands let his dong work by it-
self it wasn't a bad-sized dong neither must go at least
five soft, six-seven hard hell now he was startin' to sound
like Jimmy LaForce he laughed an' shook it off not a damn
bit more'n he had to neither.

He washed his hands. He wondered if other men washed
their hands because they had to or so they could sneak a
look at themselves in the mirror over the washbasin like he
did sometimes. Funny thing he didn't like other men to
see him lookin' at hisself in the mirror but now there wasn't
any others so he looked as long as he felt like even took
out his comb an' combed his hair another thing he'd never
do if somebody was in there.

His hair was goin' pretty good there in front. Another
few years those two tunnels diggin' in from each side
would meet then he'd have nothin' left there in front but
one'a those funny lookin' tufts standing' there all by its
lonesome look like ole Abe the cattle-dealer for chrissakes
never takes his hat off even when he eats.

Maybe if he could make it stand up there a little more
'stead'a layin' down so flat'n scrawny. . . .

Russ took a couple'a paper towels from the deal shot one
out ever' time he pushed the button an' rubbed his hair
real hard almost like he was kinda mad at it leanin' way
over so the dandruff wouldn't fall on the shoulders of his
deerskin jacket when he straightened up looked in the
mirror he woulda laughed out loud if it wasn't so sad sure
as hell was standin' up all right looked like Phyllis Diller.

He hurried up an' pushed it into place again this time
workin' it around with his fingers so it'd look like more
pushin' it forward some down over his forehead like he
saw the young guys was doin' nowdays hurryin' like crazy
before somebody walked in an' caught 'im at it christ he
felt hot'n sweaty all of a sudden—

There . . . ! It didn't look half bad . . . fact is, he looked

pretty goddam good. Shit he was only a little past thirty
with his new hairdo he didn't look a day over twenty-
five. Man he had a good strong face too not soft'n pussy
like those faggots you see nowdays maybe even a little
mean that didn't hurt none neither the broads ate that
up 'course they always liked his kind.

Kinda like Brando. Yeah that's who he looked like—
like Brando in that old flick on TV the other night. The
one where he played the Nazi with the blond hair combed
down on his forehead. Yeah Brando had hair just about
like his 'course Russ was quite a bit bigger Brando wasn't
much taller'n that blond Captain's wife screwed her way
through the war.

Man, he was some cat though. That other old flick
where he ran around in a undershirt rippin' dresses off
that goofy cunt dresses that looked like somebody's old
lace curtains man why he'd wanna bang her in the first
place Russ'd never know—'course then Brando might never
screw Carol Gore neither . . . then again he might.

Wonder if Carol's here tonight . . . ?

Russ liked him best in that Nazi one though he had
more class in that one. Them sharp uniforms the Nazi's
wore Brando looked like he had to be zipped in them
tight boots all the way up to his knees man the way he put
on his hat kinda bendin' his head into it real graceful like
cockin' the brim over one eye a little wearin' his gloves all
the while the way he kinda pranced down that long row'a
steps in Paris his body straight his waist not even bendin'
like one'a those Tennessee walkin' horses the smooth way he
held his drink two fingers underneath steadyin' it with just
his thumb sippin' real cool-like the way he talked his lips
barely movin' kinda puckered up never raisin' his voice
man he didn't have to particularly with that blonde the way
he slapped her around when he came back the second time
grabbin' her by that blonde mane hell if it hadn't

been no movie he'd'a probably put 'er right down on her knees made her eat it . . . the way he died at the end he even had class rolling down that hill hell he let hisself be killed smashin' his gun'n all hell he had to know that rich yellowbelly Martin an' the faggoty Jew what's his name the little skinny guy that died a couple'a years ago all fucked-up on dope'n all man he had to know they was somewhere right around there but he didn't give a shit he'd rather be dead then whipped by a couple'a guys like those two.

Hell he could'a just climbed back up on top'a that hill hid hisself behind one'a those big trees picked them off one by one then lit out for home laid low till the fightin' was over. . . .

"Nein, I vould razzer be kaput 'sen vipped by you."

Russ just kept starin' in the mirror Brando kept starin' back at him maybe it was the other way around.

"See, I am ze young lion . . . I am ze young lion!"

Russ-Brando let his voice spiral the second time he said it the almost scream seemed even louder then he expected here in the men's room the Russ-Brando finger was still stickin' in the face'a the other guy who was also him—

"Sir, would you mind tossin' me over a little toilet tissue?"

Russ wheeled when he heard the voice. There was this young face fulla shaved-off pimples kinda starin' at him over the top'a the first shithouse stall Russ felt like an asshole.

"Ah, this one's . . . out."

Russ mumbled somethin' about rehearsin' his part for the church play an' got a roll outta the other stall an' tossed it over to the kid who musta sat back down Russ couldn't see his head no more he heard the kid say thank you very much as he damn near run out the door.

His seat was still open when he got back. He slid into it took a hard pull on his drink didn't stop until the ice cubes started burnin' his lips. He looked around nobody was watching. Jimmy LaForce was gone he just sat there clutchin' his glass waitin' for the power waitin' for it to run down his legs down his arms out his fingertips. . . .

He could almost feel the ball. He rotated it till the tips of his three middle fingers was layin' across the seams it cradled against his thumb his little finger splayed out to guide the nose that was one of the reasons he always asked for a tall glass.

And the power was back now. It was there all the way down through his legs. Right now he coulda run for six hundred yards an' twenty touchdowns. The power was there wangin' its way up'n down'n sideways touchin' him him touchin' it man he could feel it man it could feel him.

All of it was there—that other feeling too. The one where he was high not high-drunk just high. Like his barstool was growing an' he was sittin' right there in Dobchek's higher'n everybody else higher'n the D.A.'s wife higher'n the bartenders higher'n the whole crowd higher even than the liquor island sittin' up there somewhere on the top shelf with Napoleon Seven-star an' the Ambassador 25 sittin' up there right under the ceilin' lookin' down.

Lookin' down . . . feelin' that warm-sad feelin' . . . feelin' that warm-sad feelin' for hisself an' the rest of 'em . . . maybe a little sorry for the poor miserable bastards . . . maybe even Jimmy LaForce.

The ache gone from over his heart the pressure sissin' out from inside his head from behind his eyes from inside his ears man he was loose again.

Loose . . . like after a hard game. Like he'd just had his hot shower an' Charly'd rubbed him down an' he was sittin' there laughin' shootin' the shit with the boys even the principal the big shots that could crowd their way into that steamy little locker room down under the stands everything he was sayin' being taken down by the man from the *County Post* even that one time after the Hudson game the D.A. was talkin' about that guy all the way from the *Times-Journal.* . . .

It was then that the guy with the orangeish face walked in. He walked up to Clyde whispered to him Clyde came over to Russ makin' on like he was helpin' him pull off his jersey whispered to Russ, "There's a scout here from Arizona State. Wants to talk to you. Don't say nothin'. It ain't exactly legal yet. Meet me at my car—after ever'body else clears out."

They did. Clyde sat behind the steerin' wheel of his brand new '59 Chevy Impala funny thing he'd just got it a couple'a days before nobody ever figgered he could afford a car like that Russ sat alongside him the scout with the orangeish face looked a little like Ralph Kiner on color TV sat in the back seat offered Russ a full ride two hundred bucks a month on the side for sweepin' an aisle in the college bookstore at six o'clock every evenin' but the bookstore closed at five at first Russ didn't even catch on he wondered how he'd ever be able to get into the bookstore to sweep his aisle if it was already locked up but then the scout laughed an' Clyde laughed an' poked Russ in the ribs an' said, "Get it, get it," an' Russ did.

He got the deal too. Clyde said he should take it so he did. Funny thing, Russ never did find out which aisle in the bookstore he was s'posed to sweep.

Right now though he could use a little piece of ass.

Hell not a little one one'a those great big juicy pieces one'a those with the initials C.G.

"Fill me up here, Buddy."

Russ hadn't seen her around yet tonight though—not that he'd been lookin' all that much 'course ever' once'n awhile he had took a little peek around the bar an' dining room just lookin' around 'a course not lookin' for nobody special but if Carol woulda been there he'd'a noticed her.

'Course she was probably still back in the banquet room at the reception. Yeah the foldin' door was still pulled shut probably locked from the inside the sign over it said NO STAGS—BOYS OR GIRLS . . . 'course there was another door to the banquet room opened out into the main parkin' lot she could'a gone out that way went right home . . . !

Nah she never went straight home—Carol Gore? Chances were the reception was still goin' on hell it was only 'leven o'clock already man most receptions were over by that time the foldin' door pulled open the people streamin' out to the main bar besides he couldn't hear the band.

"Hey, Andy, give me some change for the jukebox."

Andy gave Russ four quarters for the one Russ couldn't tell for sure if he was happy or not Andy had one'a those kinda faces.

"Well, so far, so good, Russ."

"Have a drink, Andy—get drunk an' be somebody."

"No thanks—I got enough drunks around here now."

Russ took his quarters an' headed for the jukebox. Andy was a lot nicer when he had a few under his belt didn't always walk around like he had a stiff back an' a mouthful of alum fact is he'd been quite a pain in the ass since he quit drinkin' always walkin' around with a glass'a milk in his hand so he could tell customers he had colitis like Bloodclot said, "There's nothin' worse'n a tavern keeper that don't drink less'n it's one that don't buy an' Andy you're both."

Russ dropped in two'a his quarters played J9 Mary Hopkins *Those Were the Days, My Friend* S5 Johnny Cash *Born To Lose* H6 Engelbert Humperdinck *Release Me* an' O2 Kay Starr *Your Cheatin' Heart*. The jukebox

was right there by the foldin' door to the banquet room.
Before the little blue light whirred over to J9 an' the first
one started playin' he stepped over to the foldin' door
leaned his ear against it made like he'd stopped to tie his
shoelace just then he realized he was wearin' his boots so
he stuffed in his pants leg instead.

There was still laughin' and talkin' goin' on back there.
They was still there Carol too probably it even seemed
like he heard her voice there one time but just then *Those
Were The Days, My Friend* clicked in an' he couldn't hear
nothin' but Mary Hopkins maybe Carol Gore would hear
her too an' come out she knew he always played it the
other songs too funny thing he always played the same four
songs an' so did she.

Russ walked back to his stool feelin' even better now
the power still there wangin' away inside him that sweet
little ache down in deep an' low his balls even startin' to
crawl a little now the head of his dong warm feelin' like
he had to take'a piss even though he'd gone not much
more'n fifteen-twenty minutes ago.

He sat back down an' sipped his drink slow'n easy. He
had his edge right where he wanted it now he wanted to
hold it right where it was shit yeah he was ready.

For anything. Right now he coulda gone any direction
so long as a broad was at the end of it hopefully Carol
Gore but if she didn't show that bushel'a tits down at the
end would do man he'd like to run barefoot through an
acre'a those 'course he'd have to figger a way to spring 'er
from that faggot she was with didn't look like he'd know
what to do with her if she sat down on his hand lookit
the way she's wigglin' around her legs crossed tight her
jackin'-off leg pumpin' three beats faster'n the music man
she was probably all lathered up already one twelve-inch
chop would take out the faggot—

Nah, he better watch hisself. Sip slow'n easy hold the

good edge Nick meant what he said Russ could see it in his eyes besides maybe she was hot for the guy maybe he wasn't too bad a guy for a faggot maybe she was even married to him funny thing nowdays how some'a the best-lookin' broads end up with those skinny four-eyed faggots shit the way they let their hair grow to their shoulders both wear the same clothes half the time he couldn't tell one from the other hell they probably never even got around to screwin' just sit there sippin' wine in them little glasses an' talkin' about it.

Yeah, he better stick with Carol Gore least she knew what she had one for not just somethin' to piss through or talk about neither to tell the truth Russ had never heard Carol mention hers once Carol never swore.

She didn't have to. Man the way she talked that little whispery voice comin' straight from her pussy breathin' in his ear all the while hell even her breath was hot not just warm like most broads—hot!

An' dancin' with her was somethin' else again. That hot breath in his ear him askin' her to meet him out in the truck her answerin' in that whispery voice, "oh, Russ, oh, I couldn't do that, you know I couldn't do that, don't ask me to do that, you know I shouldn't do that, what about Cathy" hell she couldn't an' shouldn't but he knew she would an' she knew she would hell that made it even better like he was such a great guy she just had to do it for him no matter what it just wouldn't be right to turn down Russ Simpson, Jr. hell she couldn't say no to him shit she couldn't even spell it, "oh, Russ, oh, I couldn't do that" breathin' hot in his ear her body kinda flowin' around his dancin' the two-step slow both steps between her crotch her body kinda flowin' around his dancin' close but not dirty not dry-humpin' like he'd seen some do just their bodies kinda flowin' around each other's his body askin' her body answerin' back.

Man dancin' with Carol Gore was better'n screwin' most women.

"Gimme one more, Andy."

"For the road?"

"Nah, for me'n my truck."

"That'll be . . . about it, then, won't it, Russ?"

"Yeah, I'm ready. 'Course maybe my date ain't."

Andy was still standin' there with the empty glass in in his hand lookin' at Russ.

"You . . . sure you're feelin' allright, Russ . . . ?"

"Shit, yeah . . . ! C'mon, don't just stand there with your bare face hangin' out, fix me a drink."

"I dunno—"

"Whatsamatter, Andy, can't you take a joke—hell, I was only kiddin'."

"I see you lookin' at that young blonde down the bar—"

"What the hell—is it against the house rules to look now too?"

"I got nothin' against you lookin', Russ—but don't you be thinkin' about goin' down there an' tryin' to make a pass at them young college girls."

"Furthest thing from my mind, Andy . . . furthest thing from my mind."

"Yeah, I'll bet it is—shit, if they ever cut your head open ten to one they'd find it stuffed full'a snatches."

"Nah, tits'n asses."

Andy had been leanin' way over the bar talkin' close to Russ now he grabbed Russ's arm an' squeezed it.

"Play it cool, huh, Russ."

"Got to."

"Do it for me'n Nick—you know who that bunch is down there, that blonde?"

"Nope."

"She's the daughter'a that big New York City writer just

bought all those farms up in West Ghent—the rest are friends'a hers she brought up from the city."

"She go?"

Andy gave Russ his disgusted look like he'd never think'a anything like that hisself shit Andy'd screw a snake if it'd lay still.

"Russ, what I'm tryin' to say is we're finally startin' to get some high-class people in here—an' I ain't talkin' against you, I mean, we're gettin' some *money* people, the kind we need to pick up the nut around here—"

"I got it, Andy, I got it—there ain't no need to foam at the mouth—"

"Russ, promise me you won't go down there an' try to horn in . . . ?"

"Shit yeah, I promise . . . you just go ahead an' fill that empty glass'a mine you're holdin' there in your hand."

Andy did an' when he handed it over Russ gave him a little wink.

"Shit man, I got somethin' better'n that comin' anyway."

Andy just nodded an' headed down the bar through the swingin' kitchen door probably goin' back to report in to Nick.

Russ sipped his new drink listened to the jukebox hell all his songs musta played through while he was listenin' to Andy's bullshit some'a that new rockshit was playin' now hell he couldn't even make out the words sounded like a bunch'a scalded cats howlin' through a culvert probably some'a that rich writer's daughter's crowd played it.

Shit, she wasn't so much. Probably just one'a those rich little bleached Jews from the city shit yeah if her father's a writer an' they're from the city she must be a Jew hell gettin' so Andy'd rather have Jews in here than him 'course he'd take niggers if they had the price of a tap nah he wouldn't not since he remodeled.

Hell she couldn't touch Carol with a ten-foot pole. Sure

the blonde had ten years or better on Carol maybe even
fifteen Carol was a few years older'n Russ even he'd still
been in high school when he first started puttin' the blocks
to 'er she was already out workin' at the Farmer's State
Bank had to quit that job Fearless Fosdick the President's
son kept tryin' to cornhole her in the vault.

Russ couldn't say that he blamed him though he'd'a
probably been tryin' to do the same thing if he hadn't've
already had her tied up funny thing she could'a had anybody around she wanted Fearless Fosdick Stan the Man
the eyedoctor Pete Drivel owned the drugstore she had
to quit him too caught him tryin' to spike her milkshake
with Spanish fly shit there were two-three other young
doctors lawyers one of 'em already married come from
one'a the biggest families in town married into the other
biggest finally knocked her up man there was a big stink
about that Carol was workin' for him she was his secretary there was a lotta talk he came back from the Country
Club drunk one men's night raped her right there in his office Carol never would let on though just went ahead an'
had the baby that was one'a the things Russ liked about
Carol she never would let on to nothin'.

Just went ahead an' had his baby had it all by herself
upstairs in the room she was rentin' from ole Mrs. Petersen
hell nobody even knew she was knocked-up she'd been
strappin' herself in maybe that's why it came the seventh
month just a little bitty runt of a thing Russ stopped
by to see her a week or so later told Cathy he was goin'
to town to grind feed just like he did tonight Carol had
the boy just a few months after him'n Cathy were married.

Yeah, Russ had to hand it to her all right she was a
gutty little devil. Had the boy upstairs all by herself just
went upstairs after supper laid down an' had the boy ole
Mrs. Petersen never could get over tellin' the story claimed
when she got home from the movie she walked in the

back door from her garage heard some whinin' wailin' commotion upstairs when she got up there there was Carol dragged herself in the bathroom ole Mrs. Petersen could see the blood trail on the floor there was Carol in the bathroom . . . she'd been bitin' on a roll'a toilet paper to keep from screamin' . . . after the boy come she got herself sittin' up God help her she lifted him up bit off the cord with her teeth.

Nah that young bleached blonde couldn't hold a candle to Carol Gore.

"Hey Buddy, slip me one more quick one before Andy gets back from the kitchen."

"Russ—"

"Buddy . . . please . . . ?"

"Oh . . . sonuvabitch!"

Buddy whipped a bottle off the bottom shelf the first one his hand touched poured some straight into Russ's wash glass with the beer that way Andy couldn't tell.

"Thanks, Buddy, I 'preciate it."

"You won't tomorrow."

The D.A. slid more like fell back on his stool his wife glarin' at him outta her little pig eyes didn't look to Russ like she'd moved a glob since the D.A. left just sat there waitin' for him like a walrus ready to pounce.

"Where have you been, Joseph?"

"Can."

"For an hour . . . ?"

"Fell asleep."

"I see the District Attorney also managed to vomit on himself again."

"Possibly next time I can arrange to do it on you, dear."

The D.A.'s head started sinkin' down toward the bar Grasshopper Fats just sat there starin' at his sinkin' head looked to Russ like she was kinda hopin' he'd pass out show his jugular for a split second.

The D.A.'s forehead was kinda restin' on the bar ridge now Russ started talkin' in the ear nearest him.

" 'Course my farm ain't—isn't—exactly small . . . 2000 acres."

The big Drambuie head just kinda wavered where it was for a minute there then started back up real slow-like kinda swivelin' toward Russ all the while.

"Who'r you . . . ?"

"Hell, I'm Russ Simpson, Jr. . . . 'member, '59—the Hudson game . . . 54 to 14—?"

"Russ Simpson, Jr."

"Yeah, I'm the guy bought up all those farms up in West Ghent—got me one'a those conglamorous mergers you hear talk about nowdays—'course the farms are just part of it."

The glaze lifted a little off the D.A.'s eyes his head held steady now'an he tried to focus on Russ's face.

"Thought I heard it was some big-shot Jew from down in the city—"

"Nah, that was me—I just started that Jew story for a cover." Russ nudged the D.A. in the ribs with his elbow. "Don't ever pay to let your left hand know what the right hand's doin', I always say."

The D.A. didn't say nothin' to that his head just started sinkin' again only this time it was still swiveled toward Russ.

"Hey, Buddy, give my ole friend the D.A. here a drink. . . ."

Russ didn't wanna lose the D.A. now not when he was just gettin' into some good serious talk. Didn't seem like Buddy heard Russ he just stood there lookin' straight ahead hell he was only two feet away.

". . . Hey Buddy, catch the D.A. here, get his wife too —hell, catch my whole crowd here one."

Funny thing Buddy still didn't hear him just turned an' headed the other way looked like he'd just remembered he'd forgot somethin' an' had to get after it in a hurry just then the D.A.'s head jerked up his big gravelly Drambuie voice reached out an' snapped Buddy back.

"Say boy, don't you hear good—my ole friend Russ Simpson Jr. here says he wants to buy a round'a drinks!"

Wasn't much Buddy could do but set 'em up. Russ pulled out his roll an' slapped a couple'a twenties on the bar. Buddy made a little sighin' sound didn't even look at Russ when he picked one up but he didn't ring it up neither just walked right past the cash register an' through the door marked OFFICE (*Private*).

"Yeah, D.A., one hand feeds the other, I always say— you scratch my back I'll scratch yours, har, har, har."

The D.A.'s head was sinkin' back down again looked like he'd about burned all he had left hollerin' at Buddy so Russ gave him a pretty good shot between the shoulder blades the D.A.'s head came back up but he caught a fit'a coughin' along with it. Russ picked up his wash glass gave him a swig the D.A. couldn't hold that deuce-mixture he sprayed it out over the bar caught Buddy just comin' back Buddy didn't like that a bit he was a pretty snappy dresser drove all the way up to the Robert Hall's at the Colonie Shoppin' Center just to buy'a pair'a pants.

Yeah, Buddy'd just about had it for the night he had that haunted starey look in his eyes an' that little vein jumpin' in his forehead.

"Russ, Andy wants to see you for a minute in the office."

"Buddy, tell Andy I'm a little pressed for time right now . . . tell you what, Buddy, you tell him to call me at my office first thing in the mornin'—set up a 'pointment with my secretary."

"What . . . ?"

" 'Matter 'a fact, you tell him I'm 'vailable for lunch tomorrow. Tell him I'll meet him here for martinis lobster so forth an' so on at twelve sharp high noon—you think you can remember that, Buddy—?"

Buddy was already movin' down the bar toward the door marked OFFICE (*Private*) he had a look on his face like he'd just been pecked in the head with a sharp rock.

Russ called after him.

"Tell Nick to be there too—I gotta little deal I wanna discuss with both of 'em."

Russ didn't know whether Buddy heard him or not Buddy just kept goin' through the door didn't even look back. Russ turned to the D.A. he was down takin' a little nap again this time his head was propped up by his Drambuie glass. Russ gave him another fairly good jab with his elbow an' the D.A. came up a circle on the middle'a his forehead where it'd been layin' on the Drambuie glass.

"The boys here wanna invest in another little deal I got cookin'—'course I'm not 'xactly sure I wanna cut 'em in at this stage'a the game, I mean, after I've gone out an' did all the heavy brainwork . . . laid out two-three hundred thou down."

"I . . . know . . . what . . . you. . . ."

The D.A.'s head sunk down again this time it didn't stop till it hit the bar with a pretty good whack. On the way down his nose grazed his Drambuie glass knocked it over an' the Drambuie spread out in a little pool around his head. The D.A.'s wife waited till he started snorin' then one'a the creases 'round her left eye moved for just a second there kinda looked like she was tryin' to wink at Russ but he acted like he didn't notice.

"Hi, Russ."

"Hi, Carol."

Seemed like neither one of 'em knew what to say next so they both grabbed for somethin' an' started talkin' at the same time.

"What you doin' sittin' here—"

"How you been behavin', Carol—"

"Go ahead."

"Nah, you go ahead—ladies first."

"All right—what you doin' sittin' here all by your lonesome?"

"I ain't. I'm with my ole buddy here."

"Him?!"

"He's just the D.A.'a the whole goddam county's all . . . !"

"That . . . ?!"

"Sure—me'n him's ole buddies from way back."

"Don't you think somebody ought to . . . help him out a little?"

"The D.A.s' all right—just takin'a little snooze's all."

"Least we can do is take his face outta—"

"You keep your hands off my husband!"

"Sorry lady, I just thought—"

"Slut!"

"Carol, this here's Mrs. . . . ah, the D.A.'s wife—Mrs. D.A., this is Carol Gore."

Carol let the D.A.'s face sink back into the Drambuie.

"Pleased to meet'chou."

The D.A.'s wife just humphed an' pulled her chain'a minks up tighter around her neck.

"Carol, ah, maybe you'd rather stand on the other side'a me. . . ."

Russ leaned in close an' whispered in Carol's ear leastways what he thought was a whisper.

". . . they're drunk."

"No kiddin'. Looks to me like you've had a few yourself."

"Couple."

"Where's Cathy?"

"Right where she's s'posed to be."

"What'sa matter—you two on the outs?"

"You might say that."

"What happened?"

"Cathy's leavin' me."

"Russ . . . you're kiddin' . . . !"

"Ain't. She's . . . hung up with somebody else."

"Cathy?"

"Yup. Some English faggot over to the school."

"I don't believe it. . . ."

"Hell, its' been goin' on for a long time—why'd you s'pose she took that job in the first place?"

"Why . . .I thought . . . just to help out. . . ."

"You sayin' I can't support my own wife . . . ?!"

"Of course not, Russ—"

"Of course not! Well, you just better bet your sweet ass I can—"

"Please, Russ, not so loud—"

"You just ask the D.A. here what I'm makin'—go ahead, ask 'im?!"

"Russ, I know you're doin' fine, Russ—"

"You just better believe it—2000 acres'a the best goddam land in West Ghent—"

"Sure, you have, Russ, everybody knows—"

"Eight thousand head! Black Angus! Hell, I got cows I ain't hardly ever seen!"

"I know you have, Russ, please, Russ—"

"Give us a round here—give 'em all a round! Buddy, buy the house a drink!"

"Russ, please—"

"Buddy!"

"Russ, Buddy isn't here."

"Where'd he go—where'd that ole woman go?! Back there whisperin' in Nick'n Andy's ear, that's where he is —spreadin' lies about me!"

"Russ, Buddy's gone home—it's after midnight—"

"Midnight? Hell, I gotta get to the mill!"

"Russ, sit down—"

" 'Fore it closes—"

"Russ, you can't drive—"

"What'a'ya mean, I can't drive?!"

Carol leaned in real close to his ear Russ could feel her hot breath hear the whispery voice talkin' fast'n low.

"Russ, you want me to go along with you, do something real . . . nice for you?"

"Yeah."

"Then sit down, real nice'n quiet . . . I'll go along with you . . . see you get home . . . safe."

"Promise?"

"Promise."

Russ sat back down.

"You gonna drive?"

"Yeah, I'll drive. What's so funny?"

"I got the truck—with a load on. . . ."

"So? I drove it once before."

"By God, you did, didn't you . . . ? Nice warm night, wasn't it Carol?"

"Yeah, Russ . . . a real nice warm night."

"On the grass."

She didn't answer.

"Won't be quite so warm tonight, Carol. Ain't no grass neither. Think you can take it in a snowbank?"

She spoke low but her voice wasn't so whispery no more.

"One more remark like that, Russ Simpson, just one more . . . you'll be twice as cold in that truck."

"Aw, c'mon, Carol, I was only kiddin'—have another drink . . . Buddy—"

"Russ, Andy's looking over."

She started talkin' low'n fast again.

"Look, Russ, you've had enough—remember what happened that one time you had too much to drink—"

"Yeah, I couldn't get it up—"

"Shhhh. I gotta go, Andy's gettin' suspicious—"

"But you said—"

"Don't worry, I'll meet you. Now you let me go back to the reception for a few minutes—give me time to say a few good-byes—but you go right out to your truck the minute I leave, just set in it, get the motor running, warm it up a little . . . I'll slip out the side door an' meet you there."

She started to leave but Russ reached out an' grabbed her arm.

"You don't know where I'm parked."

She had to grin a little at that herself.

"Across the highway—way in back. I already checked it out."

Russ waited till she'd gone through the slidin' foldin' door then he stood up real casual like figgerin' he'd stretch a little maybe even yawn let everybody know he'd had it was headin' straight home for bed but the heel'a his boot caught on the rung'a the stool an' he almost went to his knees managed to catch the ridge'a the bar with his hands hold hisself up just collected his things an' stuffed them in his pockets.

Outta the corner'a his eye he could see Andy watchin' him. Now Andy strolled over.

"Russ, I'm proud'a you."

"Hell, she's no big deal—"

"Nah, I mean gettin' outta here so early—hell, you ain't even started no fights or busted up any furniture yet."

"I kin stay a little longer if you want, Andy—"

"No, no thanks, Russ."

Andy pulled out his big roll an' peeled off a twenty an' slipped it across the bar to Russ.

"Tell you what I'm gonna do, Russ—for you bein' such a good fellow, stickin' to your end'a the deal—here's your twenty back."

Russ picked up the twenty an' slapped it back down on the bar speakin' up nice'n loud so the bad breath Doc an' Grasshopper Fats an' the rest'a the D.A.'s crowd was bound to hear.

"Give my crowd here'a drink, Andy . . . keep the change."

Russ turned away from the bar before Andy had a chance to let go what was buildin' in his face an' gave the snorin' D.A. a good jolt to the shoulder.

"Keep your nose clean, ole buddy."

It was colder'n hell outside twice as cold in the truck. The cold air seemed to clear his head a little he had a quick jolt said somethin' about startin' the truck drivin' right home Cathy'd have the bed all nice'n warmed-up but then he started to shake so he started 'er up an' turned the heater on decided he better warm up a little before tryin' the drive home.

It had been nice'n warm in Arizona. Too warm. No fit weather for a white man to be playin' football in—not that that was it he could'a made it big no matter how hot it was if he'd'a just felt like it.

He hadn't felt right down there from the start. Hell they don't even have no decent country to look at it wasn't even green in the summertime 'ceptin' a little dinky patch here'n there they keep pumpin' water on shit in all the while he was there he never did see one oak tree or maple nothin' but those scrawny little palm trees with a little bitty tuft on top looked like a telephone pole with a Dennis the Menace hairdo.

Man they could keep that desert so far as he was concerned. Everybody comin' down there oohin' an' ahin' about how beautiful it all was all them beautiful mountains shit a mountain ain't nothing but a big pile'a rocks beautiful cactus beautiful sand shit yeah they had sand all right sand in their teeth in their beds he never would forget the time after the team barbecue he tried to put the blocks to one'a the pom-pom girls out in the desert someplace between Buckeye an' Apache Junction man he like to ground his down to a raw bleedin' pulp hate to think what hers musta felt like it ain't no joke gettin' a ream job with sand they finally had to give it up it was hurtin' her so bad.

An' that coach was somethin' else again. Wasn't a bit like Clyde. Mean little fellow didn't much more'n come up to Russ's shoulder probably never amounted to a pinch'a shit as a player hisself Russ always figgered that's why he wanted them to be so great.

Man he was a slave driver. Russ could see it comin' right off the bat he barely got down there hadn't even had a chance to rinse off put on some dry clothes he was all hot'n sweaty from comin' out on the bus from Phoenix 'course he'd been sweatin' a little on the plane comin' down from Albany first time he'd ever been on a plane funny thing it was nice'n cool on the plane but he was sweatin' anyway then the plane landed at Sky Harbor he stepped out through the door down that little ramp he didn't notice it right off the bat he was still lookin' back tryin' to see if the stewardess had her eye on him too but she wasn't then it hit him like to put him right to his knees shit man it was hot. Hundred'n ten in the shade if it was an ounce hot an' there weren't no shade he could see 'ceptin' a few'a those Dennis the Menace telephone poles over along the big woven wire sheep fence they had strung all around the airport heat bouncin' up off the concrete runway the airport buildin's he was walkin' toward startin' to shimmer'n shake he felt a little dizzy felt like turnin' and runnin' right back up that ramp to Albany catchin' the first bus headin' down to Iola.

But he didn't. He just set down his imitation alligator suitcase stood there lookin' around a little. Stood there halfway between the airplane an' the gate the rest'a the other passengers had already gone through. Just stood there lookin' around not really seein' nothin' least nothin' he could put a fix on just lookin' around shiftin' now'n then from one foot to the other when the hot asphalt got to burnin' up through the sole'a his blue suede shoes he'd got on sale at Pop Harrington's to go with the old gray flannel suit an' royal blue silk shirt somebody had donated. Just stood there lookin' around.

Then he picked hisself up walked through that gate got on that bus marked *Tempe—Arizona State* rode it till it got there when it did there was that mean little coach waitin' never even give Russ a chance to find out where he was bunkin' maybe rinse off a little change into a pair'a Levi's short-sleeved shirt or nothin' just told him to get his ass over to the stadium they was havin' a team meetin'.

Man that mean little coach was some gung-ho. He started right off the bat at that meetin' he never let up so long as Russ was there. Hell he didn't give a shit if it was a hundred'n twenty in the middle of a sandstorm a player had three broken legs he said hit the field that player hit the field—Russ had to say one thing for him though he won ball games yeah he won ball games all right.

He never would forget that first meetin'. It wasn't a bit like the ones Clyde used to have ever'body laughin' grab-assin' around makin' little jokes about Clyde behind his back hell sometimes Clyde would even catch them at it laugh right along with them not this guy the minute he walked in shut the door behind 'im all them big guys hell most of 'em outweighed that mean little coach by a hundred pounds or better come jumpin' to their feet they didn't sit back down neither till he told them to.

Then he started in. Things were gonna be different around there now they hadn't done worth a shit the year before they had lost one game an' that was one game too many what'a'ya think this is some kinda country club we're gonna hit this year boys an' after we hit we're gonna stomp an' after we stomp we're gonna grind an' so on an' on an' on Russ couldn't remember everything he said but he could still remember the feeling in the room an' the feeling in him he didn't much like either one an' he didn't like that mean little coach at all that much he knew for sure.

All he kept thinkin' was what the hell was he doin' there.

An' then meetin' all the other ballplayers. There was so many of 'em hell there must'a been a hundred most of 'em bigger'n Russ from all those big city schools High School All-Americans varsity guys who'd lettered two-three years already hell some of 'em Russ had even read about in the *Times-Journal* ever'body said Mackey the quarterback was sure to make All-American that year.

He had felt kinda . . . small. Sure he was 6'2"-210 he'd been workin' with the weights all summer buildin' up his chest an' shoulders wore a size 46 jacket 32-inch waist ever'body said he looked like Lil' Abner blond hair fallin' down over his forehead leg muscles bulgin' through his Levi's that come from runnin' up an' down the stairway of bales he'd stacked up to the rafters in the hayloft runnin' behind the cows when he went to bring them in for milkin' ole Orville Dibdahl the foreman woulda liked to kick his ass for that if he dared hell that summer he never walked a step if he had a chance to run by the time he hit Arizona he could do the hundred in ten flat in pads never even break a sweat.

But he still felt kinda small.

Then that first day'a basics. They were out on the small practice field behind the stadium just runnin' some drills it was 110 in the shade as usual all they had on was gym shorts 'cept the butterballs they was in sweatsuits some'a the blimps even had on the rubberized jobs the mean little coach had split them into different color teams Russ was on the red one he wore a red T-shirt said ARIZONA STATE ATHLETIC DEPT. across the front he really thought he was hot shit till he fumbled the first hand-off he had a crack at.

The mean little coach blew his whistle hard even the whistle sounded mean. Ever'body stopped in their tracks Russ had his head down he didn't see him comin' but he knew he was he could feel him gettin' closer nobody sayin' a word fifty-sixty men out there not a sound closer closer fifty-sixty men not a sound closer closer now Russ could hear cleats scuffin' the turf now he felt the kick.

He almost went down. He had been standin' there kinda humped over he wasn't expectin' no kick in the ass he almost went down.

Then he heard the laugh. At first there was a kinda suckin' in'a breath then there wasn't no sound at all then came the laugh.

Just here'n there at first kinda a titter here'n there first one then the other kinda jumpin' from one part'a the practice field to another more'n more—. .

"Shut up!" The sound roared loud in the cab for a second there Russ thought that mean little coach was right there in the truck with him then he realized who it was said it.

"Next one who laughs gets his ass kicked too."

The little bastard meant it too 'course he didn't have too much to worry about wasn't likely anybody was gonna take him up on it the rest of 'em was there on a scholarship too all he had to do was point a finger they'd all be back on that Tempe-Arizona State bus headin' the other direction.

So nobody laughed again then. They all stood stock still fifty-sixty men not a sound not even shiftin' from one foot to the other Russ could hear the doves cooin' up under the stadium roof somebody practicin' on a cornet in one'a the

houses across the highway sounded like maybe the guy
oughta switch to drums—

"Where'd you ever learn to play ball, boy?"

It took a second for Russ to figger out he was talkin' to
him there was fifty-sixty men there but he was talkin' to
him standin' there lookin' up at Russ holdin' the football
Russ had fumbled in one hand lookin' up at Russ straight
in the eye.

Russ couldn't tell him. He could feel the pain over his
heart runnin' around down under his left arm the pressure inside his head pushin' against the back side'a his
eyeballs the wet inside his mouth his throat dry the
buzzin' in his ears . . . but he couldn't tell him.

"I said where the hell'd you ever learn to play ball, boy?
Whoever taught you to take a hand-off like that?"

Russ couldn't tell him.

"Look at me, boy—don't give me that ostrich act—
where'd you go to high school?"

"I . . . I . . . can't . . . remember."

"You puttin' me on, boy . . . ? You are, next time my
boot don't just tickle your ass, it ends up between your
shoulder blades—"

"Honest, I can't . . . remember . . . I promise—"

"He can't remember—you hear that, boys, har har this
little dodo bird here can't remember where he went to
high school har har—"

Now the rest of 'em had the signal they could laugh too
so they did.

"Har har—here, I got a hard one for you, boy—what's
your name? Think you can handle that one?"

"Russ . . . ah ah Russ Simpson ah Junior."

"Well, well. Very good, Mr. Russ Simpson, Junior—with
that startling bit of genius, that intellectual tour de force,
you have passed the entrance exam to Arizona State, you
have passed your football boards with honors."

Everybody was laughin' hard now everything he said

they laughed harder it seemed like to Russ they all wanted to make sure the coach heard them laughin'.

"Tell me, Jooouunnyur, did your mother ever have any children?"

"I ain't got no . . . mother."

The coach looked at Russ a little while longer just looked at Russ seemed to Russ like now it was the coach's eyes kept slippin' down toward the ground the rest'a the team tried to laugh but it came out kinda strained so they dropped off one after another now only one big tackle from Hoboken was laughin' Zuzu Zuhowski they called him Russ found out about him later caught him out at the Palms truck stop cleaned his ass for him good.

"Shut up, Zuzu."

Zuzu did.

"All right, you dodos, get at it—same drill, run it again."

The coach started away but he hadn't gone more'n a few steps when he came back to Russ still standin' there in the same spot slammed the football back in his middle Russ's hands automatically dropped down to take the hand-off.

"You better sign yourself up for one'a those English tutorin' deals, boy—you don't talk worth a shit."

Then he blew that mean whistle'a his started across the field after somebody else.

It wasn't just that. Sure that was part of it that kinda thing but it was more the . . . feelin'—that sorta . . . empty . . . lost feelin'—like he was on the field all the resta the players all around laughin' jokin' grab-assin' sayin' little things dint mean a shit . . . so he would say something too somethin' kinda funny he thought . . . but they never seemed to hear his just laughed right by his to the next guy's lookin' right past him to hear what Fran Kraus was sayin' even givin' him that "shut up, Fran's sayin' somethin' " look that look that said "yeah you're here but not really an' we'd just as soon you weren't" an' so did he.

But he kept on tryin'. Man he laughed ever' time Fran opened his mouth sometimes even before he did got so he never opened his mouth 'cept to laugh at somebody else's jokes. An' he grab-assed. Man he grab-assed anytime anyplace you name it baby he'd grab-ass he didn't give a shit if he was fallin' down tired one'a the boys wanted to grab-ass all he had to do was give Russ the word. An' he ran for Cokes. An' he stood in chow lines shit he'd be in that breakfast line afore that beastly Arizona sun ever showed over the telephone-pole palms all Fran or Mackey had to do was roll out five to seven an' stroll down there Russ'd have a place saved for 'em right there by the chow hall door.

He even stole for 'em—for Lucky. Course he didn't really steal he just did it on a dare that ain't the same as stealing. Shit yeah Lucky the captain on the defense had to have that pair'a cordovans for the sorority ball or whatever the hell it was Sally Lasher invited him to in Joe Bellow's window but he didn't have the gelt but he really had to have 'em Sally was just about the richest girl in school pretty too if you don't mind thick ankles but they didn't bother Lucky he was apeshit over her thick ankles maybe the rest'a Sally too her old man's thick checkbook for sure.

So Russ got 'im the cordovans. They was all laughin' around one night grab-assin' about how Lucky could go to the ball if he only had them shoes it just popped outta his mouth, "You got any balls you'd go after 'em, Lucky."

"What'aya mean, go after 'em?"

"Steal 'em."

"Shit, who could lift a pair'a shoes right outta his shoe window?"

"I could."

"Yeah, I bet."

Bet.

It wasn't easy. He hung around that shoe store so long before he finally got 'em Joe musta thought Russ was workin' for 'im. Got so Russ almost thought he was—it was like goin' to a job, ever' day after classes he'd run back to Irish Hall Jockstrap Jungle the civilians called it throw his books in his room head for Joe Bellow's shoe store.

He finally got 'em. He had to it was Friday the day before the ball Lucky was already startin' to polish on his old loafers didn't look none too happy about it neither.

There wasn't really nothin' to it. Joe just walked back in the stock room an' Russ just walked out the front door with the cordovans under his arm no box or nothin'.

Lucky couldn't believe his eyes when Russ handed 'em to him. He couldn't believe the size neither when he went to try them on shit Russ just took the cordovans in the window those'r the ones Lucky said he liked they was size 8 Lucky wore 13 shit he shoulda he weighed 265.

Nothin' Russ could do but take 'em back an' exchange 'em. Man he didn't wanna but there was nothin' else he could do Lucky was countin' on 'em now for the ball with Sally besides "what's the big deal takin' back a pair'a shoes an' exchangin' 'em once you already got 'em?"

Wasn't nothin' he could answer to Lucky on that so he took the shoes an' headed back down to Joe Bellow's shit he didn't even have no box they was s'posed to come in hell what was he gonna tell Joe?

Wasn't nothin' he could. Joe already knew. He'd stood back there in the stock room an' watched Russ take 'em through his peephole.

"You must'a needed a new pair'a shoes pretty bad, Russ."

"Yeah, I guess I did, Joe."

"One'a the sorority girls invite you to the ball tomorrow night?"

Guess Joe knew most ever'thing went on up there at the school had Russ figgered all along.

"Yeah."

"You didn't have to steal 'em, Russ."

"I guess . . . I needed 'em pretty bad."

Joe took the shoes from Russ an' put 'em back on their little stand in the window.

"I'd'a given 'em to ya."

"Yeah . . . ?"

"Yeah."

Joe just kept arrangin' them shoes this way an' that seemed like he wanted to make sure they was showin' just right.

"Still will . . . if you need 'em that bad."

"I . . . need 'em pretty bad all right."

"Better get a pair your size then—be a long night dancin' in those."

Joe was lookin' down at Russ's feet so Russ jumped in fast.

"Thirteens."

"Thirteens . . . ?!"

"Yeah . . . Thirteens."

"Yeah . . . looked to me like about 'levens."

"Yeah, people'r always sayin' my feet look smaller'n they are."

"Yeah . . . ?"

Joe turned an' headed back into the stock room Russ angled closer to the door so he'd be able to get goin' soon as Joe handed him the shoes.

Joe was carryin' his measurin' gizmo when he come back.

"Russ, you just set down there a second I'll—"

"Joe, kin I have my shoes?"

"Sure. I said so, didn't I?"

Russ took the box out of Joe's hands.

"Thanks a million, Joe, I won't ever forget this honest

. . . see, I gotta run now, ah, Sally, see she's my date, ah, she's waitin' for me."

Russ ran out the door. Joe was a good guy. Musta liked football pretty good too Russ always saw 'im around after the games far as Russ knew Joe never mentioned a word to anybody about the shoes just smiled an' gave Russ a little wink whenever he saw him.

After that he didn't try so hard to be one'a the boys. Got so that didn't bother him much anymore anyway hell he didn't have time to waste thinkin' about that he got to missin' Cathy so hard.

God he got to missin' her. Got to be a pain he could put his hand right on a pain the same as though somebody was punchin' him over'n over right there below his Adam's apple kept punchin' him over'n over till the pain an' the lump got bigger'n bigger an' colder'n colder . . . he could still feel it right now.

She'd always been the only one he could ever really talk to about anythin' that meant anythin'. Like all the things he was gonna do when he got through college an' got to be a lawyer'n ever'thin'. How he used to stand there when he was just a kid on the Farm standin' there barefoot an' raggedy in the pickle-patch watchin' the new cars go by figgerin' out which one he'd buy when he was a lawyer'n all one'a those new Buicks maybe even a Cadillac convertible like that rich guy from the city's got a summer place over by Long Lake Les Cohen trades in for a new one ever' two years shit the old one wouldn't even'a lost the new smell yet Russ knew that for a fact use'ta go over there ever' Saturday wash all his cars hell he'd have five-six of 'em all at the same time use'ta give Russ fifty cents a car shit he could afford it people said he was at least a multimillionaire.

Yeah, he could tell her anythin'. Talk about anythin' he felt like. She wasn't a bit stuck-up like some'a the girls from town. He didn't have to always watch what he was sayin' when he was with her tryin' to always think'a somethin' to say didn't remind them where he lived—hell, sometimes when he knew he was gonna be talkin' to one'a the other girls he'd go ahead an' think'a somethin' beforehand and make sure he'd have so much to talk about they'd never have a chance to think like maybe somethin' from Current Events or the big game comin' up or somethin'.

Cathy was never like that though. Hell he'd have a helluva time gettin' her off the subject. Seemed like all she ever wanted to talk about was what it was like livin' on the Farm how it felt not to have real parents tellin' you what to do did they really work the boys as hard as people said did they get enough to eat did it really bother him havin' to wear clothes other people wore before did he really get whipped with a harness strap if he didn't do what he was s'posed to?

Things like that. Man she was full'a questions—they'd be sittin' there in her little car the motor runnin' the heater makin' it nice'n cozy he'd be tryin' to put the make on her a little not too strong but a little about the way she liked it pretty soon she'd come poppin' up right in the middle of a big smooch to ask him if he'd gotten enough to eat for supper?

"Sure. Why, am I actin' weak tonight?"

Cathy laughed her little giggly laugh.

"You'd act the same if you never ate. What'd you have tonight?"

"You. On toast."

"C'mon, be serious."

"I dunno—the usual, meat, potatoes, vegetable—"

"What kind of meat?"

"I dunno, some kinda pork, I guess."

"Couldn't you even tell?"

"It was in some kinda gravy."

"Oh. Doesn't sound very appetizing."

"It was all right."

"Russ . . . are you sure?"

"Sure I'm sure—hell, I had three helpings. . . ."

She didn't say nothin' for a minute or so just sat there lookin' out through the windshield at the dark he could see her face it was lit up a little from the radio light he could see she was thinkin' hard she was bitin' on the corner of her lip.

"Russ, do me a favor . . . promise me . . ."

Now she turned to look right at him.

". . . if there ever are times you don't get enough to eat I want you to come right up to me and tell me."

He couldn't help but laugh there was such a serious look on her pretty little face her little button nose quiverin' in the air her jaw stuck out ready to take on the world.

"Hell, I get plenty to eat—Christ, I'm almost the biggest guy in school, ain't I?"

"Well, you don't have to swear about it. . . ."

Russ could see her feelin's were hurt he figgered it must be about the swearin'.

"Look, I'm sorry about that swearin'a mine . . . I'll try to watch it a little better."

Her nose was still flarin' out a little on the sides so he kept on talkin'.

"Hey, Cathy, I . . . I ah . . . 'preciate it an' all you're worryin' about me'n all . . . but iffen you don't mind . . . I'd 'preciate it just as much you don't. See ah, I get plenty to eat . . . an' them kinda questions don't jest . . . set too right with me—iffen you know what I mean."

She laughed a little then shook her head a little then laughed a little more harder this time then turned her face back toward his he could see it again in the radio light it was nice'n soft'n pretty now just the way he liked it.

"Russ Simpson, when are you ever going to learn to speak English?"

He just sat there lookin' at her happy to see her face like that but he didn't laugh or nothin' just sat there lookin' at her.

"Maybe you best come over here an' learn me a little."

She didn't laugh that time just started crawlin' over toward him that other look he liked so well on her face—

"Slide over."

The door beside him whipped open the one he'd been leanin' against an' he almost fell out woulda if he hadn't got hold'a the steering wheel just in time.

Somebody was standin' out there. Somebody tryin' to push him over, talkin' in a fast whisper—

"C'mon, Russ, slide over—hurry up, before somebody turns on their lights an' sees me!"

Then he remembered it was Carol comin' just like she said she would so he slid over from behind the steering wheel an' she climbed up in the driver's seat.

Just before she pushed in the clutch an' dropped 'er into low she looked over at Russ.

"You sure you want to go?"

"Roll 'er."

Yeah, that was one'a the big things down at Arizona State not havin' Cathy to talk to. Hell, if a man ain't got his girl to talk to about all the big things he's gonna do someday then it ain't quite so easy to get 'em done.

Seemed like nowdays he couldn't talk to her no more about a lotta things. Not that it was her who couldn't do no listenin' it was him who couldn't do no talkin'.

Carol drove pretty damn good for a woman. She didn't fool around just went ahead an' whipped 'er in an' outta gear shiftin' down on the upgrades shiftin' up on the downgrades holdin' her steady on the level.

Russ was feelin' kinda funny. He couldn't tell for sure

if he was drunk or not. Sometimes it felt like he was his mind kept wantin' to slide off go someplace else maybe back to Arizona then again to high school zoom away to some little piddly thing happened way back on the Farm now an' then home even here'n there almost everywhere so long as it wasn't in the truck.

Almost everywhere. But in the almost time it was here in the truck an' then he felt cold sober. Then he knew who he was an' where he was an' who was sittin' over there behind the wheel. An' where they was goin' an' what they was goin' to do when they got there.

Then his mind would slide away again. He'd feel drunk again. Only this time it didn't go so far kinda stayed halfway between the almost an' the everywhere.

First time he ever nailed 'er was on the football field. First time he ever nailed anybody for real. If he could call it that he barely got it up against her pumped a couple'a times before he blew all over her skirt she didn't even get mad just went ahead an' wiped it off with her hanky then laid back down on the grass took his head in her arms kinda pressin' his head up against her tits kinda rockin' his head back'n forth kinda hummin' a little way down deep in her throat.

Yeah, he guessed he could count that first one. He'd got the head of it there once that much he knew for a fact that's what made him blow the minute he knew that baby was goin' in that's all she wrote.

Christ he'd liked to'a pissed his pants he was so scar't. Not when he blew he wasn't thinkin'a much'a anythin' right then not even when she was sittin' up wipin' it off he was still too busy congratulatin' hisself yet it was after they was layin' back down her kinda rockin' his head against her tits when it hit 'im what the hell happened to his rubber?!

How the hell could he blow all over her her skirt too when he had his rubber on?

He reached down real slow'n careful like so she wouldn't know what he was doin' . . . his hand hit somethin' mighty wet'n slimy . . . sure felt like his own . . . sure couldn't feel nothin' that felt like rubber . . . there was the ring the ring was still there that's all there was the sonuvabitch had bust . . . !

Then the real doozy hit him.

What if he'd got some in her . . . ?!

Shit he musta. No way he couldn't.

Shit man he'd knocked her up!

Then his mind came joltin' back in the truck there was Carol jes' drivin' along pretty as you please shit she wasn't knocked up he could see that much even in the light from the dashboard.

That first one was really somethin' though. She was workin' at the K an' L restaurant then. He couldn't'a been more'n fifteen sixteen at the most hell he was only fifteen it was in the early fall fair time he wouldn't be sixteen till January fourth he was going to be a sophomore that fall.

She musta been already close to twenty or better. . . .

He opened his eyes an' peeked over at Carol he wondered just how old she really was hell he never could tell about a woman he shut his eyes back down again.

. . . Yeah, maybe better she'd already been outta school a few years by then he'd gone in the library one time looked 'er up in one'a the old yearbooks seemed to him now he'd figgered then she musta been five-six years older probably still was hell he was startin' to feel drunker again anyway he couldn't figger out what she saw in somebody as young as him what with all them older guys chasin' her ass all over town but she picked him.

Yeah she picked him. Came right up to him an' asked him one day. He was just sittin' there tryin' to suck the last suck'a Coke outta the ice meltin' in the bottom'a his glass when she come up an' leaned across the counter to him all the while makin' like she was cleanin' up some dirty dishes an' asked him.

"Russ, would you like to meet me after work tonight?"

"Meet . . . you . . . Carol . . . ?"

She smiled a little at him just the corners of her mouth kinda crinkled.

"Yes . . . meet . . . me . . . Russ." . . . .

"Well, say . . . say, I don't . . . really know, Carol—I mean, I gotta go back out to the Farm an' help with chores."

He said the last like he was really hot to get back out there an' git with them chores. The corners of her mouth crinkled an' she mocked him again.

"Then you just better not meet me."

Russ could feel his ole tillywhiz start to move lookin' around for'a little stretchin' space he could feel it then an' he could feel it now.

" 'Course maybe I could hurry up . . . an' get 'em done. . . ."

She didn't smile this time just hurried up an' picked up the rest'a her dishes seemed like she was in quite a hurry now an' when she spoke her voice had that whispery sound.

"I'll pick you up at the Farm—where your road turns in off the highway. You know where I mean?"

"Yeah."

"Will you be there?"

"Yeah."

"Nine?"

"Yeah."

She picked up her tray'a dirty dishes an' headed for the kitchen never even looked back or smiled or winked or nothin' just headed for the kitchen with that tray'a dirty dishes.

Russ stood up looked around a few times to see if anybody was watchin' shrugged his left shoulder a few times real casual-like like maybe he had a little crick there or somethin' even rolled his neck a couple'a times like it had crawled up there too an' walked out on the sidewalk stood there for a couple minutes lookin' up an' down the street like he wasn't none too sure just exactly which direction he'd be goin' then finally started walkin' down main street toward the highway leadin' out to the Farm.

Wasn't until he'd cleared the highway intersection he realized he still had the Coke glass in his hand straw'n all.

First thing he did when he got home was get his rubber on. He kept it hid behind a loose stone in the foundation of the barn he could practice putting it on there had it down to seven seconds flat twelve with one hand the way he figgered it most'a the time one would be all a guy would have to work with he'd be holdin' her down with the other 'course Carol looked like a two-hand job. He took some udder disinfectant washed it out extra clean checked it over real close for tears he even filled it with water to make sure it didn't leak no way that baby could'a had a hole in it when he put it on.

He felt better after he got it on. Least now he was ready. Weren't no doubt in his mind she had to be one'a those nympho whores like Pete was always talkin' about he wanted to be damn sure he was protected in case she happened to jump him right off the bat soon as he got in the car 'fore he had a chance to get his rubber out of his billfold get his tillywhiz out get it on he'd practiced so much it didn't roll up nice'n tight like it did when he first bought it off Terry Franzer hell knowin' him he'd probably used it a few times hisself 'fore he sold it to Russ hell how would he go about puttin' it on in front of a woman anyway even a nympho whore like Carol did he just say excuse me go ahead put it on what would she be doin' while he was?

Still he damn near chickened out though. All through chores an' supper he was thinkin' about what he had layin' ahead'a him what he'd probably be goin' through before that night was over.

Maybe he wouldn't'a gone at all if the Ox hadn't come along. Shit once Russ told him about the deal he couldn't'a kept him home with a two-by-four. Ox was a couple'a years older he'd really been around had his rubber on ready'n waitin' in nothin' flat wore his all through milkin' an' supper too.

They was out there an' waitin' by 8:30. Carol was a little bit early herself.

She seemed a hair surprised to see Ox along. Didn't say nothin' about it though till after they'd both hopped in the backseat Russ got his side scraped on the door latch both tryin' to squeeze in back at the same time an' were headin' down the highway.

"You goin' in to the fair, Ox?"

"What fair?"

Ox's voice seemed awful loud there in the backseat seemed like he jumped up off the seat a little when she said his name. Russ could see Carol flick a look at them in the rearview mirror he couldn't see if there was that little crinkling around her mouth or not he didn't think so though her voice sounded kinda tight.

"How many fairs we got around here?"

"Oh, the fair . . . !"

Ox didn't say no more finally Carol flicked another look in the mirror.

"Well . . . ?"

"Nah."

Nobody said nothin' more Carol just kept on drivin' didn't even look in the rearview no more Russ hadn't said word one yet started to figger it was about time.

"Ox kinda thought . . . see, Ox kinda thought. . . ."

"I hope he didn't strain himself."

"No, no he just kinda thought . . . it might be nice to ride along."

"Really."

"Yeah."

Ox musta figgered Russ could use a little help Russ could feel him give one'a his little shrugs like he always did before he talked. "I don't mind."

"Possibly someone else might."

"Nah, Russ don't mind neither—hell, he was the one asked—"

Russ's poke with his elbow got him stopped in time Russ figgered it might be a good idea to change the subject a little.

"Nice night, ain't it?"

"Lovely."

Things weren't goin' a bit like they figgered hell all she kept doin' was drivin' straight ahead down 9H lookin' straight ahead out through the windshield shit they'd driven by three-four side roads plenty'a empty fields she could'a pulled in any one of 'em but she didn't just kept drivin' down 9H lookin' straight ahead not even lookin' for a turnoff Russ could see her face a little from the side in the light from the dash seemed like her face looked kinda funny kinda wild kinda sad kinda lonely all at the same time.

Funny thing even though she wasn't doin' nothin' to make it happen just them looks on her face Russ could feel his dong start to stiffin up fightin' with his Levi's shit he should'a put on his dress pants Dale give him they was still a little big for him—

She whipped that big old Pontiac Silver Chief right around in the middle'a the highway U-turnin' so tight them old worn-out shocks on the low side set down flat on the springs the tires squealin' all the way around for a minute there Russ thought sure she was goin' to roll 'er.

She didn't. Rocked 'er a few times from side to side but then she got 'er straightened out an' runnin' hard down 9H only now straight back the way they come!

He finally got hisself untangled off the top of Ox all Ox kept sayin' was "hey! . . . hey!" Russ couldn't think'a much more hisself Carol she wasn't sayin' nothin' just drivin' hard.

Finally Russ kinda leaned over the seat toward Carol restin' his arms on the back'a her seat.

"You're headin' back . . . the same way you come."

Ox joined him leanin' on the back'a her seat only on the other side'a her Russ couldn't help but think'a two crows he'd seen in the orchard once both perched on the same branch both reachin' as far as their necks could go peckin' away on both sides'a the same cherry neither one of 'em got it he felt his hard-on drop like that cherry.

"Yeah, you're headin' back . . . the same way you come."

"How come?"

"Yeah, how come?"

Russ couldn't tell what the look on her face meant now.

"I'm no twins."

"What'a'ya mean, Carol?"

"Yeah, what'a'ya mean, Carol?"

"Just what I said. I'm no twins."

Russ knew what she meant but it was Ox who said it out loud.

"You mean you don't wanna take us both on, Carol?"

Russ could see Ox's comin' right out an' sayin' it like that hurt her pretty good her head kinda jolted back a little an' she tried to pull herself up a little straighter when she answered but it didn't work too good Russ could'a beaned Ox that big dumb bunny never did have no couth at all.

"I dont' remember ever sayin' I was gonna . . . take either one of you . . . on."   . .

She didn't say it mad more sad. Russ was startin' to feel a little sorry for her right now he mighta just let 'er go forgot about the whole thing but Ox just kept right on peckin' away he musta still had his hard-on the more he talked the more Russ could see that cherry droppin' away 'course this one wasn't exactly a cherry neither she still had the box it come in though.

"Hell, you don't have to worry none 'bout me'n Russ sayin' nothin'. We don't ever tell nothin' on nobody, least of all each other. Besides, we always screw together, we got a lotta broads we screw together, shit we always share our broads, I wouldn't think'a gettin' some an' not cuttin' Russ in, neither would he."

She couldn't help but laugh a little at that Russ felt like crawlin' under the seat pullin' it in after him. 'Course she must be nothin' but a nympho whore even to talk to Ox after that.

"You're sure some smooth, Ox. What'a the girls over to the high school call you—Smooth Dog?"

"I get by."

"I'll bet you do—way by."

"Better believe it."

Russ could see Ox was really eatin' it up he figgered he had 'er on the run now when he asked her he was already lookin' out the window checkin' around out there in the moonlight for a likely spot looked to Russ like they was gettin' awful close to home though.

"Well, Carol, what'a'ya say—let's fuck."

Carol just pulled over off the highway a little a few feet down the Farm road just about the same spot she'd picked them up.

Ox didn't even see where they was figgered he had a lock on her leanin' way in across the back'a her seat whisperin' sweet nothin's in her ear Russ figgered they could probably hear 'im way down to the house.

"What'a'ya say, Carol, let's get at it, ain't no point in fiddlin' around you know you wanna I kin hear the way you're breathin' hard you know I got you all hot'n bothered what'a'ya say let's fuck."

Funny thing was she was breathin' kinda hard Russ

could see her tits risin' up an' down more'n they had to
every time she took a breath looked to him she was havin'
quite a time keepin' her voice normal when she answered
couldn't even make her little laugh come out straight.

"Not tonight, Smooth Dog. Time for you Bobbsey Twins
to get tucked in."

"You ain't pronouncin' that quite right, Carol. . . ."

Smooth Dog reached right over that front seat an'
gave Carol's right tit a big squeeze Russ ducked automatically he didn't wanna have his head in the way when
she swung.

". . . you ain't pronouncin' that right atall."

When Russ didn't hear no screams or wild flailin' around
he stuck his head up an' took a peek. By this time Ox had
both his arms around her from behind one hand on both
her tits kinda rollin' them around slow inside her sweater
damnedest thing Carol wasn't doin' nothin' just lookin'
straight ahead her face showin' pale-white in the moonlight comin' through her side window her breathin' deep'n
slow'n heavy when she started to talk Russ wasn't even
sure at first it was her he thought for a minute there some
little girl had crawled in the car there with them.

"What are you doing to me, you big boy you . . . what
kind of a girl do you think I am . . . no, no . . . I'm not
that kind of girl . . . you shouldn't be doing that, I
shouldn't be letting you . . . oh, oh . . . whatever will
you think of me . . . you mustn't, no, no, you mustn't,
I mustn't let you . . . honest, I'm not that kind of a girl
. . . oh, oh . . ."

She just kept goin' on like that in that soft low whispery
little girl's voice lookin' straight ahead out the windshield
like she was talkin' to some guy sittin' out there on the
hood'a her old Silver Chief her face pale in the moonlight
Ox almost standin' up now standin' up as far as he could
his back up against the roof of the car leanin' way over

her from behind his hands workin' up'n down the front'a
her body like pistons first grabbin' high then grabbin'
low then high then low looked to Russ just sittin' there
on the edge'a his seat takin' it all in like Ox figgered hand
speed was the big thing there was three-four spots there
to rub an' he had to hit each one as often as possible makin'
sure not to slight any one of 'em keepin' 'em all about the
same temperature all that steady hand-flailin' musta cost
Ox plenty though sounded like he was about pooped
breathin' hard through his mouth like a horse with the
heaves still his hands didn't slow down none Russ leaned
over the seat a little more he wanted to make sure he had
her hot spots down pat so he'd know where to grab when
his turn come—

"Oooooohhhhhhhh . . . ! Oohhh!

Just that fast Carol's sound changed. Here she'd just
been goin' along sayin' her same old baby-talk things in
her whispery little-girl voice the next thing Russ knew her
sound got about forty years older an' quick's a whistle she
started to move too her body slidin' sideways on the seat
landin' flat on her back her legs flashin' up through the
moonlight streamin' through the window at the same
time her hands whipped up an' grabbed Ox by the shoulders him still leanin' way over the front seat his hands
tryin' to follow her body along still beatin'a tattoo on her
hot spots hell she let out another cat-scratchin' yowl an'
snaked him right over that front seat smack down on top'a
her!

Russ like to shit his pants. Looked like Ox was squeezin'a
little too he let out a howl even louder'n her yowl startin'
thrashin' around in that front seat like he was drownin'
or somethin' workin' like hell just to stay above water her
pullin' him back down again her bare legs vise-locked
'round the small'a his back her hands rip-tearin' away at
his Levi's workin' an' jerkin' away at them like she'd

flipped her gourd both of 'em howlin' an' yowlin' all the while goddamnedest thing Russ ever did see looked like a bronc gone plumb loco tryin' to buck its rider an' undress 'im at the same time the rider tryin' to buck hisself off hangin' onto his pants for dear life all the while.

Man Carol turned out to be some strong woman. Ox was no slouch when it came to muscles he was the arm-bendin' champ'a the whole high school but she whipped him she got his pants pulled down Russ could see his big white ass gleamin' in the moonlight.

Not for long though. Just then Ox gave one last mighty heave broke through her leg-lock snapped open his side door went rollin 'out head over heels on the ground picked hisself up went runnin' stumblin' down the dirt road toward the house all the while tryin' to jerk his Levi's up his ass still gleamin' in the moonlight as he went around the bend.

Guess Carol turned out to be a little more'n the Ox had figgered even for a guy been around as much as him.

At first it got awful quiet there in the car. Then she started to cry.

Actually it was more like wailin'. Those long low wails like a little girl makes when she falls down an' hurts herself.

She musta forgot Russ was still there. When he talked she cut it off like a knife an' when she answered it was in her grown-up voice.

"Don't cry, Carol . . . I'm still here."

"Get outta here."

"No."

"I said get outta here."

"No."

They was quiet for a minute or so she fumbled around for her purse found it took out a hanky an' blew her nose real soft like a girl does when somebody's around.

"You'll run too."

"I don't run from nothin'."

They was quiet for a while again she was lookin' straight ahead out through the windshield again an' when she talked her voice was startin' to get a little whisper again too.

"You sure . . . Russ?"

"Yeah . . . I'm sure . . . Carol."

"Where . . . shall we go?"

He said the first place that popped in his mind.

"The . . . football field."

"You sure you don't want to go to my trailer?"

At first he couldn't tell for sure where the memory ended an' the now began but then he realized he was hearin' her louder now her voice was comin' from outside he was hearin' her with his outside ears an' then he was back in his truck again she was still over there behind the driver's wheel he sat up straighter an' looked around it was real moonlight outside tonight too.

"No . . . the football field."

"How can we . . . do it there—it's all covered with snow."

"In the truck."

She turned in past the stadium cuttin' the lights in case anybody was watchin' pulled on through into the parkin' lot they'd plowed off on the field for the skatin' rink.

She stopped the truck took it outta gear an' set the hand brake. He reached out his arm an' she slid over toward him. He put his arm around her shoulders an' she laid down on the seat. He lifted his body and crawled on top of her. He could feel her motherly body under his. It felt good.

While he screwed her she talked to him in her whispery little-girl voice. He thought about that Hudson game the D.A.'d been talkin' about.

Saturday

HE WOKE up scared. Cold awake scared. Light just breaking through the window the pain over his heart the pressure inside his head the sick taste in his stomach the dry craving mouth clammy sweating skin. Scared.

Wondering where he was scared.

Knowing he had done wrong scared.

Remembering scared.

My god was he still there scared.

Feeling the body next to his scared jumping away from that body scared jumping up off the bed scared feeling around on the floor for his clothes scared scared scared scared—

For a minute there Russ thought he was going to have a heart attack maybe he was already having one his heart started pounding like crazy big thumping hurting pounds the breath swooshin' up outta his body hangin' up there in his throat startin' to feel dizzy man he was stranglin' he couldn't seem to get enough air no matter how hard he tried—

Then he smelled her perfume. Cathy's perfume. He must be home.

Sure he was home. There was the old chair with the blue cushion he sat on every morning when he pulled his boots on. There was the dresser they picked up at the Wogslund auction when they was first married. There was the lamp he sent for to Sears for her birthday one year. Sure he was home.

Hell he had to be Carol didn't even have a house she lived in a trailer shit yeah they hadn't even been in her trailer he'd taken her in the truck he had to be home.

Even so he lifted the shade a couple'a inches enough to let the light come fallin' in on Cathy's face just enough to be sure.

She was sleepin' curled up on her side that almost smile on her face her little hands huggin' his pajamas up against her titties like she always did when he didn't come home huggin' them up against herself so he'd have to wake her up to get them when he finally did come home.

But last night he hadn't took them from her last night he had slept in his clothes hell he couldn't even remember gettin' here.

He'd better get out of there before she wakes up smells Carol on him.

He didn't feel like goin' just yet though funny thing he just felt like standin' there lookin' at her face lookin' at that same face he'd been lookin' at for thirteen, fourteen years now seemed like he just had to keep standin' there lookin' at that face keep lookin' at it an' hopin' she'd never wake up an' see him.

Really see him.

Things seemed real clear now. Real clear like they always did when he'd hung one on an' woke up cold awake the light just breakin' in.

One thing for sure he was no damn good. Rotten clear through. To the core. A goddam phony bullshitter. Drunken bum. Dirty filthy sex fiend. Dumb shit. Stupid fuckin' loser. Liar. Bragger. Mean. Bullheaded. Sewermouth. Chickenshit. Unfaithful. Failure.

Shit he didn't even have the right to stand here lookin' at that face. A face like that shouldn't even be in the same bedroom with somethin' like him.

Yet he couldn't go. Seemed like he just had to hang on to that face. Like there was somethin' in it he needed real bad.

It didn't look a day older. Looked just as young an' pure as that freshman day. Peaceful. Smooth as a baby's ass. Every hair she ever had the same shiny color too. She could come bustin' up outta that bed right now do the sis-boom-bah. Pure. Peaceful. Full'a . . . love.

That face knew where it was.

Why'd he have to go'n drink an' play around when all he wanted to do was get down on his knees an' put his head where his pajamas were?

Then last night came hammerin' back full bore an' he couldn't stand to be in the same room with that face no more.

He was out in the hall an' halfway down the steps to the kitchen before he remembered he was still wearing his good clothes. The hall light was on they kept it on all the time the kid was still afraid of the dark.

Russ went back up the stairs to the hall an 'carefully shut both bedroom doors. Then he took off his clothes an' held them up to the light to see if there was any come on them.

He couldn't find any. There was a little spot near the knee but it looked more like booze maybe some'a the D.A.'s Drambuie darker not chalky white like dried come.

He was startin' to shake a little now. The pain an' the pressure was back again too. His mouth an' throat was suckin' dry cold sweat was startin' to pop his stomach was queasy he needed a drink at least a beer.

But what about his clothes? He couldn't just leave them layin' there in the hall she'd think that was kinda funny might even suspect somethin'.

Nothin' to do but sneak back in her bedroom an' hang them up in the closet. That way he could always tell her if she asked he'd just come in a little late an' took off his good clothes an' hung them up an' went to bed just like normal.

He did. She never woke up just rolled a little more over on his side flung one arm over on his pillow all the while still hangin' on to his pajamas for dear life the almost smile still on her face.

The pajamas! What could he tell her about them she'd wonder why she still had them when she woke up in the mornin' why he hadn't took them from her put them on when he came home!

He really felt whoozy now he couldn't seem to think straight the sweat was poppin' all over cold clammy sweat but his body was burnin' the pain poundin' the pressure pushin' seemed like he could even hear ringin'n buzzin' in his ears ever'time he looked over at her huggin' the pajamas it got worse.

Should he try to slip them away from her? What if she should wake up she usually did what could he tell her it was damn near broad daylight now Dobchek's been closed for hours him standin' there in his shorts'n boots!

He had to do somethin' though. First thing he did was set down on the floor'n take off his boots it wouldn't look quite so goofy him just in his shorts sittin' here on the floor—hell what the hell was he doin' sittin' on the floor?

He got up real careful-like an' crept over to the chair with the blue cushion where he usually took off his boots an' took them off an' set them there under the chair in their regular spot.

Lord now if she woke up he'd just be standin' there in his shorts—would that look right? Didn't he usually take off his shorts too before he pulled his pajamas away from her or did he usually still have them on when he did?

He couldn't think straight he was gettin' dizzy as hell seemed like now he was havin' all kinds'a hot flashes felt like he almost wanted to just set down there on the edge'a the bed beside her an' cry.

But he couldn't do that. That'd be some kind of a sure sign'a something. He had to get a grip on hisself get those pajamas away from her some way without wakin' her up givin' ever'thin' away the last thing in the world he wanted to do was hurt her feelin's.

Man it'd kill her if she ever knew he was layin' up with somebody else why the hell'd he ever have to go an' do it?

He started toward the bed. He started toward the bed then he stopped an' took off his shorts an' started again all the while fightin' down the hot little cries that kept tryin' to get up through his throat fightin' them back all the while he leaned over her an' took the pajamas away from her as gently as he could.

She never woke up. Just once reached out her hand a little like she was tryin' to take them back but he held his breath and her hand dropped back on the cover.

He flung the pajamas on the chair with the blue seat like he usually did when he took them off. He remembered to pull the shade back down before he snuck outta the room.

He was breathin' easier now. He went back down the

stairs through the kitchen to the pantry where he kept his barn clothes an' put them on. It wasn't until he pulled up his Levi's an' felt the cold rough denim against his bare ass that he realized he had no shorts on but he thought to hell with it an' just finished dressing.

He felt better once he got his barn clothes on. Safer. More like he had his hands on things again. Like now there was somethin' he could grab ahold'a.

He went back in the kitchen. He didn't feel like puttin' on a light so he just sat down at the kitchen table watchin' the phony light that comes just before the sunrise come creepin' through the window. The old shed was still out there. Just like it was ever' other mornin'. But now when he tried to look at it his eyes went right past it to the other things.

Maybe he better have one drink—at least a beer or somethin'. Better for her to see the drink in his eyes than the other.

Better for her not to see him at all. Better for her if he took the six-pack to the barn sipped on it a little while he was doin' chores then maybe by the time he came in for breakfast he'd be straightened out enough to fake it through.

But it never did work out that morning. Even though he drank the whole six-pack it didn't seem to help much he couldn't seem to get his mind off the other things.

No, that Saturday morning he never could seem to get straightened out. The first thing he did when he got in the barn was count Cathy's money there was thirty-six bucks missing that set him back a little too. An' when he finished milkin' an' was rinsin' out the milk pails there in the milk house he could see Cathy through the kitchen windows movin' around there by the stove funny thing he felt like cryin' again hell he never even cried when he was a kid. That used to get ole Mrs. Olson so goddam mad when he wouldn't cry one time she broke a broomstick on 'im tryin' to make him but he never did but seemed like lately he could anytime he wanted to if he just let hisself. An' right now he felt like lettin' hisself stand here in the milk house window holdin' a milk pail in his hands watchin' Cathy cookin' breakfast through the kitchen window movin' around real fast in that chipper way'a hers bet a dollar she was even singin' low to herself low so's not to wake the kid maybe even *Those Were the Days, My Friend* she could sing it almost as good as Mary Hopkins. Christ he wanted to sit right down on the coolin' tank an' cry but he didn't he just set that last milk pail upside down the way it was s'posed to be on the driprack an' walked outta the milk house an' got in his ole red truck still sittin' there with the load on from last night an' started 'er up an' gunned 'er right out the driveway.

Gunned 'er right out the driveway right past the house right past the kitchen windows he could see Cathy wavin' like mad outta the corner'a his eye but he kept his head straight ahead made like he didn't see 'er damn near hit a car turnin' onto 9H his eyes seemed to be cloudin' over he didn't see the car comin' too good.

Seemed like he couldn't see nothin' too good right now. They'd been clear's bell when he first woke up but now the whole damn works was cloudin' over again.

One thing he knew for sure though he was goin' to get hot an' do some good things for her before she laid eyes on him again—like get his dirty rotten no-good ass right straight down to the mill to grind feed pay Ole Man Wiff some on his bill better not pay quite so much as he planned last night though or now there wouldn't be enough left to go around to some of the others—that way he'd have something to tell Cathy it wouldn't look so bad when he came pullin' in with'a load'a ground feed he could say he'd decided to get right up an' at it get the feed grindin' outta the way before breakfast besides he wasn't too hungry this mornin' anyway he'd say givin' her a little wink "if you know what I mean" then she'd maybe laugh an' say "I knew you'd stop and have a few" an' he'd say "yah, my truck couldn't get by, they had a big magnet in there" or somethin' kiddin' like that but she'd just laugh again happy he'd just stopped an' had a few happy he hadn't started on a binge like he did most Las' Fridays.

Then they'd laugh an' joke all the way through the rest'a the breakfast. Then when they'd finished that he'd horse around with the kid a little maybe even ask him to get his coat on come along give 'im a hand diggin' out the spreader—

Shit! He'd forgotten to cover the spreader last night! Now the whole damn works'd be frozen solider'n a well-digger's ass in the Klondike. He'd have to get Tommie with his big diesel to pull the whole damn works tractor'n all over to the shop thaw'er out that'd cost eight-ten bucks more maybe fifty if a couple'a seams popped when she froze shit he oughta have his head examined!

He stopped for the crossroad at Dobchek's. There weren't any cars comin' from either way but he stopped anyway.

Maybe he could catch Tommie at Dobchek's. Hell if he was out hittin' it las' night chances are he'd be in there right now suckin' up a few mornin' taps. 'Course Russ hadn't seen 'im las' night but that didn't mean nothin' he could'a been up the road at Skinny's lotta times Tommie'd drink one place one day another place the next.

Yeah, he'd better stop in see if Tommie was there. No point in drivin' over to the shop or callin' if Tommie was out hittin' 'em las' night he'd never get 'im there the mornin' after.

Yeah, he'd better get in there'n catch him early get Tommie out on the job afore he had'a chance to suck up too many he didn't catch Tommie afore he got goin' good they'd never get that spreader outta the snowbank today not to mention fixin' that reduction gear on the tractor probably have to pay a twenty or so on the bill first though.

Yeah, he'd better get right in there he'd sure's hell hate to see that load'a frozen shit sit there all weekend. Come Monday mornin' every seam'd be sprung.

Russ parked the truck in the lot behind the building. He didn't like people drivin' by seein' his truck sittin' out front of a tavern this time'a day.

The front door wasn't open yet so he went around through the kitchen. Nick was behind the bar moppin' up his trusty shaker right close on the bar where he could get at it when he needed to. When he saw Russ come through the swingin' kitchen door he straightened up leaned on his mop his face was fire-red sweat poppin' pretty good straight grain 180 proof.

"Mornin' Nick."

It was a little early in the mornin' for Nick to be talkin' so he reached out a paw for his shaker an' oiled his gullet first.

"Mornin' Russ. Come over to see how us rich folks live?"

"Tommie been in?"

"Which Tommie?"

"Weldin' Tommie."

"You mean last night?"

"No, this mornin'."

"Hell, the milkman aint' even been here yet."

"Oh. Well, I . . . jus' figgered . . . he mighta stopped by."

"No, we don't usually get too much business before we open."

Nick took another slug then set down his shaker wiped his mouth started moppin' again. Russ just stood there watchin' him kinda shiftin' from one foot to the other

kinda wonderin' what to do with hisself next. When Nick
finally did get around to sayin' somethin' more he didn't
even look up.

"You want Tommie call 'im up—should be openin' up
about now."

Nick had already mopped hisself around the liquor
island before Russ answered.

"Yeah. S'pose I could do that."

Nick just grunted an' swung his head in the direction
of the phone booths.

"Phone's over there."

Russ didn't answer or make a move. Nick finished moppin' behind the bar then straightened up again leaned on
his mop lookin' steady at Russ all the while.

" 'Course I guess you know where the phones are."

"Cathy's . . . Cathy's leavin' me, Nick."

"No shit, Russ . . . ?"

"No . . . shit, Nick."

Nick laid down his mop come toward Russ his big
paws reachin' out to touch him all the way. Russ never
did know why he said it he was just standin' there lookin'
at Nick's shaker an' his mouth opened an' the words
come out.

He felt like cryin' again when he felt Nick's hands
pawin' around his shoulders. Nick musta noticed it too he
took his hands away reached up an' took down one'a the
stools sittin' there upside down on the bar set it down
beside Russ kinda motionin' at it with one hand.

"Better . . . grab a seat there, Russ . . . ole buddy."

Russ did like he was told. Nick went around behind the
bar picked up the other half'a his shaker threw in a few
ice cubes set it down in front'a Russ picked up the V.O.
poured 'er full.

"Take a little snort'a that. Put a little hair back on your
chest."

Russ did like he was told. It felt good havin' Nick take over. He took a healthy cuff'a the straight booze. When it hit bottom it felt so good he wasn't even sorry he'd said what he did to Nick.

He felt even better when Nick came around the bar to his side again took down another stool sat down beside him put his arm around his shoulders for just a second there.

"Drink up. You're better off drunk than the way you are."

Russ did like he was told again. He didn't feel like arguin' this mornin'. The way he felt today he'd'a gone along with most anything. Beside it felt good anyway. All he wanted to do right now was just what he was doin jus' sittin' here alongside Nick listenin' to his voice it didn't matter if it went right by his ears or not all he wanted to hear was the sound there beside him know that big ole friendly bear was sittin' right there drinkin' away with him just like they used to do feelin' the straight booze workin' its way down inside'a him lettin' all the shit roll off his back forgettin' about Cathy an' the kid an' money an' Tommie an' broken tractors an' frozen shit an' all the rest jus' sittin' there waitin' to feel like a man again.

Only thing today Nick wouldn't let him. He kept sayin' things Russ couldn't help but hear things that no matter how hard he tried jus' wouldn't keep goin' right by his ears.

". . . tell you the god-honest truth, Russ, I can't really say I blame 'er. I mean, shit, I hate to say this to you, but you been fuckin' up somethin' fierce these las' couple years—ain't too many women would'a put up with you this long. 'Course that Cathy'a yours is one in a million."

"Yeah, she's . . . really somethin' all right."

"You better believe it. They threw away the mold when they made her. You'll go a long way before you find somethin' better."

"Yeah, I . . . guess you're right, Nick."

"You gawddam know I'm right."

Nick reeled in his talkin' hand long enough to drain about half his shaker. Russ tried to do the same but he came up coughin' so he set his shaker down an' turned toward Nick.

"What's so great about her?"

Nick let out somethin' that sounded like a growl then steadied hisself with the bottom half'a his shaker. He couldn't answer till he set his shaker down an' got his hands movin' his trigger finger in its usual spot about two inches off the end'a Russ's nose.

"Buddy, you don't know that answer yourself, I can't tell it to you."

"No, I'm serious, Nick. What's so goddam great about her?"

Nick snorted an' when he couldn't think'a nothin' to say right off the bat he had ta reach for his shaker musta been pretty excited he didn't even notice it was empty jus' tilted 'er up an' swigged off the ice cubes.

"Well . . ." The "well" came out more like a growl than a word. ". . . she's prettier'n sum'bitch for one thing. I mean, mine's a dog compared to her in looks."

"What the hell you talkin' about—Jackie's pretty's hell!"

"Nothin' like Cathy. I mean, you stand the two of 'em side by side out in the bright light, say about noon, maybe two o'clock—"

"All right, so she's prettier'n a sum'bitch—what's that prove?"

Nick waited until he had filled his shaker. This time he didn't even bother gettin' up an' goin' for the ice cubes.

"Proves she's pretty. I mean, you gonna look at the same woman ever' day for fifty years she might just as well be pretty."

He took a slug his eyes following the shaker up'n down stayin' on it even after he started talkin'.

"I mean, why take a bitch mongrel if you get a chance for one with papers . . . for the same price?"

"It'd still be a dog."

"Yeah, but'a different kind'a dog. An' it ain't just that she's pretty—hell, a lotta women are pretty—Cathy's got—class—yeah, real class."

Russ looked over at Nick seemed like he was actin' kinda funny this morning for one thing he wasn't talkin' with his hands now they was just layin' there on the bar beside his shaker red'n round looked like a couple'a front shoulder hams for another most'a the time he was talkin' straight ahead Russ started to get the feelin' it didn't much matter whether he was here or not Nick'd be sittin' there sayin' the same things.

"Tell you the truth, you hadn't'a had 'er locked up all along, right from the start, right from the time we was jus' kids . . . tell you the truth, I might'a taken a little run at her myself."

"Why didn't you then?"

"There was plenty'a times . . . when you was away down to college . . . when I felt like makin' a move . . ." It almost seemed like for a minute there Nick forgot what he was talkin' about but then he took another slug an' rallied. ". . . but you know Cathy, she had to go'n stay . . . faithful."

Seemed to Russ like Nick hit that last word a little harder than he had to maybe it was all just in his mind.

"What the hell'd you expect her to do?"

Seemed like Nick gave that a lotta thinkin' too but he never did answer maybe he was just gettin' sleepy he hadn't had enough yet this morning to pick him up an' carry him both.

"What the hell'd you expect her to do?!"

Russ surprised himself when he asked the question again he wondered why he did hell he sure's hell never worried about Cathy say nothin' about Cathy an' Nick!

"Nothin'."

Nick finally did turn toward Russ looked him straight in the eye funny thing his hands stayed right where they was layin' there on the bar.

"That's the trouble with you, Russ, ever'thing always come to you too easy."

Russ couldn't believe his own ears comin' from Nick Dobchek shit he had the whole goddam works handed to him on a silver platter.

"I mean you was lucky to get her in the first place."

Russ damn near swallowed his shaker on that one it'd been anybody else but Nick he'd'a gut-punched him off that stool Nick just kept on talkin' in that low steady voice lookin' Russ straight in the eye his hands still layin' there on the bar that shook Russ up as much as anything he couldn't ever remember Nick jus' sittin' there talkin' calm like this—

"You never would'a neither you hadn't been such a big honcho carryin' the ball big scholarship an' ever'thin' good-lookin' besides—"

"Nick . . . you best watch . . . what you're sayin'."

"Why? It's all true, ain't it . . . ?"

"Shit no! Nothin' ever come easy to me—like it did for some."

"I ain't talkin' about money."

"Nobody ever left me a hundred-thousand-dollar business, set me up for life—"

"I ain't talkin' about money—"

"All my old man ever left was Russ Simpson, Junior. Hah, 'Jr.'—that's a laugh!"

Nick took a long pull on his shaker a longer look at Russ.

"Russ, you ever gonna quit feelin' sorry for yourself?"

Russ didn't know why they did it but before he could stop them his hands jumped out like maybe they was thinkin'a takin' a poke at Nick but somewhere along the line they changed their mind ended up just slappin' his half'a the shaker off the bar it went bouncin' along over the fancy carpet didn't hurt nothin' it was metal an' empty anyway.

Nick waited till it stopped bouncin' came to rest over against one'a the planters with the plastic flowers didn't even move just swung his head an' watched it go.

"Go pick it up."

He said it patiently like he was talkin' to one'a his kids he had seven of 'em. Russ did while he did Nick just sat there watchin' him.

"Russ. if there was ever a guy around here had it knocked it was you."

Russ just brought the shaker back set it on the bar picked up the V.O. poured some in. Nick reached over tapped Russ's shaker with his trigger finger.

"Don't you ever come in here tryin' to take it out on me, Russ."

"What's that s'posed to mean?"

"I ain't the one diggin' your hole for you."

Russ slammed his shaker down on the bar but not very hard didn't even slosh any whisky out.

"Nick, you ever thought'a talkin' straight—so's a man can understand you?"

"Maybe it's you that's listenin' crooked."

Nick had his finger up Russ's nose again he held it there a little longer then dropped it an' turned away walked away like he liked to when he thought he'd dropped the big clincher that was one'a the things about Nick pissed Russ off plus he was pissed at him right now to begin with christ someday somebody's gonna reach out'n grab that finger break it off at least fracture it a little in a few places man Russ wanted to be around when it happened he'd just walk away like Nick was now.

Nick was back over to his mop by now picked it up

looked at it awhile like he'd never seen it before then leaned it back against the bar an' walked back to Russ started stabbin' at him again.

"Russ, the last couple'a years you been diggin' yourself a hole faster'n you or Cathy or anybody else around here gives a shit kin keep it shoveled in—"

Russ's mouth opened to say somethin' he didn't know what he hadn't really thought'a nothin' too great to come back with yet shit it wouldn't'a done no good nohow there came that finger again an' Nick rode right through whatever it was goin' to be—

"—an' you know it!"

They just stood there eyeball to eyeball funny thing Russ had time to say somethin' now really cut Nick every way but loose but damned if he could think'a anything now neither finally it was Nick who started in again.

"Tell you the truth, Russ, I'm beginnin' to think you won't rest till you've pulled it in after you."

Nick turned away real sudden-like picked up his shaker like he was mad at it or somethin' drained it right down empty slammed it back down on the bar quite a bit harder'n Russ had took a deep breath wiped his mouth with the back'a his hand like he always did Russ could see the strength of the straight whisky rise up in Nick's eyes they kinda watered over then he turned away from Russ headed fast for his mop grabbed it up started moppin' again like there was no tomorrow then all of a sudden he slowed way down the mop just swishin' around swishin' around swishin' around.

Then Nick did somethin' Russ had never seen him do before. Talk with both his hands clamped around somethin'. An' the words came out kinda funny too. Not like Nick's voice at all. Low'n slow'n broken. Kinda just keepin' time to the swishin' of the mop.

"See . . . the thing is . . . Russ . . . this is . . . somethin' . . . I know a little somethin' . . . about . . . myself."

Russ drained his shaker an' poured hisself another jolt of the straight booze. There was nothin' to listen to now 'cept the slurp-slurp swish-swish'a Nick's mop an' the talkin' of his own mind an' he sure's hell didn't need that so he took a pretty good haul on his shaker went over an' plugged the juke punched J9 whole quarter's worth.

"Those were the days, my friend, we thought they'd never end, we'd sing and dance forever and a day. . . ."

Russ went back to his shaker. Nick just kept moppin' away.

Funny thing now that he'd played it a whole quarter's worth he didn't much feel like listenin' to the words of the song no more. Trouble was his mind didn't wanna 'xactly sing along with those words seemed like now it'd rather sing along with its own tune only 'bout twice as loud.

Goddammit it wasn't as though he hadn't given it a fair try. Not that he couldn't'a tried harder . . . longer.

'Course it wasn't all his fault neither—Cathy could'a dropped outta Normal an' come down there an' married him or somethin' like he asked her to. Hell she coulda went to school down there with him got her teachin' certificate down there with him just as well but no she hadda listen to her parents "she was too young to get married" besides "they couldn't afford to send her outta state to school" like hell they couldn't "they could just wait to get married when he got his degree" like maybe they was afraid he never would which he didn't.

But he coulda! Ain't nobody could ever say he couldn't'a! Shit he coulda been the best damn lawyer in Columbia County sure's hell better'n that Drambuie-head D.A.!

'Course her folks'd never thought he'd amount to a hill'a beans. He could tell that in her old lady's mean-eyed pinchmouth face ever' time she tried to look at him —hell in all the years they'd been married now that woman'd never looked him square in the face. Like she couldn't even stand to look at him—like ever'time she tried it made her think'a Freddie the Contractor Cathy coulda married the ole lady never missed a chance to tell how he always sent the old lady for chrissakes flowers ever'time the calendar showed red not to mention how he always traded Cadillacs ever' two years even called up Cathy an' wanted her to pick it out one time when Russ was away down to Arizona Cathy had wrote an' told him about it like it was some kinda big joke hah some big joke all right hell the sonuvabitch even offered to build a house for her let her draw up the plans an' everything Christ that's a helluva thing to offer a seventeen-year-old girl her first year in college her boyfriend two thousand miles away her mother busy whisperin' in her ear yeah that's why the old lady never could look him square in the face ever' time she tried she thought'a Freddie the Contractor's money an' it gagged her she hadda look away.

Not that her father ever fell all over him neither. But at least once'n awhile the last few years he'd jack his recliner chair to a sittin' position let Russ see his face maybe even talk fishin' an' huntin' with him for a few minutes—leastways till ole mean-eyes would walk in the room then he'd jack his chair right back down again go to starin' at the ceilin' again his hands crossed over his belly like he was already on the slab just layin' there waitin' for her to put the pennies on his eyes.

'Course her parents always were big people around here least they thought they were so maybe they were.

'Course they never expected their only daughter'd run off'n marry one'a the boys from the County Farm even if he was Russ Simpson Jr. who carried the football who didn't even know who Sr. was.

Not that Russ gave a shit. Hell he was thirty years old the fourth of January what difference did it make now who Sr. was? Or Mrs. Sr. for that matter?

The jukebox clicked off now so did the other tune. It was so quiet there in that empty bar Russ could hear the Budweiser clock over his head turnin'. He hadn't even noticed Nick finish moppin' an' go out somewhere. The stools were still sittin' atop the bar ass-end down there was somethin' about them bare legs stickin' up in the air reminded Russ of the West Ghent graveyard. He could smell whatever it was Nick used in his mop water smelled like Top Job Cathy used at home. The sun was gettin' higher now slantin' in the new plate glass windows on the tables where the lawyers an' doctors ate.

Seemed to Russ like there was no place in the world lonelier'n a empty barroom the sun comin' pourin' in.

He poured hisself another straight one this time about the size'a Nick's walked over an' plugged the jukebox this time a whole dollar's worth'a J9.

He walked back to his stool sat down took hisself a little sip. All of a sudden he didn't feel like sittin' there no more so he picked up his shaker walked over by the plate glass windows sat down in one'a the lawyers' chairs just sat there feelin' the sun come shinin' in on him.   . .

Just sat there feelin' the sun lookin' through the plate glass windows at all the snow on the hill across the road.

Thinkin' nothin'. Just stupid things like how a guy sittin' up there on top'a that hill with a deer rifle could pick off most anybody sittin' here in one'a these chairs.

He never would forget the day he left Arizona. He stuck it out till spring the last day'a spring training the day'a the spring intrasquad game. It was cooler then there was still a little snap in the air that afternoon when he walked across the field to the locker room the dew that passed for the spring rains was already heavy on the grass.

The letter he'd got from Cathy the day before was in the back pocket of his Levi's he stuck his hand back there an' felt of it just to be sure.

She sounded so happy about everything at Normal an' he wasn't even there but way down here how could she be so goddam happy?

It was hot'n stuffy in the locker room. He walked over to the locker said RUSS SIMPSON JR. on it sat down on the bench in front. He sat there for as long as he could just starin' at the concrete floor then he looked at the big electric clock on the wall above Charlie's door the big hand was already five minutes past ten ever'body else was already out so he stood up an' opened his locker took out his gear laid it on the bench.

He put on his plastic cup first then his hip pads then his shoulder pads then his jersey then his pants then sat down again to pull on his socks.

He was already seven minutes late so he just sat there that way for awhile just lookin' at the concrete floor again. Finally he put on one shoe just sat there with one shoe on one shoe off thinkin' all the while how happy she sounded an' how happy he wasn't an' what difference did it make if he went out there an' threw his body up against another man's an' come in all sore'n achin' just to carry that little piece'a pig leather filled with thirteen pounds'a air across a little bitty line'a chalk there on the ground?

Then the last bell rang so he went out an' did what he was told. What he was down there for. It never seemed so bad once he got out there an' they started knockin' heads. Then the juice started to run an' the ball was in his hands he always felt better when the ball was in his hands. Then he had an excuse to run over them. To drive his cleats down on Zuhowski's hand. To straight-arm Pagnetti with a doubled fist. To bust through with his knees driving high in Lucky's face. To bring a shoulder down in Hefner's gut. To wait on his punt till Jensen broke through an' he could kick it right in his big-shot face.

Christ that mean little coach was really pissed that day. Particularly after his big-deal end Jensen walked over to the sidelines with his nose all over his face.

He pulled Russ then. Sat him down. Russ didn't give a shit he had a feeling he wasn't too long for this place anyway.

An' then when he walked outta the locker room that evenin'. It was just gettin' dark. There was that little snap in the air. The sky was high an' streaked with pink the way it is down there. An' then against the pink he saw them flyin' high. An' they kept comin' closer. An' he could hear them callin' one to the other that hootin'-hootin' sound come wailin' down wailin' down. An' then the shaky V passed over him. An' the stadium. An' the field. An' everything.

An' he stood there watchin' until he couldn't see them anymore . . . the big honkers headin' home.

He went too. He didn't even stop to pick up his things tell anybody yes-or-no just headed right down the road to Phoenix got on board that Greyhound bus. . . .

He musta dozed off. He hadn't even noticed Buddy come in put on his red tendin' vest go over an' unlock the big double glass door.

He couldn't sit there anymore. Pretty soon the lawyers'n such would be comin' in to claim their chairs for lunch they always liked to sit here along the plate glass windows drink their martinis look out at the snow on the hill across the road man a good shot with a scope could sit right up there pick the olives right outta them goddam dinky little glasses.

Russ laughed right out loud picked up his shaker headed for the bar. Buddy was standin' there by the service bar slicin' fruit when he saw Russ comin' he dropped his knife turned an' scurried through the door marked OFFICE (*Private*).

Russ sat down in his usual spot. By the time he took

one sip Andy came hustling out through the door marked
OFFICE *(Private)* Buddy trottin' along at his heels.

"Where the hell you come from, Russ?"

. . "Didn't come from nowhere."

"What'a'ya mean—didn't come from nowhere—?"

Buddy jumped over alongside Andy he couldn't wait to
get his two cents in seemed awful excited about somethin'.
"I'll guarantee you one thing, Andy, he didn't come in
from outside, I just unlocked the doors. I was over here
behind the bar, cuttin' my fruit, fillin' my olive trays, the
next thing I know I look up an' here he comes carryin' a
drink in his hand—"

"Buddy . . . go finish settin' up, I'll handle this."

Buddy backed off but not very far just stood there
gawkin' one hand in an olive jar the other in the cherries
about every five minutes he'd remember an' fish one out
then stand there holdin' it another five his fingers turnin'
red on the end.

"Russ, you been in here all night?"

"Shit, no."

"How'd you get in then?"

"Walked."

"I mean, where?"

"Kitchen."

"Kitchen's locked."

"Wasn't when I come in."

"When was that?"

"Oh, along about . . . seven."

"Seven! This mornin'?!"

"Shit yeah."

Andy's face started to look like it was catchin' on.

"Nick here then?"

"Yeah."

"You two been sittin' here drinkin' all mornin'?"

"Nah, Nick was moppin' part'a the time."

"That dumb bastard!"

"Nick ain't so dumb."

"He ain't very smart. How the hell's he gonna cook all day'n night if he was drinkin' all mornin'?!"

"He was moppin' part'a the—"

"I told that big hillbilly fifty times to hire a porter—hell, I even sent for some porter jackets like you see down in the city, got a whole bundle of 'em layin' back there—you know why he won't hire a porter?!"

Wasn't enough Russ had to go along with Nick stickin' his finger in his nose now his little brother was doin' it too.

"Maybe he enjoys moppin'."

"Sure, he gets his rocks off moppin'. Moppin's his thing —so long as he can drink a half a quart while he's doin' it! You know that silly sonuvabitch gets up five o'clock in the morning comes down here sits all by himself in the dark drinkin?'"

"Relax, Andy, hell, Nick's all right—"

"Like hell he is! Neither are you. Lookit you—you smell like you come here right outta the barn, swam through a distillery on the way—"

"I had to do my milkin', didn't I—?"

"Yeah, but you didn't have to come down here. Now get outta here, we got luncheon to serve—least go home'n change, take a shower or somethin' . . . maybe then you can come back—"

"Can't."

"What'a'ya mean, you can't?"

"Can't. Cathy locked me out."

"Locked you out!"

"She's . . . leavin' me, Andy."

"No shit, Russ?"

"No shit, Andy."

Buddy came lopin' down the bar his ear to the ground. "What was that, Russ—?"

"Buddy, this is somethin' private, between me'n Russ—"

"Cathy left me."

"No shit, Russ?"

"No shit, Buddy."

Andy stepped in pushed Buddy aside a little.

"Just a minute here—you say she's leavin' you or already left?"

"Left. Jus' . . . locked up . . . an' left."

"Christ. Look, I'm . . . real sorry, Russ."

"That's all right, Andy—ain't your fault."

"Me too, Russ."

"Don't mention it, Buddy."

They all just stood there tryin' not to look at each other looked for a second there Andy was gonna reach down an' pour Russ a drink but he stopped hisself Russ figgered he better lay it on a little thicker.

"Took my boy with her too. Every dime I had in the house. Even threw my clothes out'n a snowbank."

They both looked mighty sorry but neither one of 'em reached for the V.O. bottle maybe they was too busy thinkin' how it coulda happened to them.

"Yeah, she even turned my cows outta the barn—"

"What?!"

"Cathy turned your cows out?!"

"Yeah, I don't know what got into her . . . I come home last night—you seen me leave, Andy, cold sober—I go straight home there's the lights all on, house all locked up, clothes stickin' outta the snowbank, cows bellerin' out'n the barnyard—"

"Here, you better have yourself a little touch, Russ—put some hair back on your chest."

"Thanks, Andy . . . I kin use it."

Andy set the bottle back down in the rack stood leaning on it looking down at it like it just made him think'a somethin'.

"Man, that don't sound like the Cathy I know. . . ."

Buddy glanced over at Andy like he just thought'a

somethin' too. "Don't sound like the Cathy I know neither. . . ."

Andy looked up at Russ, didn't look him right in the eye though.

"You wouldn't . . . fib—be kiddin' us, would you, Russ?"

"Would a man lie about somethin' like this, Andy?"

"No. No, I don't guess he would."

"I mean . . . why would he?"

"Beats me."

"You don't believe me, call 'er up."

Andy grinned. "At home . . . ?"

"Go ahead. When that don't answer try her mean-face mother."

A couple'a the lawyers came in sat down at their table over by the window. Andy waved at them his saloon-keeper face slippin' into place then turned the other one back to Russ.

"Awright, stay here, in the corner—we'll figger out what to do with you later . . . don't move."

Andy came around out from behind the bar grabbed an order pad from one'a the waitresses' stations by the service bar started toward the lawyers to take their order as he passed Russ he stopped.

"Say . . . where'd you sleep last night?"

"Barn."

"Thought so."

Andy flicked on his mater-dee face headed for the lawyers. Russ sniffed a couple'a times he couldn't smell nothin' Andy was probably just makin' it up to make him feel bad.

The next thing he knew for sure the game was on the bar half-filled with men their heads all screwed 'round toward the big color TV the little men in blue an' gold flickin' back'n forth across the screen the big men watchin' callin' bets sayin' "Hey, you see that!" "Run you black mutha," "Get 'im, get 'im, for chrissakes get 'im," "All the way, c'mon, all the way!" "Wowww, did he get cold-cocked!"

For a second there Russ thought he was back at Arizona State. He could almost feel the guy gettin' hit hisself.

But he wasn't. He was here in Dobchek's. Just one of the watchers.

Not feelin' too good right now neither.

The lump startin' to grow in his belly. That hard cold lump he always figgered was colored gray. Lay there low on the left side. Had somethin' to do with bein' afraid.

"Buddy . . . can you spare me a drink . . . ?"

Buddy didn't say nothin' just went ahead an' poured the drink his old woman's lips pressed tight together the boys musta give Russ the green light today.

What the hell was there to be afraid'a? Here he was just sittin' here in Dobchek's. Jus' sittin' here all these guys around him most of 'em guys he growed up with jus' watchin' some old college football game havin' a few drinks. . . .

It didn't use'ta come when he was drinkin'. Hell what was the use'a drinkin' when it come then too?

'Course he shouldn't be spendin' the money. Shouldn't'a said what he did about Cathy.

Shit what was the big deal crime about gettin' drunk once'n awhile?! Spendin' a few more bucks than he should'a maybe?! Sayin' some goofy things?! Maybe even if he got drunk enough endin' up givin' ole mattressback Carol a fast jab or two—so what's the big deal crime about that?!

Nothin' to be afraid about!

But the lump was still there. Growin'. An' he was still afraid.

Funny thing seemed like the longer he watched that stupid ole college game he didn't even give a shit about the bigger the lump got.

He kept gettin' scareder an' scareder too. He looked down he was grippin' the bar with both hands, just to keep from runnin' right outta there.

Runnin'. Yeah, that was part of it. He felt like runnin'. Maybe runnin' away? Or jus' runnin'? Jus' runnin' right outta Dobchek's an' down the road 'round the corner by Johnson the vet past the Red Barn Luncheonette 'cross the bridge up the hill by his place up his driveway past the house past the barn out through the fields back in the woods . . . runnin' . . . runnin' . . . like he use'to.

Like he use'to when he was a kid growin' up on the County Farm an' he had that sick ashamed feelin' an' he would run until he couldn't run anymore until he was suckin' hard an' he couldn't make it no farther until the pain in his lungs was bigger'n the one in his guts . . . then he could fall down an' wanna cry but be sick in a pile of leaves instead.

Where nobody could see him.

"Hey, Buddy—fix me up here, will ya?"

Yeah, but that was then an' now was now. An' he wasn't all alone anymore now he had Cathy an' the kid an' maybe they still loved him no matter what he did least liked him quite a bit an' he wasn't on the County Farm no more sick ashamed to his guts he had his own farm dinky small eighty acres only twelve cows milkin' second mortgage financed to the nuts but it was his—goddam you, it was his!

But he was still afraid.

Why? How come the cold gray lump kept comin' back more'n more nowdays? The one he thought would be gone forever when he got Cathy an' the farm.

The one he didn't even wanna think about.

But it was there.

Maybe he ought'a think about it. Let hisself feel it. Like he did sometimes when he'd been drinkin' hard an' woke up when the booze wore thin cold awake his mind cryin' his body crawlin' the little cricklin's right there under his skin.

Like now.

Maybe that's why he went on the binge. So maybe he could ketch a glimpse'a cold gray lump.

Find out what was . . . wrong . . . with him.

Yeah, maybe there was somethin' wrong with him. Maybe he wasn't quite all there . . . or somethin' . . . ?"

Shit there had to be! It ain't right is it for a big guy 6'2-190 to be scared all the time? Scared even when he's scorin' the big ones the crowd jumpin' up an' down Cathy turnin' cartwheels the cannon goin' off him trottin' over to the sidelines pullin' off his helmet before he got to the photographers answerin' the roarin' stompin' crowd with a little wave of his hand. . . .

No, that's wrong—that's all wrong. He wasn't scared then. Not when he was runnin' the ball the holes openin' before him. Not when he could see that end zone not when he felt that daylight not when he had the ball runnin' by them through them around them over them no goddam it all to hell ain't nobody can stop Russ Simpson Jr. when he had the power an' was runnin' with the ball!

When he was runnin' with the ball an' had the power.

Seemed like those two were all tied up together there somehow.

Was that right even? Maybe he'd even been scared then too . . . ?"

It's hard for a man to keep track of just when he was or wasn't when he's scared so much'a the time.

Seemed like he was a little. In a different sort'a way. When he got all the way to the sidelines an' he sat back down on the bench an' the roarin' quieted down.

Wonderin' if he'd be able to do it again the next time.

Particularly at the end. After the game was over. Walkin'

across the field to the locker room the crowd pourin' out on the field the kids jumpin' around hammerin' him on the back the grown-ups just standin' there waitin' to touch his body as he walked on by.

After the game was over. That scared dead feelin' already creepin' in.

A whole week to go before that other feelin' came again.

A whole week full'a nothin'. Jus' gettin' ready for the next time. The lump growin' bigger an' bigger an' colder an' grayer . . . waitin' for Saturday.

Then it would come. Then it would come an' they'd be warmin' up on the sidelines doin' little sprints high-kickin' shoulder-pad-crackin' the band playin' Cathy leadin' cheers sis-boom-bah that buzzin' in the stands louder louder the cold gray lump bigger bigger the huddle around the coach Clyde talkin' low with that little catch in his voice maybe he was scared too when he finished the roar come from their throats their hands clappin' shoulders their hands grippin' each other's Clyde sayin' his little prayer the cold gray lump bigger bigger startin' to choke his throat the crowd singin' *The Star Spangled Banner* the crowd's roar buildin' on the last few notes drownin' out "of the brave" rollin' down upon him standin' there alone in the middle of all his teammates standin' there alone amongst them fightin' down the puke fillin' his throat waitin' for the whistle an' the runnin' an' the power.

It always came. The boy on the other end of the field would bring down his signal finger move ahead that little hop step one two three kick . . . then they'd all be coming at him the ball coming first closer closer goddam goddam please christ please let him catch it don't fumble it please christ got it! Now runrunrunrunrunrunrunrun-runrunrun—

"You all right, Russ?"

"Andy . . . ? Yeah, sure, Andy—sure, I'm all right."

Andy was leanin' in lookin' at him close Russ figgered he'd better say a little more.

"How's the wife an' the kids, Andy?"

"Shirley? All right, I guess—right back there in the kitchen makin' salad."

"That's nice. She's sure a good worker."

"Yeah. You wanna see her or somethin', Russ?"

"No. No, just wonderin' . . . how she was. Your kids too."

Andy backed off a couple'a steps still lookin' at Russ real close-like then came steppin' close again.

"You mad at me or somethin', Russ?"

"You mean 'cause I asked after your wife an' kids—?"

"You know what I mean . . . las' night, what I said about postin' you?"

"Nah. Why should I be? It's true, ain't it?"

"Nahhh. We ain't gonna post you—"

"No, I mean . . . I should be posted, Andy."

"You . . . kiddin' me?"

"Honest, I'm serious. Post me, Andy."

"C'mon Russ . . . nah, you know me'n Nick was just tryin' to scare you, for your own good'n all—"

"Post me, Andy . . . please."

"Cut it out, Russ. C'mon. Look, I kin see you're tryin' to do better—hell, you wasn't bad at all last night 'cept for that little joke you pulled on me with that twenty an' today . . . hell, today you been nice'n quiet as can be, just sittin' here watchin' the game—hell, you ain't even said a word—'

"Post me, Andy."

Andy backed up stood lookin' at Russ hands on hips.

"You mean it?"

"Yeah."

"When?"

"Come . . . come Monday mornin'. Give me time . . . time to run this one out first."

"Sure, Russ . . . Russ, you sure—"

"Yeah, Andy . . . I'm sure."

"OK . . . if that's what you want. Just remember one thing, Russ, it was you asked me—see, all that talk yesterday . . . well, we all got together, Cathy too yesterday, an' talked it over—see, we knew you'd be comin' in soon as you got your hands on Cathy's check an' . . . look, all we was tryin' to do was scare you. . . ."

"I'm scared, Andy."

"Oh, c'mon, Russ, it ain't nothin' to worry about—"

"I'm scared."

"Sure, Russ . . . sure. Hey, Buddy, pour Russ a little drink on me."

Andy turned an' headed for the door marked OFFICE (*Private*).

Russ went back to watchin' the football game. He watched a few plays watched the team in white spring the halfback for thirty on a black fox sweep around the weak-side end looked to Russ like they could run that play all day all they had to do was pull the guards let one take the end outside the other one turn the linebacker in just enough time for the back to break through get that little bit'a daylight sidestep the cornerback shit he could'a run right over that deep safety just showed 'im a little hip crossed his leg over dropped his shoulder spun right by 'im. . . .

Russ turned away. Took a sip'a his new drink. Funny thing seemed like nowdays every time he watched a game he started feelin' guilty he wasn't up there playin'.

He'd been scared ridin' the Greyhound home from Arizona. Scared maybe the Greyhound would crack up he wouldn't make it home to her. Scared that it wouldn't an' he would.

What if she was so goddam happy like she wrote an' wouldn't be to see him?

Wonderin' how she'd act when she saw him. Wonderin' what she'd show on her face or hide in 'er mind. Wonderin' if she'd be wonderin' what he was doin' there why he'd left Arizona an' come on home.

Maybe even thinkin' he was a quitter. A quitter didn't even have enough guts to fight it out get to be a lawyer or nothin'. Maybe even thinkin' he wasn't good enough to make the team.

Had she? Been really glad to see him? When he walked into her sorority house told the ole housemother with the blue hair white around the roots he had come to see Cathy Suring so would she please call her tell her a friend was here to see her? An' he had stood there with the blue irises wiltin' in his hand an' all the snooty little sorority girls goin' in an' out lookin' at him like he had cowshit on his shoes he even thought he saw some gigglin' an' whisperin' behind their hands an' he felt like turnin' around an' runnin' right back to that Greyhound bus depot but there she was comin' down the stairway with the red carpet on it an' she saw him an' he couldn't run nomore.

She didn't run up to him an' throw her arms around him an' kiss him like he'd seen in the movies though. She just kept comin' at him real slow-like down those long red steps comin' real slow her mouth kinda open takin' those short fast flarin' breaths just kept comin' closer reachin' out her hands to take the flowers like he brought them ever' day takin' him by the hand not even squeezin' just leadin' him like he was a baby toward the big blue couch her eyes hooked deep into his her eyes askin' askin', "Is something wrong? Is something wrong?" his eyes answerin' answerin' . . .

"I quit . . . I quit. . . ."

"You talkin' to me, friend?"

"Yeah, I quit."

"You . . . quit?"

Russ turned his head to the voice his eyes seemed filled with water all he could tell for sure was the guy was wearin' a red'n black checked mackinaw shirt.

"Football."

"Yeah?"

"Yeah."

The older man turned back to his tap his hand reached out to lift it to his mouth Russ's hand reached out an' caught his mackinaw sleeve.

"Honest—for that team up there."

The man looked at his tap then at Russ's hand still clutching his sleeve then he put his tap back down on the bar an' turned to Russ again.

"Yeah . . . ?"

"The ones in white. But I quit."

"That's what . . . you was sayin'."

"Just got . . . sick of it . . . ! Sick'a playin'!"

The man nodded his head not really like he understood more like he couldn't think'a nothin' else to do but figgered he ought'a do somethin'.

"That's the way she goes, I guess."

"Yeah. Kinda a shame too. See, I was good—I mean, damn good."

"Hm-hm. Say, boy, you mind lettin' loose my sleeve?"

Russ did. The man took a long pull on his tap his eyes swivelin' up an' down the bar like he might be lookin' to find another stool.

" 'Member the Hudson game? '59? 54-41—I went for seven touchdowns four extra points three field goals 446 yards rushin'—"

"Boy, tell you the truth, I don't give a fart in a whirlwind about football—jes' stopped in for a quick one—"

"From around here?"

"Poughkeepsie. Rollin' a semi to Albany an' back—'course I ain't s'posed to be drinkin' beer, p'tic'ly when I'm rollin' heavy—"

"What the hell, a man's gotta stop'n wet his whistle once'n awhile—ain't no big deal crime. . . ."

"That's 'bout the way I figger it."

The big man drained his glass pushed his stool back started gettin' to his feet Russ's hand jumped out an' grabbed the red'n black checked sleeve again.

"Don't go . . . I mean, kin I buy you one for the road?"

Lumberjack Shirt looked down at Russ's hand then at Russ's face thought about it for awhile then shrugged an' sat back down.

"Guess one more won't kill me."

"Nah, do you good—put some hair back on your chest. Hey, Buddy, give me'n my friend here a drink."

Buddy came growlin' over reached out for their empty glasses.

"Well, Russ, you *been* doin' pretty good so far today."

"Just pour the drinks, Buddy."

Buddy did an' went back to the far end of the bar. Russ lifted his glass an' clinked it against the big truck driver's.

"Skoal."

"Ostrovia."

The man started to turn away again.

"Yeah, I don't mean to brag but I was pretty damn good—just about the hottest thing ever come outta this part'a the country. Had just about every college in the country after me—shit, I coulda gone to anyone'a those fancy Ivy League colleges, course my grades weren't so hot so I took Arizona State. But I coulda went! I coulda been a doctor, lawyer, one'a those business ex-xecutives —any goddam thing I wanted to be . . . !" Russ stuck his finger in Lumberjack Shirt's big red beer nose held

it there makin' little jumpy pointy motions like Nick did.
"You know why?!"

"Well . . . no."

"Because I could carry that ball, that's why. You're goddam right, I could! You just better believe it! Weren't
nobody could touch me . . . nobody! You hand me that ball
my power clicked in shit man it was all she wrote!"

Russ had been drivin' home each point with a stab at
the big man's nose he kept leanin' further'n further back
now he was about to fall off his stool so he ducked to one
side an' leaned in close to Russ.

"Say, boy, why don't you sit a spell, take a little pull
on your drink? No point gettin' too carried away."

"You think you could bring me down?"

"Bring you down . . . ?!"

"Yeah, bring me down. I mean, I'll take my drink tuck
it under my arm like this see then I take'a run at you—"

Russ's foot got tangled with his stool he almost went
down but the big red'n black checked arm shot out an'
caught him in time.

"Boy, you bes' sit down before you get hurt."

Russ did. Seemed like all of a sudden he felt all burned
out an' when he started talkin' again he sounded that way.

"Man, all I had to do was play ball. Goddammit, I
could play ball, I could always play ball, any kinda ball
you jes' name it I could play it . . . but. . . ."

Lumberjack Shirt took a fast squint at Russ then a long
pull on his tap looked like he was hot to get his rig rollin'
again.

"Never had time for damn fool games myself."

While he was sayin' it he started pullin' himself together collectin' his change shovin' a quarter in the well
for Buddy Russ just kept on talkin'.

"That's why I quit. Ain't nothin' for a grown man to be
doin'—see, I hadda get back up here'n settle down, my

girl was buggin' me to get married, you know. An' then'a 'course, somebody hadda look after the big farm my folks left me. See, they was both killed in a big car accident when I was down to Arizona playin' football."

Lumberjack Shirt stopped where he was halfway standing up.

"That's . . . tough break."

He didn't sit back down though just stood the rest'a the way kept gatherin' together his things hat'n pigskin driving gloves Russ started to talk a little faster.

"Yeah, it happened right up 9H here. She was drivin' her Caddy convertible east toward here an' he came around the corner there by the Red Barn goin' west in his Continental . . . they met head-on right there on the bridge."

Lumberjack Shirt sat back down.

"Christ . . . !"

"Yeah, killed 'em both deader'n mackerel. I . . . I was the first one there . . . pulled 'em out."

"Must'a been . . ."

"It was, man."

Lumberjack Shirt scratched his head looked sideways at Russ put on his brown checked permanent crease hat looked sideways at Russ again.

"Thought you said you was down south playin' ball when it happened . . . ?"

"Yeah, I was. See . . . they was missin' for awhile, few days, nobody knew what happened to 'em—so they called me down to college an' I flew right up here—"

"Missin'? Didn't you say they was killed in a wreck?"

"They was. See the cars both went off the road inta the crick . . . nobody noticed 'em."

"You mean that little bitty crick up north'a here a mile . . . right past the Red Barn?"

"Yeh. See, they ended up under the bridge—"

"Look, friend, I gotta get rollin'. Thanks for the beer—"

"Don't go . . . please . . . have another beer—hey, Buddy, another round here—"

"Look fella, I gotta get that stock to Albany—"

"Please. . . ."

"Well, if . . . iffin' it means . . . that much to you—"

"Thanks."

The big man sat lookin' straight ahead his big thick hands layin' before him on the bar the hands already curved to grip the wheel the fingers squeezin' down ever' once'n awhile when he talked lookin' straight ahead down the road to Albany.

"I got a boy'a my own—little younger'n you maybe. Mighty proud'a that boy. Went to college'n all like you did. Worked his way through—wouldn't take a blasted dime from me'n ma—not that we had any money to give. Took 'im almost seven years but by godfrey he made 'er. Got to be one'a them big engineers, civil I guess they call 'im. Got a big job up at the G.E. plant in Troy."

"What's his name?"

"Peter. Pete I call 'im but he likes to be called Peter."

"That's nice. Real nice. 'Course I'd'a been a lawyer . . . that's what I was headin' for . . . iffin' a . . . iffin' a . . . my folks . . . had'n'a got . . . killed . . . in that big . . . accident."

The big man in the red'n black checked mackinaw shirt put his big thick hand on Russ's arm for just a second there gave it a little squeeze. It was just a second there but when he took his hand away Russ could still feel where it had been.

"Buck up, boy, it'll . . . work out."

"No. No, it won't. See . . . if . . . somebody'd just been there . . . to tell me what to do—see, sure . . . sure, I was six-two two-hundred-ten but see . . . I still wasn't big enough . . . but see . . . nobody was ever there to tell me what to do. . . ."

The big truck driver stood up kinda leaned his body across Russ so the rest of 'em couldn't see but Russ kept the tears that was right behind his eyes from comin' out anyway.

"I'm . . . all right."

"Sure you are, boy, sure you are. Don't you let nobody tell you no differ'nt neither."

The big man in the red'n black checkered shirt drained his tap in one pull set it down put his hand on Russ's shoulder left it there a little longer this time.

"I gotta roll."

"Kin I maybe . . . ride along—to Albany an' back . . . ?"

The hand patted Russ's back two times seemed like his back felt real small under that big thick heavy hand two times an' then it was gone.

"Sorry, son . . . law says I can't take no riders."

Now the game was over. The little men had quit runnin' across the screen an' the big men had gone back home.

All but Russ. He was still left after the other ones had gone still sittin' there in his usual spot just sittin' there lookin' up at the empty screen.

It had got awful dark out all of a sudden too. All the candles were lit the tables along the windows fillin' up Russ could see the big neon sign DOBCHEK'S flickerin' spooky throwin' sparks against the windows along the snowbanks beneath it the smaller letters STOP! GIVE YOUR- SELF A BREAK waverin' back'n forth back'n forth never would stand still. . . .

Next thing Russ knew Nick was on one side'a him Andy on the other him tryin' to walk between 'em more like they was carryin' him through the door marked OFFICE (*Private*).

They laid him down on the couch spread his old barn

mackinaw over him Russ could smell the coat made him
think to himself he oughta get up go home do his milkin'
must be gettin' mighty close to milkin' time but he didn't
just laid there let them tuck the coat around him pull his
boots off all of a sudden he felt like reachin' out an' grabbin' hold'a their hands keepin' them there but he didn't
didn't do or say nothin' just laid there made like he was
sleepin' feelin' them hoverin' over him listenin' to them
talk in their hospital voices hearin' the sorry they felt
for him feelin' the rough softness of their hands watchin'
them tiptoe to the door closin' the door marked OFFICE
(*Private*) only this time with him inside. . . .

Russ woke up his eyes wide staring open—
"Cathy, I forgot to milk the cows!"
He reached over to grab ahold'a her but she wasn't
there. There was nothin' there no other side'a the bed just
him laid out on a narrow slab—
"Cathyyyy!!!!"
The door opened a light was switched on it wasn't
Cathy he wasn't dead he could see Nick standin' there
in his cook apron dirty spots'n all his shaker in his hand.
"Cool it!"
"Nick . . . what you doin' here?"
Nick just stood there just inside the door lookin' at
Russ a kinda funny look on his face now Russ remembered
where he was how he got there he groaned inside an' laid
his head back down.
" 'Bout the same as you, I guess."
Nick walked over to the desk took a bottle outta the
drawer poured some into his shaker handed it to Russ he
didn't take it just turned his head toward the wall.
"Better take some. Chase some'a them rabbits away."
"Nick . . . I gotta get home . . . milk my cows. . . ."
"I called Cathy. Said she'd get Phil down the road to
help 'er—"

Russ sat up his legs droppin' to the floor he started feelin' around under the couch for his shoes.

"Shit, he don't know my cows—Stumptail's got a bad hindquarter, he might put the milker on it—"

"Gotta hunch they're through by now. . . ."

Russ quit feelin' for his shoes looked up at Nick.

". . . it's past midnight."

"No shit?"

"No shit."

Russ stood up then sat back down again. The cold gray lump was there so big now he hadda feelin' it might never go away.

"When'd you eat last, Russ?"

"I dunno. Yesterday. Where the hell'r my shoes at anyway?"

"On your feet. Wanna bowl'a soup? Got some good homemade split pea, lotta ham in it—"

"Nah."

"Oughta eat somethin'."

"I . . . can't."

"Oughta. I always try to eat at least one good meal a day."

"Maybe . . . later."

Nick pulled out the chair by the desk sat down in it lookin' at Russ.

"Andy tells me you want us to cut you off come Monday."

"Yeah."

Nick took a swig of his shaker.

"Might be a good idea for you, Russ. Don't look like you'll ever learn how to drink. See, you're one'a those guilty drunks—sit out there on that nothin' farm'a yours eatin' yourself out because'a what you are or what you ain't, what you did on your last binge, tellin' yourself you'll never touch a drop or a broad again . . . till you get so

filled up you gotta come down here an' spill your guts.
End up doin' 'er up again, twice as bad."

Russ reached over took the shaker outta Nick's hand took
hisself a little swig funny thing he couldn't even taste it
must be he still had so much booze left in him it tasted
like sugar water.

Nick kept on talkin'.

"It's that kinda thinkin' that gets you. Me, I never let
myself sober up enough to do any thinkin'."

He took the shaker back from Russ an' took one.

"Thinkin'll kill yuh."

Russ sat lookin' at his shoes awhile they were his old
barn work shoes scuffed an' cracked here'n there Cathy
hated 'em tried to throw them away a few times but he
always fished them out on the way to the dump.

"It ain't just that way, Nick. Sure, I feel bad about . . .
what I do . . . to Cathy'n all—but then, then after a week
or so . . . see, I work awful hard to make it up, goin'
without things I might need—I mean, maybe I need a new
pair'a shoes or somethin' but I don't get them see to make
up for the money I blew . . . I even kinda keep track in
my head over the whole year, make myself go without
some piece'a machinery I might need, hell, last year it
was the front end loader—do all kinds'a things, try to be
extra nice to her an' the kid, bring them little surprises I
might find in the woods or the fields, might just be a
little bird's nest or somethin' . . . a pretty stone . . . but
then . . . then after I figger I'm about even, maybe two-
three weeks . . . I get . . . this thing . . . this thing buildin'
up in me, this kinda wild feelin'—like I'm pumpin'
up inside an' I can't hardly hold myself down on the
ground an' I can't stand them around me touchin' at me
grabbin' at me always wantin' somethin' from me . . . !"

"Like what?"

"Like . . . I dunno, Nick. Somethin' . . . more! But

. . . whatever it is . . . maybe I just ain't . . . got it. Maybe I just ain't got it, Nick."

Nick didn't say nothin' just handed Russ his shaker never even looked at Russ when he did it.

Russ didn't take a drink right away just sat there starin' at the shaker in his hand.

"Then I wanna come down here an' give . . . what I got . . . to somebody else. Nick, maybe if I could just . . . never come here nomore . . . ?"

Now Russ took a drink. He even had time to take a second one before Nick looked up at him an' said somethin'.

"Go someplace else? Sneak around corners? Be a closet drinker? Lay out in your barn dead ass drunk two-three days atta time?"

"I mean . . . quit. For good."

"Nah, you'll never quit. You gotta blow it off some way. You're just talkin' this way now 'cause the lid's off an' you're feelin' sick an' sorry."

Nick took a fast hard slug'a his shaker then handed it to Russ. He waited until Russ was takin' one before he put the finger on 'im.

"Russ, you'n me, we got the mark on our foreheads. The X, the fuck-me sign. The ones who got the mark don't ever quit—leastways, not till they got the hole pulled in after them."

"I am, Nick. Come Monday mornin'."

Nick reached over grabbed the shaker from Russ took a slug wiped the back'a his mouth with his hand.

"Yeah, so am I."

"I mean it though."

"Sure you do."

He took another slug an' handed it to Russ who did the same. Lately Nick had been talkin' real slow'n quiet serious-like he wasn't even usin' his pointin' finger must be he was there had his quart in him by now an' didn't need it.

The booze was pickin' Russ up a little too. Oh the cold

gray lump was still there but it had got him up off the slab. At least Cathy an' the kid weren't sittin' there starin' at him anymore starin' at him layin' there all dressed out on the slab touchin' at 'im grabbin' at 'im shakin' their heads that funny little look in their eyes.

Seemed like lately he'd been seein' that funny little look in their eyes more'n more. When they looked at him— or maybe when they shoulda but didn't an' looked away. Then he'd catch a glimpse of it . . . reminded him'a that doe he'd shot last fall wasn't quite dead when he caught up with it that look was in her eyes too when he leaned over her throat with the knife—

Russ tried to laugh but all that came out was a funny little croakin' sound so he reached over for the shaker took a little nip then a half-assed laugh came out.

"Maybe we oughta switch to dope, Nick—they say that marywana ain't half bad."

"Shit. This way I at least know part'a the time what's happenin' to me."

Nick finished off the shaker put the bottle back in the drawer staggered a little when he straightened up looked to Russ like he'd just about had the course.

Nick hooked his thumb at Russ.

"How 'bout givin' me a shot at that couch?"

Russ stood up Nick laid down closed his eyes pointed his finger where he figgered the door oughta be.

"Now you go on out there have you a few . . . get yourself relax. Hell, you ain't done nothin' so bad—shit, while you was sleepin' in here Wolcott fell asleep at the bar pissed his pants . . . ran down his leg . . . inta Mrs. Highberg's shoe . . ."

Russ took his old barn mackinaw covered Nick with it the best he could.

Saturday night was really swingin' by the time Russ got out there the jukebox poundin' sounded like Ace Cannon the talk an' laughin' boilin' through the swirlin' blue air.

Russ's spot was open it usually was most people didn't like to sit way back in the corner so close to the service bar.

"Give me one, Andy."

Andy hadn't seen him coming when he heard Russ's voice he turned put his hands on his hips stood lookin' at 'im.

"Wow."

"What'a'ya say, Andy?"

"What is it, full moon? They're all out tonight—Christ, I got Wolcott one end'a the bar now you on the other . . . what am I, haunted or somethin'?"

"You got nothin' to worry about from me, Andy—I'm on my way home."

"Yeah, that's what Wolcott said when he came in. What the hell is it, he gets drunk spends all his money down at Hansen's then comes wanderin' in here with a assful broke—shit, assfull is right."

"Yeah, Nick was tellin' me about it."

"Christ, I offered him five bucks to go back to Hansen's —but no, he had to go sit down next to Mrs. Highberg!"

Andy flung his bar-rag in the rinse tank stepped a couple'a fast steps away.

Russ could see Andy wasn't gonna be too easy to crack tonight his head jerkin' around one eye on the clock the other on the crowd drinkin' his colitis milk with both hands his other eye checkin' ages as the younger crowd kept streamin' in.

"Yeah, I'm all set now—that nap sure straightened me out. Say, while I'm thinkin' about it . . . thanks a lot, Andy."

"What for?"

"For . . . takin' care'a me."

"You don't do much for business layin' here stinkin'."

"Well, guess I better have just one before I go. . . ."

Andy didn't move.

"Gotta get up early tomorrow. Get Tommie over there, dig out my spreader, get it in his shop so she'll thaw out—"

"Tomorrow's Sunday."

"Still gotta get up early—get my milkin' done so's I can get my kid to Sunday school on time . . . it's our turn for early services this month, you know."

Andy shrugged like he didn't much give a shit but he did move back in front'a the whiskey-well stood there lookin' at Russ his grumpy colitis look on his face.

"Nick say you could have one?"

"Yeah. Honest. . . ."

"What's he doin' now?"

"Sleepin'."

"That figgers. . . ."

Andy hadn't reached down for the V.O. bottle but he hadn't moved away neither.

"Well, I don't guess you'll be seein' much'a me after tonight."

"What'a'ya, movin' or somethin'?"

"Don't you remember—you're postin' me come Monday mornin'."

"Oh, yeah."

"I ain't shittin', Andy—tomorrow's my last day. Only reason I say Monday, figgered I might come in a few hours tomorrow afternoon, watch the game 'fore I hang 'em up."

Andy smiled his who-you-tryin'-to-shit smile but he didn't move away 'course he didn't reach for the V.O. bottle neither.

"Your TV broke?"

"Nah, it's workin'. 'Course Cathy don't like football on TV—says she can't see what's the big deal if you don't know none'a the players—"

"Thought you said Cathy was gone . . . ?"

"Oh, yeah . . . forgot about that. . . ."

Andy smiled his shit-eatin' smile leaned in patted Russ on the shoulder.

"Buck up, ol 'buddy, she's back. Me'n Nick talked to her about the milkin'.."

Andy made a big show'a lookin' at his watch then checkin' it with the big one on the wall.

" 'Course that was six hours ago. The way she's been comin' an' goin' lately maybe she's gone again by now. . . ."

"Well, she was!"

"If you say so, Russ."

Neither one of 'em said nothin' for awhile Russ didn't feel much like lookin' at Andy he could feel Andy still lookin' at him he figgered he might as well get it over with.

"What'd she say . . . when you asked 'er?"

"We didn't. We knew all along she wouldn't leave yuh."

"I'm . . . glad you didn't mention it."

"We figgered you would be."

"I am."

Russ glanced up at Andy he caught Andy with the nice look on his face the one Russ remembered from when they was younger together before he was Andy the Businessman.

Andy reached down picked up a glass off the drainboard with one hand the V.O. bottle with the other set the glass on the folded catchcloth dropped in a couple'a ice cubes poured in a healthy slug'a V.O. topped it off with the same'a water slid the drink across to Russ.

"Who you like in the game tomorrow?"

"The big Pack with the Bears?"

"Yeah. Should be a helluva game."

"Always is. Be colder'n'a mother out there."

"Who's home?"

"Packers."

"Man that's the worst. Remember that game we watched a few years back—somethin' like thirty below wasn't it? Helluva wind besides?"

"Yeah. I took you for twenty that day."

"Wasn't the first time. Maybe I'll take the Pack to-morrow—that frozen ground'll cut down the Bears' run-nin' attack."

"Packers play on the same field—besides, they got that heatin' system under the ground now."

"Yeah, might even be worse for the passers tomorrow. Hard to grip a football in that kinda weather."

"Packers got the edge if Starr plays—that cagey old bastard can make the weather work for him."

"He's gettin' pretty old."

"He kin still get up for the big ones."

"Bears got the runnin' though."

"What'a'ya talkin' about—Packers got the depth, Gra-bowski, Hampton, the Roadrunner . . . an' don't forget Donny Anderson, he's some helluva ballplayer—"

"He ain't no Gale Sayers."

"Who is? Maybe Anderson can't run with Sayers but I'll guarantee you one thing Sayers can't kick, catch, or block with Anderson neither. . . ."

"Hell, he's nothin' but an overrated college stiff—shit, the Packers give half a million bucks an' he sits on the bench half the time, ten-thousand-dollar-a-year guys playin' ahead'a him—"

"He wouldn't be if I was coachin'. In my book he's a money ballplayer—"

"Yeah, in the bank. Hell, Russ, he's nothin' but a flash in the pan—got himself a big name at some little dinky school down south, never lived up to it again. Hell if the Packers hadn't gone so far in hock for him in the first place he'd be on the bench all the time. Man, they've been tryin' to unload him for years, they'd trade him in a min-ute if they could find some other team willin' to pick up his contract."

"Man, for a guy never got past third string high school you sure got all the inside dope, Andy."

"Now don't start givin' me that big honcho routine,

Russ. Just because I sat on the bench don't mean I can't tell a real live ballplayer when I see one—an' I still say Anderson's a big overrated stiff couldn't cut it with the big boys."

"What'a'ya mean—he's there, ain't he?"

"He wouldn't be if it weren't for his reputation and his contract."

"Jesus Christ, he made the pro bowl game two years ago—"

"Ahhh, Lombardi got 'im that."

"Andy, you're fulla shit."

'Not as full's you. Or Anderson. What the hell's Anderson to you in the first place?"

"What's he to you, Andy?"

"Ahhh, bullshit!"

Andy stomped down the bar slammed a couple'a taps in fronta two longhairs.

Russ pulled out his wad held it down low between his legs while he counted it. A hundred-thirty-seven bucks. He musta started with pretty close to two hundred that means he'd blew sixty-three.

That wasn't good. It wasn't as bad as it could'a been though there'd been times when he was hittin' it hard he'd gone through a hundred in a single day here it was almost the end'a the second day he only had one more to go.

'Course he could go home right now start his straight kick right off first thing tomorrow mornin' 'stead'a waitin' for Monday. That way he'd be sure to hang onto the 137 bucks he had left put it together with the 100 or so Cathy was still holdin' they'd be in pretty fair shape that'd make close to 250 give ole man Wiff 40 or so on the feed bill Tommie 20 the first mortgage payment's a little over 100 'course he owed for month before las' too les' see the first's Monday it's set up in advance so actually he owed for three months with the one comin' up October November December shit that'd be over 300 bucks!

Maybe they'd hold for a hundred though. They'd did it before 'course they said they wouldn't do it again but maybe if he told them about his health kick his goin' straight from now on they'd hold off one more time.

Say they hold for 100. That'd be 100, 40, 20 equals 160 from 250 leaves 90 shit that ain't too bad 90 bucks to live on till secon' Friday Cathy gets the first half'a December's check they should be able to make it easy on 90 bucks for two weeks thirteen days actually one'a these days is gone already shit they ain't in so bad shape . . . !

Seems like there was somethin' else hangin' though. Yeah the gas bill. Bryant said he couldn't go another goddam pint on the gas he had to live too Christmas comin' an' ever'thin'.

Carl'd wait though. Russ had gone to grade school with his son Dougie. If Russ went around to the house took Cathy an' the kid Lillian'd break out the coffee an' the doughnuts he'd get Carl aside give 'im the straight scoop he'd let 'im go least to the fifteenth Cathy got the first part'a December's check. . . .

That all went to her old man though. On the second mortgage. Only way her ole lady'd let him lend Russ the money was for her secon' Friday check to go straight to him shit Russ never even got to see it she'd swing in there on her way home endorse it over to him.

Maybe just this once. Christmas comin' up an' all . . . nah! He'd jerk off in The Farmers' State Bank window at high noon on the Fourth'a July before he'd crawl on his belly over to ole Mrs. Meanmouth ask her to let it go a month yeah he'd bet his ass she'd be the one he'd have'ta end up askin' she wore the pants in that family when it came to money least one leg.

It'd be a pretty tough Christmas. Christ he wished to

hell he woulda thought'a Christmas 'fore he took off Friday night. Bet a thousand bucks he wouldn't'a gone'n done it then.

What the hell difference would 63 measly bucks'a done? Add 'em to the 90 still only makes 153 how the hell could anybody three people live on 153 bucks the whole goddam month'a December Christmas comin' besides an' goddamit ta hell he was plannin' on gettin' Cathy that fur-trimmed coat she'd been wantin' for three years Jesus Christ he'd promised the kid a bicycle!

He had to get 'im that bicycle. He'd looked the kid straight in the eyes the kid made him do it crossed his heart hoped to die too a red'n white one with the high handlebars an' the banana seat.

Shit.

Christ he was nothin' but a pig. A dirty hog. Here he'd gone'n blew a red'n white bicycle with high handlebars an' banana seat an' a good start on a fur-trimmed coat she'd been waitin' on for three years—

His milk check! Hot damn his milk check! Shit yes he'd have a milk check comin' again around the twentieth be just in time a few days before Christmas hell they could live on the 153 bucks till then it wasn't much there were only seven milkin' good this time'a year but it would be enough enough for a red'n white bicycle a fur-trimmed coat Christmas with all the trimmin's!

Let's see he better figger it out again he din't wanna let hisself get too excited maybe there wa a monkey wrench in there somewhere—100 on the mortgage if the bank would go for it 40 to ole man Wiff 20 to Tommie . . . oh yeah the telephone an' 'lectricity they was four months old already they'd already got the cutoff warnin' from the telephone 'lectricity wouldn't be far behind better figger 'bout two months' worth on them probably run around 20 apiece that'd be 40 more bring it down to 113 still could make it if they squeezed bought a lotta chuck roasts liver shit yeah he could butcher that bull calf he'd been raisin' make nice meat for Christmas—

Dickman! Goddam there was Dickman lookin' over his way too Dickman Fuel & Heating, Inc. Rum'n Coke Dickman face as red as one'a his trucks he'd carry a guy longer'n anybody around.

He'd already carried Russ goin' into his second winter Cathy didn't even know it he hadn't paid Rum'n Coke a penny in fifteen months not since spring before last then he hadn't cleared that winter all the way up.

Las' time Rum'n Coke mentioned it was creepin' mighty close to a thousand. Been two-three months'a furnace weather already this year goddam winter came plenty early this year had ta be over a thousand by now—

The extra Saturday night bartender his name was Dicky or Ricky somethin' like that came over stopped across the bar from Russ set down a drink.

"Drink's on Mr. Dickman."

Russ just nodded he knew that much already looked over at Rum'n Coke lifted the drink to him he lifted his drink back started pickin' his way through the crowd toward Russ Russ knew he'd do that too.

" 'Lo, R.C."

" 'Lo, Russ."

"How they hangin'?"

"Low."

R.C. straightened up took a sip'a his drink looked around slow at the crowd studied his own drink for a while took another sip screwed up his face like it was full'a his own number ten fuel oil set it down again Russ could tell he wasn't likin' it a damn bit better'n he was.

"Rough winter, Russ. That ole Timkin'a yours is suckin' it like water."

"You don't have to tell me, R.C."

"I . . . hope not, Russ.

He said it in a low voice never once lookin' at Russ now he picked up his drink looked way around the other way.

"By golly, there's ole Oscar Swenson, I better get over there'n say hello to him too."

"Thanks, R.C."

"What for?"

"The drink."

"You already thanked me once."

He clapped Russ on the shoulder an' started pickin' his way through the crowd Russ watched him go he felt like a shitheel thinkin' how he always seemed to make the nice guys wait till last he made up his mind right then'n there the first guy he was goin' to pay up when he got his hands on a chunk was Rum'n Coke Dickman.

Yeah, that's what he had to do get his hands on a chunk a big chunk. But where?

Maybe H.F.C. yeah the radio'n TV was always bullshittin' about them bill-payer's loans. Where you get one big loan an' go around happy as a bastard payin' up all your small ones then all you got to do is make one small monthly payment to H.F.C.

Let's see now he had about fifteen hundred maybe even two big one's to Rum'n Coke four-five hundred to ole man Wiff three-four to Carl the gas man Tommie must be around a hundred or so make it an even hundred over three hundred to the bank on the first mortgage hell closer to four round it off at four . . . let's see. . . .

"Hey, Andy, gimme a piece'a paper an' a pencil."

Andy was just passin' by with a fistful'a taps he set 'em down in front'a the pimplefaces an' came back reached over by the jewish piano an' handed over a small pad an' a ballpoint pen marked *Dobchek's Merry Christmas* on the side.

"What'a'ya gonna do, make out your last will'n testament?"

"Maybe."

Russ didn't say no more just went to figgerin' so Andy moved back down the bar ended up pretty close to the young blonde he had staked out by the jukebox he didn't have to be so careful now his wife had gone up to the house.

Let's see now say two big ones for Rum'n Coke maybe not quite but that'd give him a little cushion five hundred for ole man Wiff four to Carl a hundred to Tommie three to the bank no make it four . . . fur-trimmed coat must run around sixty-seventy the bike another forty a few more odd's'n ends peanuts candy apples might as well make it a real Christmas a hundred'n-fifty-dollar one Christ knows he owed 'em one . . . let's see . . . zero five nine ten fourteen fifteen five carry your one one an' two makes three —three-thousand five hundred dollars Jesus H. Christ!

Thirty-five hundred. Let's see he had 137 on him now plus a couple'a bucks change Cathy had another 100 or so back at the house 237—

Shit he'd even missed a few! The phone an' the lights they'd go another 100 easy . . . let's see . . . Duane! Over 400 on the mortgage-life—fuck 'em! Let 'im stick that moneygrubbin' policy up his perfumed ass with all the rest that goes there! Shit he'd paid in for eight years already that's eight times over four better than 3200 shit if he hadn't let that slimy bastard cornhole 'im with that policy he'd be clear right now. An' what had he ever got out of it? The only way the fuckin' thing would pay off was if he was dead—

The income tax! The fuckin' income tax! The fuckin' income tax he hadn't paid last year. Sat there for three nights figgerin' figgerin' they'd have something comin' back damned if they didn't end up owin' stopped on the way to the post office tore them goddam XYZ forms up real small flushed them down Nick an' Andy's john.

Fuck it!

Russ crumpled the paper an' flung it on the floor ground it to pieces with the heel of his boot. Maybe Nick mighta found it when he cleaned up tomorrow.

Shit there was no way H.F.C. would go for that big a chunk no matter what they say on the TV particularly since they was still tryin' to collect on that last little loan he got over there a couple'a years ago shit there was another one he forgot!

"Hey Dicky Ricky whatever the shit your name is gimme a drink. . . !"

He stood up started to push out his empty glass toward the bartender all of a sudden he felt so goddam empty funny thing he thought of his cows the ones that were dried up.

"The cows dried up," he said to himself, "five of my cows are dried up, I ain't gettin' much milk this time'a year, five'a my cows dried up—"

The pain came fast this time swellin' up in his chest runnin' a hot horned hand up his throat chokin' off his wind he either had to smash somebody or pass out he started to stand there was nobody close enough to smash. . . .

He musta blanked out for a little while there. Next thing he knew he was back sittin' on his stool his hands grippin' on the bar his eyes starin' at hisself in the Schaefer tap.

He looked . . . kinda crazy. His eyes looked like they was about to pop outta his head. The cords in his neck stood out like hayfork ropes goin' up with too big a load.

The rest of his face was . . . scarey. Kinda nothin' white. Like it was already dead. Just waitin' for the rest of 'im to know it.

'Course his face always looked goofy in the Schaefer tap. Shit yeah it was rounded the light was dim way over in the corner here maybe he was even a little drunk shit yeah his face always looked kinda goofy in the Schaefer tap.

He'd haf'ta try an' get a little grip on hisself though. Good thing Nick or Andy didn't see him. Better get out now while he still could.

Carol was standin' there by the jukebox eyein' him up when he walked by. When he didn't stop she turned away from him an' dropped the coin in the slot. Just as he went through the double glass doors *Release Me* came rollin' out after him, "Please release me, let me go, 'cause I don't love—"

The doors closed behind him choppin' off the rest.

It was colder in the truck than he ever remembered but he didn't do nothin' just sat there shakin' in the dark.

Funny thing he didn't really wanna go home neither. He didn't wanna go back inside but he didn't wanna go home an' he sure's hell didn't want Carol but he still wanted something but . . . but . . . he couldn't just put his finger on what.

Another drink? Nah, he was about to puke already. Some other cunt? He couldn't'a got a hard-on with Jimmy La-Force's dick. A fight? A faggot could'a whipped him with a pussy willow right now. A . . . a . . . what the hell else was there?!

But there must be somethin'. Somethin' he just couldn't think of it right off. Somethin' bigger'n cunts'n drunks'n fights—money!

Yeah, money. That was somethin' he wanted all right —shit needed!

But you don't just go pickin' up chunks'a money off snowbanks in the middle of the night.

Sure be nice though. If he could just go drivin' along in his ole red truck scoopin' up all the money he needed right up off the top'a snowbank fillin' the back'a his truck like bales'a hay—

No point in bullshittin' hisself. No way a guy could get it that way. A guy wants money he has to work for it.

Less'n he steals it.

Shit no! He weren't no goddam sticky-fingers! He might be lower'n a snake's belly but he ain't never got that low yet. Shit if he wanted to steal he could'a just grabbed a handful outta Nick an' Andy's safe when he was sleepin' back there in the office it was standin' wide open so chock full'a money it was about to come rollin' out shit he coulda grabbed two-three handfuls they'd probably never even notice it—

Nah, he weren't no goddam sneak thief. Besides . . . it wasn't just money. Sure he needed the money all right that was one'a the things but that wasn't . . . the all of it.

There was . . . some other things. Some'a those other things he couldn't think'a right now. Shit there must be!

Christ there had to be more to life then just cunts'n drinks'n fights'n money.

Like maybe Cathy an' the kid an' the farm?

Shit he had them already.

To tell the whole truth the only thing he knew for dead sure was he had to go someplace he couldn't just stay here.

Shit yeah he had to do somethin' even if it was wrong. Seemed like some kinda plan was shapin' in his mind.

He turned the key on an' pumped the footfeed a few times pulled the hand choke way out an' kicked 'er over.

She started right off. Cold as it was an' as long as she'd been sittin' there in the open she started right off.

That must mean somethin'. If she hadn't he would'a had to'a gone back inside but she kicked right in an' was runnin' smooth the pistons hardly slappin' at all the needle startin' to creep up toward the warm mark.

He flipped on the heater high. Pretty soon it was almost cozy there in the cab.

But he still didn't pull out. What was he waitin' for? What the hell was there to wait for?! There was nothin'

inside that was gonna do any big deal thing for Russ
Simpson Jr. Nothin' but an old buildin' with a few new
additions fancied up a little with neon lights a jukebox
poundin' noise smoke could hardly breathe hear hisself
think talkin' laughin' singin' dancin' bunch assholes gettin'
a nosefull throwin' away ever' dime they ever made.

But he still didn't pull out. Just sat there his motor runnin' watchin' the neon blink on an' off off an' on the electric fire flickerin' out over the snowbanks at him red an'
blue diamonds winkin' to 'im readin' the sign like he'd
never seen it before.

DOBCHEK'S
STOP! GIVE YOURSELF A BREAK

Funny thing he kinda had the feelin' he'd never be goin'
back in there again—

Shit he'd be back in there to watch the Packer game
tomorrow. Same time same station.

He slapped the ole truck in low an' gunned 'er outta
the parkin' lot pistons slappin' motor screechin' slidin'
sideways crampin' the wheels the other way the wheels
grabbin' again on the cement highway headin' east headin'
east away from home.

Down 9H headin' east away from home double-clutchin'
her into second feelin' the truck jolt forward when the
clutch plates bit together listenin' to the sprung door
creakin' the body startin' to bounce on the worn-out
shocks bouncin' worse'n worse the more he built up
speed startin' to slew from side to side droppin' her into
high the footfeed still smashed against the floorboards the
motor screamin' for mercy he wanted to give her some
but he couldn't goin' so fast the body slewin' so bad it
scared him but not enough the lights comin' at him a horn
wailin' goddammit he felt like runnin' his truck right be-

tween the headlights search an' destroy that horn an' the finger an' the body an' the eyes the horn blarin' still in his brain but he'd let it go he'd let it go but he'd wanted to get it an' that scared him.

He eased up on the footfeed slowed 'er down checkin' the load in the wide extension mirror it was still hangin' on slowed 'er down she quit buckin' slowed 'er down just rollin' along where the hell was he goin' now?

Slowed 'er down just lettin' her roll along shovin' the answers outta his head just drivin' lettin' her roll along piss on it he didn't wanna think no more just let 'er roll along ain't that ever enough for chrissakes ain't that ever enough?!

Stoppin' at the stoplight. Waitin' for the green just waitin' for the green turnin' right on 66 when it came not even thinkin' about it just turnin' right on 66 headin' down toward town.

Past the high school. Past the old high school past the diner where he use'ta get a milk-shake when he hadda quarter watch that fat Jansen girl eat J & L Specials when he didn't chocolate ice cream topped with marshmallow crushed nuts cherry watched her eat one ever' goddam day even asked her for a bite one day Christ they were good forty cents apiece she let him finish it let him finish it every day till he got too ashamed to go down there anymore.

Past the high school past the diner past Adam's IGA Superette where he bought Cathy the heart-box of chocolates that Valentine's Day chopped wood durin' noon hour sophomore winter twenty cents a cord would she ever know how hard he worked to buy her that heart-box of chocolate-covered cherries?

Past Boile the undertaker he'n Babe an' Ubby snuck in there one night looked at a stiff laid out on a slab all he could remember how blue his face was a blue face with the black beard still showin' through the blue skin in the flashlight spot they didn't stay to look too long.

Turnin' in where the neon arrow said. Turnin' in past the little-bigger-bigger-biggest then little again startin' all over again neon arrow the ole red truck just turnin' in by herself like she knew where she was goin'.

Turnin' an' parkin' there right by the front door.

He could hear the pins clatterin' the minute he opened the door. He knew it wasn't so but he didn't care he just let the feelin' come the feelin' it was then an' he had stopped after school to shoot the shit with the gang maybe even shoot a little eight ball if he had a dime. Just like it was then the piped-in music playin' somewhere he never did know from where the balls rollin' down the alley smackin' against the pins clatter clatter wowwweee a strike dancin' up'n down laughin' talkin' smoke hangin' thick drinkin' tap rackin' the balls click click chalkin' up bhammmm breakin' 'em clean one rollin' in the side pocket we got stripes.

Just standin' there inside the door lettin' the feelin' soak through. Just standin' there lookin' around slow it hadn't changed a bit. The bar was right there where it was s'posed to be. So were the two pool tables. The jukebox against the partition between the bar an' the bowling alley the kids used to play it to drown out Lawrence Welk on the piped-in music use'ta really piss ole CornPete the bartender off he was a big Myron Floren fan he'd turn the jukebox way down low the kids would bitch to Shakey the owner he'd give 'em back their dime nobody ever could figger out why he kept piped-in music an' the jukebox playin' at the same time sometimes the TV too maybe he didn't even notice he was too busy drinkin' martinis an' shakin'.

Shakey wasn't sittin' there in his usual spot down by

the end of the bar. Maybe he was dead. That didn't look like CornPete behind the bar neither. Maybe he was dead too.

But the I-jackets were still there. 'Course he knew the same guys weren't still inside them but that much hadn't changed anybody who was anybody on the team always did hang out here leastways them that was so good the coach didn't dare tell them to stay out.

Yeah the I-jackets were still here. So were the prettiest girls stickin' right close to them their I-jackets' class rings on little gold chains around their necks just like Cathy used to do stickin' right close to them their little eyes never far from their I-jacket waitin' for their I-jacket to say somethin' so they could laugh watchin' their I-jacket real close fingerin' their rings lookin' for a chance to touch him pat him rub up against him makin' sure the whole world knew which I-jacket was theirs watchin' listenin' stickin' close sometimes the ring girls even started to act like the I-jackets.

The I-jackets actin' like they didn't give a shit. Actin' like they didn't even notice no matter what their ring girl did. What the hell nobody else counted anyway they was just there for them.

Least that was the way he use'ta feel. Maybe he should'a dug out his ole I-jacket wore it tonight. Maybe then one'a those prettiest girls would smile up at him grab at his hand like that little blonde was doin' over there. Maybe then at least somebody would look over at him maybe even ask him to grab a cue get in the game laugh an' talk around grab-ass a little hell he had his dime right here in his hand—

"Russ Simpson . . . Jr."

At first he looked around to see who'd said out his name. Maybe Shakey or CornPete weren't dead after all. He didn't see nobody he knew. Ever'body was doin' just the same as they was before the I-jackets I'in' their ring girls me-tooin' Russ moved to the middle of the room closer to the bar. Heard his name real loud. This time he knew it was him who said it.

"Russ Simpson Jr."

Now ever'body was lookin' at him. Ever'body stopped what they was doin' turned their heads to look at him. The I-jackets with their cues in their hands even the ones sightin' in. All the prettiest girls rings on gold chains nestlin' there in that little hollow in their sweaters. All lookin' at him. He couldn't hear nothin' but the pins clatterin' the soft music piped in from somewhere Russ never did know where.

"You talkin' to me, mister?"

The bartender was standin' there across the bar lookin' at him kinda funny-like it wasn't ole CornPete he must be dead for sure.

"Russ Simpson Jr. . . . wants a drink. For the house."

He said it plenty loud. He couldn't even hear the pins clatterin' anymore not even the piped-in music all he could hear was the sound of his name echoin' around like it used to in the drainage culvert back to the Farm.

The bartender didn't do nothin' at first just stood there leanin' on the bar lookin' at him.

"You mean . . . ever'body in here . . . ?"

"Wall to wall. The bowlin' alley too."

The bartender's whiskey-water eyes opened up a little wider on that one then narrowed down again.

"You . . . carryin'?"

Russ reached in his pocket brought out the rest of his roll spread it out on the bar he could hear the I-jackets an' the rings start to buzz a little then.

"Roll 'em."

The bartender shrugged his skinny little shoulders kinda helpless-like started reachin' for glasses. The buzzin' whis-

perin' pokin' started up again balls clickin' but nothin'
so loud as before ever once'n awhile somebody'd sneak a
look at Russ he could see them in the backbar mirror but
he didn't let on he could.

He was feelin' better now. The noble feelin' was there
the power was there right down through his legs he didn't
even give a shit if they asked him in the game he still had
his dime out goddam bastards at least they knew he was
here!

But there was still somethin' missin'. Somethin' wasn't
quite right. Hell he'd said his name an' ever'thin' right out
loud but it still didn't really seem like they knew who he
was. Nobody's head had snapped around—sure they'd
looked his way but just like they'd look at anybody said
his name out loud.

Not that he expected them to all drop their cues the girls
pull off their sweaters start rollin' around on the floor the
I-jackets crowdin' around slappin' him on the back squeezin' his hands linin' up for autographs maybe even lift him
to their shoulders ride him around the room a few times
singin' the old school song—fact is he hadn't really
thoughta what exactly they'd do so long as it was somethin' fairly big . . . but goddam he kinda thought one just
one might know who he was what he'd done hell that
Hudson game 4 touchdowns 2 field goals 256 yards hell
that ain't exactly nothin' to sneeze at!

Shit yeah he figgered he had a little more comin' than
that. Not just smirkin' little sideways glances whispers
growin' into laughter one pimpleface imitatin' his stag-
gerin' walk his ring girl makin' the head an' finger crazy
sign. Not just reachin' out an' grabbin' the beers off the
tray soon as whiskey-water eyes set them up some even
grabbin' one in each hand comin' back for seconds not
even botherin' to look over his way maybe just lift their
glass nod their head to him.

Then forgettin' about him again. Actin' like he wasn't even there no more.

Goin' back to their pool game. The girls' eyes followin' them. The I-jackets dead serious eyein' their shots movin' around the tables on light feet takin' turns without a word movin' fast from shot to shot faces tight an' kinda mean smart alecky young faces sightin' down their cue seein' nothin' but the ball shootin' hard even when a soft shot would do drivin' their cue hard against the cue ball sinkin' their numbers one by one cleanin' the table bankin' in the eight ball . . . steppin' back takin' a quick sip'a his beer *his* beer for chrissakes settin' it back down on the rail rackin' the balls for the next game—

"Russ Simpson Jr.!"

This time the heads did snap around. This time they all did look at him not just sideways really starin' Russ back at them not just checkin' in the backbar mirror whirlin' around on his stool starin' right back at them no sound now no sound 'cept from behind the partition the balls rollin' the pins clatterin' the soft music comin' in from somewhere no sound here just people starin'.

They was the first to drop their eyes. One by one they dropped their eyes heads bowin' foot shufflin' little nervous giggles awkward turns a nothin' stab at the cue ball—

"Four touchdowns! Two field goals! Two hundred forty-six yards!"

The bartender reached over the bar an' touched Russ's sleeve Christ how he hated that touch he ripped his arm away—

"1959!"

Nothin' just the sound of a lofted ball hittin' the maple rollin' rollin' crraaakkk clatter the music from nowhere—

"My God, don't nobody here remember Russ Simpson Jr.?"

Nothin'! The music from nowhere just kept playin'. Another ball hit the maple rollin' rollin' seemed like ever'body was waitin' waitin' the crraaakkk never come must be gutter ball.

Then the bartender made a little motion with his hands. The I-jackets laid down their cues real careful their eyes still kinda down an' to the side the prettiest girls with the big boys' rings nestlin' in their little hollows sidlin' back along the wall little pink tongues lickin' red lipstick eyes flashin' too bright watchin' the I-jackets movin' in on Russ.

Movin' in on Russ. Movin' in a ragged V the honkers flyin' north their arms bent at the elbows like claws strong young bodies hunched forward eyes glitterin' mean-scared movin' in on him.

They hadn't oughta be doin' that. They shouldn't wanna do that he was one of them he was an I-jacket too—

Russ got down off his stool. He dropped to set position crouchin' over shoulders forward hands low one palm over the other leavin' just enough room for the quarterback to slap the ball in startin' forward waitin' for him to slap the ball in movin' forward there's the hole where's the ball gimme the ball gimme the goddam ball—

The hole closed up. Somebody maybe the middle linebacker shot the gap nailed him before he could get up a head'a steam the whole line pinchin' in on top of him wrestlin' him down slammin' him down on the hard frozen turf.

Why don't the referee blow the whistle? The play's over for chrissakes blow the whistle blow the whistle!

Instead they picked him up. Carried him. He didn't even struggle. Why should he he knew the play was over even if they didn't.

He could hear the crowd cheerin' an' clappin' when they threw him down on the sidelines. He lay there in the snow. Funny thing he ached all over. They hadn't hit him or nothin' but still he ached all over.

He opened his eyes. Wasn't till now he could open his eyes really see it. They were just goin' back in—their ring girls troopin' in behind. Nobody even looked back at him. The door closed behind the last one.

He heard something like a cheer. He closed his eyes again. Then he saw a funny thing. He was layin' there in the snow but he could see just like he was back inside the prettiest girls leadin' cheers jumpin' up on the pool table leadin' cheers sis-boom-bah doin' cartwheels the big rings on the little gold chains flyin' ever' which way "let's hear one for ole Russ he's our man if he can't do it no-body can" the prettiest somersaultin' over the pool table Cathy up on the bar leadin' all the others "rah rah Russ Simpson rah rah Russ Simpson yaaeeehh!"

Then he was back out in the snow. Colder'n he'd ever been in his life. Colder even than back there in the truck in Dobchek's parkin' lot. Too cold.

He got up brushed himself off a little. The truck was still sittin' there right by the door the load still on it the small bigger biggest small bigger biggest neon arrow still tellin' the people where to turn in.

He turned out. He turned the truck around an' headed out the wrong way past the neon arrow back up 66.

He'd never be comin' back there again neither.

He drove hard. Seemed like he had to get home to Cathy as fast as he could now. The road was filled with cars big cars Cadillacs Buicks must be close to closin' 'time people headin' home to nice warm beds ever'thin' just fine with them funny thing he had all he could do to keep from turnin' his ole red truck right smack dab into them lights comin' at him.

All the rest of his money layin' back there on the bar.

Cathy was sleepin' when he got there. Holdin' the not-so-little-anymore boy cuddled in her arms.

He just stood there an' watched them sleep for awhile.

They were hangin' on to each other like they really needed to.

Funny thing that kinda pissed him off. Up to now he couldn't get home fast enough to see them particularly her but now the more he watched them layin' there huggin' on each other the more it pissed him off for a minute there he felt like turnin' an' walkin' right back outta there no wonder he was such a goddam sissy faggot the way she hugged on him all the time lettin' him sleep with her an' ever'thin' when he was gone hell that was no way for a mother to treat a boy s'pose to grow up to be a man hell his ma never hugged'n kissed on him like that.

Russ pulled the kid's arms from around her neck. He never woke up just whimpered once tried to hang on to her but Russ pulled him away. Cathy opened her eyes looked up at Russ reached out to pull the kid back her eyes starin 'wide he pulled the kid away from her she took a deep breath her nostrils flarin' wide the way they did sometimes but she didn't say nothin' so neither did he just picked the kid up an' carried him into his room.

She just laid there the same way lookin' up at him when he come back. He stood there lookin' down at her she lookin' up at him neither of 'em sayin' nothin' him wishin' she'd say somethin' maybe even scream out at him come jumpin' up outta that bed slappin' at his face scratchin' at his eyes—

But she didn't do nothin' just laid there lookin' up at him that wounded doe look in her eyes.

It even surprised him when the first one came. Jerkin' up outta his guts tearin' up through his chest stoppin' it just in time in his throat. But then the next one came rip-pin' along behind pushin' the first one up into his mouth. Then the next one now he had to open his mouth let it out at first like grunts but then they came faster an' faster an' he couldn't hold them back not really words not really cries words wailing wailing words—

"Cut . . . they cut . . . they cut me . . . they cut me . . . they cut me—"

Cathy was setting up now reaching out to him but he couldn't move the fear wild in her face.

"Cut you?!"

"They cut me they cut me—"

"Russ! Where?"

"Team . . . the team . . . they cut me—"

"What team?! Russ—"

"They cut me—off the team . . . they cut me off the team—"

She was up off the bed now shaking him taking hold of him looking wild into his wild eyes.

"Russ, what's wrong?! What's wrong with you?"

"I couldn't even make the team. Lord Jesus I couldn't even make the team . . . ! Lord Jesus Christ Almighty I couldn't even make the team!"

She had him now both hands on either side'a his face holding his head together covering his face with kisses sucking away some of the bad kissing crooning crying tears running down her face telling him it was all right but he knew it wasn't it would never be all right.

"I lied. I didn't quit. I couldn't make the team. I couldn't do my lessons. I woulda flunked out just like your mother said. I was flunkin' out an' I couldn't even make the team anyway. See, I wasn't good enough. I never was that good. Never as good as they said. It was only here this dinky little high school the newspaper coach D.A. you just thought I was good—"

"Russ, you were great, you know you were great—"

"No, I wasn't good enough—"

"Yes, you were—Russ, please—"

"No, I'm not good enough—"

"Russ, stop it! Yes, you were—"

"No, I'm not good—"

"Russ, baby, yes, you were, please baby—"

"No, I'm not good—"

"Russ, baby, yes, you are, you are—"

"No, I'll . . . never . . . make the team."

"Oh, Russ . . . !"

He heard her wail now the first thing he had really heard though he knew she had been talkin' all the while her hands on both sides of his face her face pressed against his he could feel the wet of their faces taste the salt in his mouth feel her mouth against his eyes cheeks nose mouth tryin' to stop him talkin' tryin' to suck the bad from him now he felt her crazy wild strength him tryin' to wrestle free'a her she wouldn't let him go she felt stronger'n him still stickin' to him her cryin' face still pressed against his her hands still lockin' his face wrestlin' him down on the bed pinnin' him there on the bed motherin' him him still tryin' to break free'a her.

Then he let her hold him down for awhile. Let her stroke his face with her hands whisper how good he really was. It felt good. He didn't believe it but he let her do it anyway. If only she could keep him pinned down there.

Then he was cryin' too. He was cryin' hard an' each time she would say "you're good, Russ, you're good" he'd just cry harder. Funny thing he knew where he was now things were clear the plan was big in his mind he knew what he had to do. But first he just wanted to cry. Just wanted to cry an' remember the last time he'd cried that day when they dropped him off at the County Farm.

She let him cry till he was done strokin' his head like he was a big baby or somethin' liftin' up the little pink flannel nightie he had bought her one other Christmas wipin' off his face—

Just then he couldn't stand it no longer he hadda get up an' stand.

He walked over by the window stood there lookin' out he could see his ole red truck sittin' there in the moon-

light the load still on. She knew enough not to say nothin'
now just busied herself straightenin' out the bedding real
careful like she was gettin' them ready for inspection in
the army.

"Cathy, I gotta be . . . leavin' you now."

She never even looked up from her work.

"Get some sleep, Russ, it'll be . . . better in the morning."

"No, I gotta go . . . to Carol."

Now she straightened up real slow-like but she didn't
turn to face him.

"Carol . . . ?"

"Carol Gore."

"Oh."

"Yeah. See, that's . . . that's where I been hangin' out
—them Last Fridays when I didn't come home till late.
See . . . see I . . . like her a lot."

She never moved or cried out or said nothin' God she
had guts she just seemed to shrink a little for a minute
there.

"Then you better . . . go to her.'

It was hard for him he had never done anything harder
in his life never would again he just wanted to hang on
to her maybe even cry a little more lay down on their
bed one more time but he turned an' walked to the head
of the stairs.

"Cathy . . . you're still my girl. I . . . I'll always . . .
love you . . . the best, Cathy."

She didn't move. He started down the stairs. Funny
thing in all the years they'd been together that was the
first time he'd ever been able to say it right out loud like
that.

It was even colder now the moon shining brighter he
could feel it cuttin' through his clothes right to the bone
he was shaking big shakes he couldn't control.

He looked up at their bedroom window. It was nice'n warm there. Was she crying now? He hated to see her cry. All he had to do was run back inside up the steps tell her he was lyin' 'bout wantin' to leave her for Carol explain to her why he had to lie to her she'd understand she was smart she understood those things wanted to believe him wanted him to stay with her start over again tomorrow mornin' just like nothin' had happened keep goin' along together just like ever'thin' was fine an' dandy. . . .

Instead he turned an' ran to the truck. Got in started 'er up next thing he knew he was rollin' down 9H headin' east away from home he didn't even remember goin' out the driveway barely knew he was drivin' kinda feelin' like he was about to pass out.

Headin' east away from home.

Sunday

H E WAS lookin' at a flag. The American flag. He read the words, his mind hangin' on each one, sayin' each one over to himself real careful-like before he went on to the next one "America . . . Love . . . It . . . Or . . . Leave . . . It—"

He was in his truck! He was in his truck sittin' there slumped over the steerin' wheel his head up real close to the windshield his eyes right up close to his America sticker—

He must'a cracked up! He musta run off the road ended up in the ditch or somethin'—

Where's Cathy an' the kid?! They were on the way to the movie they musta got thrown out—

He jumped outta the cab started runnin' around the

173

truck all he could see was big piles'a snow the goalposts on each end'a the field—

The goalposts! The goalposts. The goalposts he was standin' in the middle'a the high school football field for chrissakes! . . . his truck standin' there in the middle'a the high school football field idlin' away the load'a sacked corn'n oats still on a few bales'a alfalfa to grind in for roughage—

Then he remembered. Then some of it started comin' back to him slow at first then faster'n faster hittin' him like a sledgehammer one to the forehead an awful one to the guts he grabbed his stomach staggered over to his truck holdin' his stomach all the way leaned against it.

It was cold. Funny thing the truck was all covered with rime frost the skin of his forehead kinda stuck to the fender where he leaned against it his hands too where he was holdin' hisself up but it was Arizona an' the sun was shinin' down—

No it wasn't. It wasn't Arizona. An' he knew it. Even though the sun was shinin' down an' he was on a football field it wasn't Arizona he had quit down there over ten years ago quit hell they'd cut 'im this wasn't Arizona no matter how hard he wanted it to be it was Iola it wasn't Arizona sun no more.

It was Iola sun daybreak sun middle'a the winter sun nothin' sun.

And he was still Russ Simpson Jr. He couldn't shake that one neither. He couldn't go back to Arizona start over again he was still Russ Simpson Jr. The biggest horse's ass that ever lived. A nothin' loser. The winter sun. A lyin' cryin' whinin' poor excuse for a man. Drunk. Alcoholic. The worst kind. Throwin' away the money. Takin' food outta the kid's mouth. Bicycles. With banana seats. Red'n white. Fur-trimmed coats. All she wanted was a little measly rabbit. Ole man Wiff. Duane. Even that faggot was

better'n him. Had no wife'n kid to torture. Just went around
dousin' himself up sellin' death insurance. He'd be better
off dead. Ever'body'd be better off. The bank. Second
mortgage. Meanmouth. Recliner chair. Tommie. Telephone company. Lights. Income tax. Rum'n Coke. Cathy.
The kid. Fur-trimmed coat. Bicycle. Fur-trimmed coat.
Bicycle. Fur-trimmed coat bicycle furtrimmedcoat bicyle-
trimmed furbananaseatred'nwhiterabbit. . . .

He stumbled a few steps away from the truck an' heaved
in the snow. Not much came just a little yellow bile string-
ing away .from his lips. He gagged again tryin' to spit it
way from hisself but it wouldn't go finally he had to take
his finger snap the yellow string into the pretty white snow.

God he wished somebody'd come up behind him knock
'im out turn off his head for awhile.

But nobody did. An' now all of a sudden the cold got
ahold'a 'im. Bent him right over again took the wind right
away from him he went stumblin' back to his truck climbed
back inside.

First thing he noticed was the warm. Then the smell.
At first he thought he'd brought it in with him he could
still taste it in his mouth but then he saw it all inside
the truck over the steerin' wheel on top the dash spattered
up on the windshield on the floorboards when he looked
down he saw it was all down the front'a him too.

He sat there in his own puke an' thought about it. Funny
thing it didn't really bother him now. He figgered it was
about right. About all he had comin'. About all he'd ever
get.

Why was he such a prick? What'd he have to go an' get
hisself all dirtied up again for?! Christ he hated feelin'
like he did now more'n anything in the world. Feelin'
so low'n small'n dirty his whole body achin' not even
wantin' to open his eyes look around him see where he
was remind hisself'a what he'd gone an' done again right

back where he was the last binge only deeper the hole keepin' on gettin' deeper just like Nick sez his whole body shakin' wantin' to cry tear big chunks outta hisself puke some more on hisself?

Dirtyin' her up too. Dirtyin' her'n the kid up too. Dirtyin' her up when she'd never dirtied him once in her life. Never done nothin' for him but good. Worked her ass off for him ever' chance she got. Cleaned an' scrubbed an' helped him outside gotta job besides comes runnin' home can't wait to get there to do some more tryin' to raise the kid up the best she knows how teach him somethin' a little more'n just how to catch a football talk shit outta the corner'a his mouth what does he do?!

What the shit does he do? Stands there waitin'! Waitin' to stick it to 'er. Waitin' for her to make some little slip so he can jab it to 'er. Some big deal slip like gettin' home from work ten minutes late or havin' one drink once'a month or kissin' on the kid too much talkin' baby talk together yeah for chrissakes some big deal crime like that!

Oh what a prick he was. Whatta no good loser sonuva-bitch he turned out to be. What a dirty rotten miserable poor excuse for a man—

How had it happened? How had he let hisself go an' do it again? How after tellin' hisself fifty times the last time makin' up all kinda new rules for hisself had he gone the very next Las' Friday fucked hisself ever' way but loose?

Why had he gone in the first place? What made him so jumpy so full'a meanness an' hate he had ta go puke it out all over the place? That made his nuts ache for an-other woman any ole pig when he had the best one in the world waitin' for him at home? Why'd he keep drinkin' drink after drink shit he didn't even like the taste'a the stuff beggin' for it lyin' for it drinkin' the best part'a his-self away drinkin' till only the pig showed? What made him want to throw his money away yeah he must want to he could never rest till he was stone cold broke in the market his ass against the wall.

Then he could work. Yeah then he could work drag hisself back his head between his legs work like a dog his eyes beggin' for mercy ever'time he looked at Cathy an' the kid tryin' like hell to scramble back outta the hole gettin' a handhold here a handhold there gainin' an inch makin' back a foot sometimes even a yard. . . .

Never makin' it all the way though. Ever'time it looked like he might start to see daylight get a whiff'a clean air he'd let go his grip slide back down again under the bottom.

Like now. Rock bottom. He'd had the course this time. He couldn't even go back home now. Not after what he told Cathy last night. No, he could never stand to see her eyes after that. Feel her eyes on him while he sat there an' ate breakfast. Catch sight'a her watchin' through the kitchen window when he came walkin' across the yard from the barn.

He should be home milkin' right now. What would happen to his cows? Old Stumptail had that bad hindquarter she should have a dose shot up it. Crooked Horn must be about due her calves almost always came headend first Cathy'd never be able to get it out you had to pull like hell ever'time she heaved to get past the front shoulders.

Maybe he should go home. Could. Just drive in the yard past the house give a little toot on his horn let 'em know he was back park down by the barn just go in an' start milkin' like nothin' had happened—

She'd already be milkin' by now. Must be at least half-past. Phil probably helpin' her. His eyes was as bad as hers worse he couldn't even look at Russ. Kept makin' lousy jokes talkin' a blue streak couldn't wait to get home to tell his pinchmouth wife the latest.

No he might as well wait now. Least till they finished milkin'. The time didn't mean nothin' now.

Seemed like ever'body looked at him that way now. Even when he wasn't fucked up maybe just meet somebody downtown crossin' the street headin' for the barbershop they'd stop nice enough an' all talk plenty maybe even a little more'n they had to their eyes lookin' over his shoulder past his arm watchin' the cars drivin' by pretty soon they'd remember somethin' they'd forgot at the hardware store an' be gone.

Or if he did look up real fast-like an' catch them that look would be there. Then they'd remember somethin' they'd forgot even faster.

Even the kid. That look was in the kid's eyes all the time nowdays.

No wonder the kid liked her better. The kid didn't trust him. Was afraid'a him. Afraid he'd hurt him. Cathy too.

S'pose the kid would ever look at him the other way again? The way he used to when he was just a little squirt. When he use'ta be his shadow on the tractor in the truck ever'where Russ went followin' him around like a little puppy dog just as cute too those big eyes lookin' up at Russ askin' ever' question under the sun—like the time Russ took him fishin' took him bass fishin' over on Dake Lake they was sittin' there in the rowboat Russ castin' for bass the kid sittin' there danglin' a piece'a string hung from a willow stick over the side. . . .

"What are they?"

"What?"

"Them."

"Lilypads."

"What are they good for?"

"Lilypads . . . oh, I dunno, just there, I guess."

"Fish eat 'em?"

"No, I don't think so."

"What are they there for then?"

"Just there. Growin' up from the bottom."

"To hold up the water?"

"Hold up the water . . . ?"

"Yeah, maybe they grow up there like that. Them big leaves spread out then God comes along an' hooks the water on 'em an' they hold it up."

Russ laughed to himself careful not to let the kid see it.

"So that's what they're for, eh? I always wondered about them lilypads."

The kid was leanin' way over the side'a the boat now his face close as he dared to the water.

"Yeah, that's what they're for. Ain't nothin' else holdin' that water up, that's for sure."

Russ shivered seemed like it was gettin' awful cold in the truck.

That was back in the days when the kid said "ain't" too. Back before she got the job teachin'. Got carried away with his "dems" an' "dose" his swallowin' the ends'a his words sayin' "ain't." Said she didn't want the kid endin' up talkin' like him. "If he is ever going to be able to compete with his peer group he must learn to speak proper English. Russ, you've just got to try to use better language —you know, he mimics your every move, even the way you speak out of the side of your mouth."

"I don't talk outta the side'a my mouth. . . ."

"You certainly do. Go watch yourself in the mirror."

"So I talk outta the side'a my mouth. So what?"

"So it makes you look . . . like a tough guy."

"You sure that's what you started to say?"

"Of course I'm sure. What else would I say?"

"Maybe lottsa things. Forget it. What's wrong with a tough guy?"

She laughed then that little tinkly laugh he always liked the one she saved for when he come up with somethin' that really tickled her.

"They're outta style, tough guy."

She said it like he woulda outta the corner'a his mouth. He answered her even tougher.

"Since when?"

"Since I got one for a kid."

"Since you got one for a husband."

"That's different."

"How?"

"Just . . . different."

"Yeah."

Christ it was gettin' cold in the truck. She'd be in from the barn by now. Probably takin' a nice warm bath she always did when she come in from the barn. The kid would bring his bowl'a Cap'n Crunch up from downstairs talk to her through the bathroom door. Probably be askin' about him. Maybe not.

He was startin' to feel sick again. Cold as hell his body shakin' his teeth even chatterin' cold sweat poppin' all over his body that sick feelin' in his guts in his mind if he coulda heaved some more he'd'a done it.

Thirsty as hell too.

Seemed like nobody looked at him the way they use'ta. Back when he was carryin' the ball ever' other play.

She never did. Not even when he came back from Ariona that time. She was already startin' to look at him different by then. Probably wouldn't even'a married him if he hadn't knocked her up. Raped her.

He wouldn't'a done it if she hadn't gone to Fort Lauderdale Easter vacation. Without him. She knew he didn't want her to go. He'd only been home from Arizona a few weeks only gettin' to see her weekends when she'd come down from Normal one weekend she didn't even come said she had to go to her sorority's spring dance Easter Ball whatever the hell she called it.

That was another thing that pissed him off. She didn't even invite him to come up there be her date. Maybe she figgered he didn't have the right kinda monkey suit maybe couldn't dance them new dances maybe couldn't afford it didn't wanna hurt his feelin's but she still coulda asked him give him a chance to say no.

But she didn't. Told him it was just for kids at the school fraternities datin' sororities an' all that. Hell he knew that wasn't so Terry Rabie from town went up took his girl from Normal he sure's hell wasn't in no fraternity he was pumpin' gas at Red's Gulf Station next to the campus that was the closest he ever got to goin' to college.

'Course he never told Cathy he knew she'd lied. He was kinda . . . afraid to.

Then she had to up an' go to Lauderdale. There was just no talkin' her out of it—"all the other kids are going. Why shouldn't I go too?"

"Why should you?"

"Why shouldn't I?"

They were parked in Lovers' Lane up by the cemetery he'd been drivin' the cool little Ford convertible her parents had bought her for her high school graduation present just comin' home from a beer blast at Dirty Pete's a lotta kids were already home for Easter break he'd felt kinda funny he couldn't wait to get outta there he drank his beers straight down fast tryin' to get a little high get with the rest of 'em they was laughin' an' dancin' all over the place Cathy as much as anybody she even led a few old high school cheers ever'body joined except him he just sat there watchin' she was havin' a ball she didn't wanna go but he said he hadda headache couldn't wait to get her outta there get her to hisself talk to her about a lotta things mostly about her goin' to Lauderdale she was s'posed to leave the next mornin' her'n some other girls in her sorority were s'posed to be drivin' down in her car.

She looked over at him kinda funny when he swung off 49 into Lovers' Lane that quick little sideways look'a hers her head tilted to one side the eyebrow on his side lifted her nostrils flarin' out one quick time a little furrow in her forehead.

"Why are we turning in here?"

"Don't we always?"

"No."

"We use'ta."

She let up a little let herself laugh.

"We had no place else to go in those days. We were too young to get in anywhere."

He didn't say nothin' till he'd stopped pulled way back in under a big pine.

"Nowdays . . . we got too many places to go. Besides, we ain't that much older."

She yawned stretched her arms way above her head it was real moonlight he could make out the just-right bumps in her sweater she'd let him play with them sometimes he felt like doin' it now.

"Thought you said you had a headache?"

"Why, you in a hurry to get to Lauderdale?"

She cut off her stretch brought her arms back down slow he couldn't see her bumps anymore.

"May I ask what that has to do with your headache?"

He felt like answerin' plenty but he didn't.

"I figger you was tryin' to say you wanted to get home to bed so you could get up early for your big trip."

"No, I was merely inquiring about your headache."

He lit a cigarette burned his finger a little strikin' the match he'd just started smokin' after he come back from Arizona might as well didn't look like he'd be playin' much more ball.

"You know, Cathy, funny thing . . . I'm startin' to get the notion girls don't exactly say just what they exactly mean."

She laughed right out loud on that one really busted out. At first it pissed him off he was tryin' to be serious there was plenty to be serious about but pretty soon he got over it had to laugh along it made him feel good to make her laugh beside she had such a pretty laugh you couldn't help but laugh along.

"What's so . . . damn funny—?"

"Russ . . . you . . . you're too much. I mean . . . you're priceless . . . !"

"Yeah, that's about how I figger it."

While he was sayin' it he started movin' across the seat toward her he also figgered it was about as good a time's any to get his hands on those bumps in her sweater.

She didn't put up no fight either just laid back on the seat put her arms around his head squeezed him so hard it pinched one'a his ears he didn't care he was too busy divin' under her sweater workin' on the latch'a that damn brassiere whisperin' into the front'a her sweater he could feel a nipple right against his mouth "Cathy, don't go to Lauderdale."

Her body stiffened. She didn't say nothin' her body just stiffened.

He didn't mean to say it an' he was mad at himself afterward but he did.

"Please . . . ?"

She hugged him tighter again.

"Why not, silly?"

"I . . . I'll—I don't want you to. See . . . I ain't— haven't been back very long."

"I'll only be gone ten days."

She might just as well said ten years what the hell was he gonna do hang around the County Farm waitin' he was stayin' back there till he found a job a place to live or somethin' shit he had no place else to go.

"Then you'll be goin' back up to college."

"Naturally."

She musta figgered somethin' was hurtin' him she said the next real soft squeezin' his head all the while.

"I've got to, Russ. Finals are coming up. We'll be . . . seeing a lot of each other all summer."

"Yeah. What's gonna happen then?"

Her body stiffened again.

"What do you mean?"

"After this summer. What's gonna happen then?"

He could feel her take a deep breath her heart was beatin' faster too.

"I . . . s'pose I'll be going back . . . to school."

Just then a crazy thought hit his head like maybe she was waitin' for him to ask her to marry him but he didn't he pushed it outta his head what if she laughed. He sat up pushed her away too slid across the seat back behind the wheel lit up another cigarette.

"What's wrong, Russ?"

"I don't want you to go."

"Is that all? Are you sure that's all, Russ?"

"Shit yeah. What else is there?"

"I'm sure I don't know, Russ. Take me home."

He did. They didn't say nothin' much on the way she didn't even snuggle over to kiss him good night just slid over behind the wheel when he got out at the Farm looked like she just meant to drive right out leave him standin' there.

"Ah . . . who's all . . . goin'?"

"Just . . ."

She had stopped there under the yard light probably on purpose he could see her shoulders shrug she didn't look over his way.

". . . just some kids . . . from school."

"Oh . . . yeah, that's right. Well . . . have a good time . . . ah, be careful."

All of a sudden she turned her face to him real quick looked like she was gonna say somethin' but she didn't just reached out through the open window touched his arm.

"Don't worry, Russ . . . I will."

Then she pulled out real fast hittin' the clutch so hard she almost snubbed 'er startin' out. Funny thing he knew somethin' was up.

Man that was the longest ten days he ever put in in his life. He'd heard about them Easter trips to Lauderdale some'a the guys in Arizona'd been there the spring before to listen to them talk the whole place was nothin' but a pile'a screwin' the motels full wall-to-wall broads just layin' there waitin' for it all a guy had to bring was a hard-on enough strength to drag hisself from room to room back out to the beach there they was layin' just as thick bare-ass under the moon the guys stripped down too runnin' barefoot through acres'n acres'a young college cunt stretchin' down the beach as far as the eye could see even out to sea there they stood goin' at it like dogs in the water hell even under the water here'n there'a foam thrashed up from down below.

An' Cathy was there. *His* Cathy! Or was she?

She hadn't exactly been knockin' herself out to see him since he got back from Arizona. Hadn't even invited him up for that goddam Sorority Ball or whatever the hell she called it—that means she invited somebody else some god-dam rich-bitch stuck-up commie fraternity prick maybe no faggot either!

Probably one'a those kind he'd seen in Arizona. Lived in the fraternity house. The big fancy houses with them half-assed Greek letters painted on 'em. Guys with names like LaVern an' Steven an' Hamilton Voss the Third the guys on the team called him Turd for short. Jewboys from Chicago their old man owned strings'a drugstores mail-order houses factories shit you name it. Roarin' around campus in their own cars wearin' their fraternity sweatshirts givin' each other the sign. Carryin' their paddles wearin' their beanies lookin' down their nose at anybody that wasn't a Teke or a Geke or a Deke. Creeps that never come around 'cept durin' football season then the only guys they asked to join was Mackey the All-American an' Golden Boy Jensen that was before Russ punted his nose all over his face.

Some guy like that. Some guy whose ole man'd been to the same college belonged to the same fraternity. The kinda guy knew where he was goin' when he got outta college knew what he was goin' to be when he got there.

The kinda guy that hadda monkey suit'a their own brought the right flowers took their dates to French restaurants knew how to order even in French hadda martini with onions before wine with the dinner like he'd seen in the movies then on to the Ball stepped right out there knew all the latest dances.

The kinda guy sorority girls invited to take them to the Spring Ball.

The kinda guy that went to Lauderdale every Easter vacation.

He was probably down there with her right now. Screwin' on the white sand.

He was too. Maybe not screwin' like she claimed. But he was down there they was together all ten days had rooms right next to each other ended up most ever' night in the same bed she told him that herself.

It was still kinda hard to believe. That fraternity creep never would'a spent six-seven nights in the same bed the trip down'n back besides without puttin' the blocks to her . . . at least once.

Funny thing Russ knew somethin' was up right along. He could feel it in his guts. That scared awful feelin' was there he'd keep tellin' his mind it couldn't be so his Cathy wouldn't do a thing like that but his guts kept answerin' the other way.

He knew for sure when he tried to call her. The sixth day he got a postcard a picture of the motel she was stayin' at on one side THE DUNES MOTEL *Conveniently Located. TV in Every Room. We Welcome Students* a circle drawn around one of the windows with "mine" beside a few lines scratched on the other side didn't even look like her writin' she musta wrote it in such a hurry no matter how many times he read it they didn't tell him nothin' he wanted to hear not how much she missed him how much she wished he was there how she couldn't wait to get back to him just the same old shit like she'd been writin' him in Arizona how happy she was whatta good time she was havin' how hot it was that day how nice the water felt crap like that even had the guts to mention some bullshit about the girls she was supposed to have gone down there with he'd thought about that plenty'a times afterward too.

He held on two more days before he tried callin' her. Two more days walkin' around the Farm hatin' it more'n ever the postcard in the back pocket of his Levi's reachin' back to feel of it ever' five minutes hidin' hisself away ever' chance he got sittin' in the silo readin' it in the barn up in the haymow out in the fields tryin' to find the good the love that was written above her name.

He called her the seventh day. Tried. Hitched a ride into town with ole Orville the foreman borrowed twenty bucks off him got off at the Trailways bus station shut hisself in one'a the pay booths started callin' nine o'clock in the evenin' didn't stop till he ran outta money six o'clock the next mornin'.

Half-crazy. He walked outta that bus station six o'clock the next mornin' half-crazy. He walked through town out past the intersection down 9H all the way to the Farm the sun just comin' up behind him the grass just startin' to grow good a patch'a snow here'n there layin' dirty in the bottom of the ditches not even tryin' to hitch a ride from the two-three cars that passed him by half-crazy just walkin' along listenin' to the voice say "I'm sorry, sir, Miss Suring's room doesn't answer, would you like to leave a message" just walking along half-crazy wantin' to bust out cryin' right there in the middle'a 9H. . . .

Russ reached up an' wiped his face off with his hands. He kinda wondered how long he'd been cryin' seemed like it'd been quite awhile now. Funny how once he let hisself get started last night it came mighty easy now.

Seemed like the next three days was kinda blurred. They was nothin' but waitin' an' hurtin' hurtin' an' waitin'. Afraid they was gonna end afraid they wasn't.

Thinkin' a thousand different thoughts all of 'em Her under Him. On the beach. In a car. On her bed. The telephone ringin' on the table beside 'em they ain't got time to answer jus' smile at each other like they know who's callin' an' go back at it. Standin' up. Layin' down. Dog style. Her ass closest to the ceilin'. Her . . . workin' her way down.

Three-quarters crazy. Tryin' to make up stories he didn't believe. Maybe she was spendin' the night with one of her girl friends her sorority sisters. She could'a drove up the highway to another beach or somethin' her car broke down. Maybe she was even dead—drowned! Eaten by sharks! Gang-raped at the point of a pistol clubbed to death afterward! Anything!

No!!! Goddam it he *knew* what had happened. He knew! Maybe not ever' little thing not just how it all happened but he knew she was hung up with somebody else his guts told him that much that feelin' down there don't lie.

Wonderin' how he'd ever get along without her. Thinkin' to hisself how he'd never thought a thought that didn't have some'a her in it since the day he met her standin' in line for their books. Never thought'a livin' a day she wasn't in someplace walkin' talkin' sleepin' eatin' laughin' her laugh wrinklin' her forehead her nostrils flarin' out her lips stoppin' kinda funny on the ends when she held them together there was a little line on the ends went up an' down—Christ oh Christ was he goin' to lose her too?

Then he'd be . . . all alone.

He couldn't take that.

He was ready an' waitin' for her when she got home. Hell he didn't even let her get home he was waitin' in the bushes below her driveway they lived on a side road outside'a town out where all them that had the money built along the lake.

She came about seven o'clock. He had got up early couldn't sleep anyway walked over there before light been waitin' there in the bushes all day. The day before he'd called her mother she didn't sound like she much cared whether she talked to him or not but he did manage to get outta her she expected Cathy sometime tomorrow she was on her way Cathy had called her from Williamsburg, Virginia, expected to be in sometime tomorrow afternoon or evening he got there early just to make sure.

He could tell it was her car even before it came around the bend he didn't know how but he could. He started to shake that cold sweat was there on his face up under his hair he felt sick to his stomach he kept tellin' hisself it was because he hadn't had nothin' to drink or eat all day but he knew better it was because it was her comin' because of what he'd made up his mind to do.

Then the mad came again the mad that had thought up his plan the mad that had made him walk over here in the dark stand here waitin' all day do what he was gonna do—the mad came again steadied him down made it better.

He had never laid a hand on her! All the years she'd been his girl Russ Simpson Jr. had never laid a hand on her for real! Sure he'd played with her titties a little and there was that one time after the Hudson game they'd been dry-humpin' on the grass for hours all of a sudden she started whimperin' beggin' him to touch her "touch me, touch me, Russ" she kept sayin' over'n over "touch me, Russ, touch me . . . touch me."

At first he wasn't just exactly sure what she meant he already had both his hands up under her sweater one in each hand squeezin' away besides he wasn't thinkin' none too clear neither she just kept sayin' "touch me, Russ touch me" finally she grabbed his hand put it down there for him! Next thing she was sayin' touchmetouchme so fast it was all rolled up together jackin' up against his hand chewin' on his ear . . .

He rolled away from her. She just laid there on the grass for awhile whimperin' to herself a little. He felt like tryin' to explain to her how it was. How a nice guy don't take advantage of his girl not a good girl like her anyway just because she might happen to let herself get carried away or somethin' hell he had Carol Gore for things like that he was savin' her to get married not wantin' to hurt her do somethin' to her she'd be sorry about later maybe even hold against him think less'a him maybe even break off with him—

But she never gave him a chance to. Just when he had it all in his mind right just when he was goin' to start she jumped up ran to her car got in an' drove away left him standin' there in the middle'a the football field!

Spoiled the whole day. Up till then it had been the

greatest day'a his life four touchdowns two field goals 246 yards the scout from Arizona State offerin' him the scholarship the Victory Ball ever'body standin' up an' cheerin' him when him an' Cathy walked in Cathy dancin' ever' slow dance with him he couldn't dance the fast ones anyway pressin' up against him lookin' up at him promises jumpin' outta her eyes grabbin' his hand at intermission he'd never felt her hand so warm'n sweaty leadin' him outta the side door'a the gym out on the football field way out in the middle of the football field layin' down on the grass pullin' him down on top'a her right out there in the middle'a the football field . . . right about where he was parked now.

They'd be gettin' ready for church about now. She'd be puttin' on her blue best dress helpin' the kid get into his suit the first one he ever had with long pants he really thought he was somethin' when he got it on tyin' his tie slickin' his hair down she'd sure look good if she hadda fur-trimmed coat to go with her best blue dress.

He stepped up outta the bushes up on the road just when she turned the corner. She didn't see him at first it was just gettin' dark she didn't slow down or nothin' looked like she was just gonna drive right by him so he jumped out in the road wavin' his hands she had to stop or run him over.

She stopped. Damn near slewed into the ditch doin' it but she stopped.

He walked over jerked her side door open she was still sittin' there her arms out stiff on the wheel her foot still pressin' down hard on the brake. First thing he noticed was her suntan pissed him off even more.

"Get over."

"Russ . . . have you gone crazy . . . ?!"

"Maybe. Get over."

She did lookin' at him all the while like maybe she really thought he had gone crazy.

"Where . . . did you come from?"

He slid behind the wheel shot the car backward cramped the wheel give 'er the gun she slewed around headin' back the way she come.

"Where . . . we going?"

He didn't say nothin' just kept lookin' straight ahead drivin' hard.

"Russ, where are we going . . . ? Russ, I've got to get home, Mummie is expecting me, so is Daddy, they'll be worried about me . . . Russ! Russ, you take me home this instant! Do you hear me, Russ, I'm getting mad now— Russ, slow down, for Gods sake, slow down!"

He took the turn off the sideroad onto 22 on two wheels he had all he could do to bring her outta the skid get her leveled out again but he did that little Ford was a pretty good car it'd do about 104 she was doin' that right now down 22.

"Russ, please slow down, please . . . I'll go with you, werever you want to go . . . for a little while, honest . . . please."

She was real scared now sittin' way over by her door her face white as a sheet through her Lauderdale tan. It was gettin' pretty dark just that time of evenin' where there's still enough light so the headlights don't do much good they came up awful fast on a semi makin' its crawl up Tompkins Hill there was nothin' he could do but try to take 'im he did runnin' flat out all the way damn near sheared off the front of another car comin' down the hill he slowed down then she didn't even have to ask him.

Neither one of 'em said nothin' till he pulled off Athletic Field Road stopped in the middle'a the football field. It was pitch dark by then. He had run in with the lights off but near as he could figger it was about the same spot.

"Get out."

"What . . . what for, Russ?"

"Just . . . get out."

"But . . . this is the high school football field. . . ."

"You've been here before. Get out."

She did the dome light went on when she opened the door he reached over an' pulled it shut got out his door as fast as he could he didn't want no light showin'.

He could just make her out standing there beside the door when he came around from his side. He walked up to her grabbed her by the arms just above the elbows started wrestlin' her to the ground.

She didn't say a word just fought him as hard as she could. It didn't take long with all he had boilin' in him right now he coulda put Rocky Marciano down.

She was down on her back now him spraddled on top'a her. He held her down with one hand his forearm across her throat his fingers clamped in her long hair. She kept twistin' her body tryin' to roll from side to side he clamped down harder with his legs. With his other hand he reached down pulled up her skirt ripped her panties off pulled out his dong he'd already unzipped his fly comin' around the car it came out easy he'd left his shorts off when he got dressed that mornin'.

"Russ . . . I'm choking—I can't . . . breathe . . . !"

He let up on his arm a little still tryin' to hold 'er down hang on to her hair keep her clamped down her legs pinned together jab it in her all the while startin' to get a little panicky it wasn't workin' out all that easy didn't seem like there was no place to put it like there was with Carol 'course she always helped him put it in.

"Spread your legs!"

"I . . . can't."

"Goddam it, I said spread your legs!"

"You're . . . holding them . . . together . . . !"

He eased up on her legs a little not too much so she

couldn't get away. She spread her legs as much as she could still didn't do much good he got it down between her legs damn near tore the skin off doin' it sure didn't feel much like Carol's—

"You're . . . too low."

He pulled up started jabbin' away a little higher damn near lost his balance it was a helluva thing tryin' to get it done what with his arm still across her throat his one hand hangin' on to her hair his knees clamped aroun' her lower legs his other hand tryin' to guide it in—

"Russ, I . . . I've got to spread my legs . . . more."

He let her do it gave up tryin' to keep her knees pinned together he'd have to take a chance on it she surprised him didn't kick or thrash around very much at all just spread her legs the head of it slipped in he like to blew on the spot it was all wet'n slippery would'a too if she hadn't spoke up.

"Russ, do you have anything . . . to put on?"

"What . . . what the hell do you mean . . . ?!"

"You know . . . one of those . . . things?"

"How . . . how you know about them?!"

"Everybody knows about them, silly."

He'd forgot hisself for a minute there sat up took the pressure off her neck let go his hold on her hair now he hurried up got a hold on her again made sure he had 'er pinned down good'n strong before he answered.

"Yeah. Yeah, I got . . . one."

"Put . . . it on . . . then."

"How . . . how can I . . . ?!"

He still had her squashed down good his face right against hers he could feel her lips move on his cheek when she answered.

"What . . . do you . . . mean?"

"How can I put it on an' hold you down at the same time?"

"I . . . won't move. I . . . promise."

Then he felt her lips move again kiss him on the cheek maybe she was tellin' the truth.

Hell things weren't goin' a bit the way he'd planned. Here he'd had it all set he was just gonna take her out here drag 'er outta the car knock her down put the blocks to 'er show 'er what was what her foolin' around with some fraternity creep after he never laid a hand on her now they was layin' here talkin' about him puttin' on a rubber!

"Well . . . ?"

"Well, what?!"

"Are you going to . . . or aren't you?"

"Maybe. . . ."

"Do it, Russ . . . do it."

She pushed up against him a little then he could feel her wet pussy against the head'a his it had gone pretty soft through all this talkin'.

He took'a chance rolled off her. Far as he could tell there in the dark she never moved once all the while he was puttin' his rubber on.

Took him quite a while too. Not so much gettin' it on he was gettin' pretty good at that by this time what with Carol'n all it was more figgerin' out how he was gonna get around it.

Then he remembered that first time with Carol. He took out his billfold took out his rubber rolled it back a few rolls got ahold of about'a half-inch'a the end put it in his mouth bit it off spit it out rolled the rest of it on over his cock makin' sure the hole was there where his juice came out.

Then he laid back down on her. She reached up put her arms around his neck kissed him all over his face. Her legs spread open his cock was hard again. She brought her legs up it slid right in. She kept huggin' him real tight kissin' him whisperin' his name over'n over. They came pretty fast. All the while he was pumpin' out he kept thinkin' how his was goin' right up in her an' he was glad it was.

Makin' a little boy.

Bindin' her to him with bone'n muscle.

Russ was cryin' again. He didn't even notice how cold it was how the motor'd stopped runnin' quite awhile ago he just let hisself sit there an' cry.

They'd be in church by now. They'd be sittin' down near the front where they usually sat Cathy singin' along with the hymns in that nice clear voice'a hers the kid standin' beside her holdin' the hymnal open his lips movin' makin' like he was singin' along too.

Maybe he hadn't exactly raped her. But he never shoulda knocked her up like that.

Didn't seem like he remembered breakin' no cherry though.

They jus' laid there huggin' on each other after they finished. Next thing he knew he felt the wet there on his cheek. At first he thought maybe it was startin' to rain he looked up the stars were still blinkin' up there all over the sky nah she was cryin' real soft holdin' it all to herself.

"I'm . . . sorry, Cathy."

"Don't . . ."

"What's'a matter, baby . . . did I hurt you, baby?"

"No, Russ . . . Russ, no . . ."

She was cryin' harder now the gulps kept comin' makin' it hard for her to talk. The whole side'a his face was wet he didn't care he just squeezed her tighter tryin' to make it up to her.

"I'm real sorry, Cathy, honest . . . I never shoulda done it—"

"No, Russ, no . . ."

"The last thing in the world I ever wanna do is hurt you, Cathy—"

"Russ, no . . . no, it's not you . . . it's me . . . !"

She got it choked out between the gulps spittin' the "me" part out like it was somethin' rotten she couldn't hold in her mouth another second.

Then she really busted out cryin'.

"Hell, you couldn't help it, Cathy, I made you do it— I . . . I forced you, hell anybody could see I forced you, no way you coulda stopped me, I'll swear on a stack'a bibles if you want me to, Cathy—"

"Oh Russss . . . !!!"

Man she wailed out his name rose the hair right on the back'a his neck. At first he couldn't do nothin' the sound'a her wailin' like that scared the livin' Jesus outta him froze him solid right there in the middle'a that football field las' time he heard anythin' like that was when his mother had one'a her wailin' fits use'ta wake him up in the night that first one would come knifin' through the blanket they hung up between their bed an' his that one froze him solid too.

He could hear Cathy suckin' in her breath her body stiffenin' up gettin' set to let the next one go. He rolled over on top'a her clamped his open mouth right down on hers took the next one in hisself.

That helped. She didn't do it anymore. Just started to shake a little he warmed her with his body till she stopped.

Then she started talkin'. Slow'n steady. Like they was back in school an' she was just recitin' the Pledge of Allegiance or somethin'. The words just rollin' out of her one after the other like a snowbank meltin' in the spring. Him layin' there listenin' the icy cold water tricklin' over him. Wishin' she'd just kept on wailin'.

"I didn't go down there with the girls. I went with Boyd Stengel, a boy from school. His father owns a big hotel in the city, a lot of other things. He's about the biggest thing up there, a lot of the girls are after him. I've been dating him almost all year. A lot of the girls asked him to our spring dance but he accepted my invitation. He asked me that night to go to Lauderdale with him so I said I would. If I had said no he would have just asked someone else. I wanted to go, everybody was talking about going, all the kids who had been there before kept talking about how keen it was, what a neat time they'd had last year . . . I wanted to go.

"At first Mummie and Daddy weren't going to let me. But I begged and begged, and finally they gave in. They know about Boyd. he drove up to visit me once over Christmas vacation, when you were still in Arizona . . . they like him.

"They don't like you, Russ. That's one of the reasons they let me go, so I wouldn't be spending the whole Easter vacation with you. I even used that to get them to let me. I told them if they didn't let me I'd spend every minute with you . . . maybe wouldn't even come home some nights. See, they've got it in their heads we've been . . . doing it together for a long time already. I know she's been checking my clothes ever since sophomore year, one time after we come home late I caught her going through the dirty clothes hamper. They're afraid you'd get me in trouble.

"So they let me go. They didn't want anybody around here knowing I was going with Boyd though so three of the girls and I took my car as far as Poughkeepsie checked it in the airport parking lot where Boyd and the other girls' boyfriends were waiting with their cars.

"We didn't stay in the same room though, Russ. That was one of the things Mummie and Daddy had made me promise so we always took rooms next to each other even after we got down there.

"But we still . . . slept together. Almost every night.

"But we never did it. Not all the way. He wanted to but

I wouldn't let him. He's a nice guy though, he never tried too hard. He'd give up when I started to cry. I'd always start thinking of you, Russ, honest I would. I even tried to let him one time by thinking of you when he was doing it—I mean, trying to do it. I just wanted to see if I could with somebody else but I couldn't. He didn't give me the same feeling. His hands didn't burn me like yours do. I'd never get all juicy inside. I've been waiting for you to do it to me, Russ. I've been waiting for you a long time."

She started cryin' real soft to herself again. He didn't try to do nothin' to stop her this time just laid there listenin' to her lookin' up at the winkin' blinkin' sky feelin' the cool spring breeze blowin' against his face dryin' the wet around his eyes funny thing all of a sudden he felt the cold of the early spring night felt the cold of the still damp winter earth under the small weak sprouts of spring grass felt the chill workin' his way deep into his bones workin' deep into his bones up through the thin layers of thaw an' grass workin' up from the part froze solid way down in the deep below.

"But I never did it all the way with anyone else before, Russ. Honest, I didn't. Not like we did it tonight."

He couldn't hear her breathin' now he couldn't even hear hisself they was both holdin' their breath.

"Why'd you make me wait so long, Russ?"

"I won't never . . . make you wait so long again, Cathy."

They let out their breaths an' rolled together again. Now the thaw was deeper the spring grass thicker the part froze solid back down in the deep below.

The chill leavin' his bones.

"Did you . . . put it back on?"

"It's . . . still there."

Church would be about over now the minister finished

with his sermon they'd be down on their knees sayin'
the Lord's Prayer maybe the Twenty-third Psalm Russ
said both just to make sure got hung up on that "walkin'
through the shadows of the valley of death" part yeah
he was afraid Russ Simpson Jr. believed in God all right.

Well he couldn't just sit here in his puke all day though.
He had to do somethin' even if it was wrong. Didn't make
some kinda move pretty soon now he'd freeze to death first.

He got down on his knees on the floorboards an' reached
down under the seat. Pulled out the monkey wrench. An
old beer can. Empty. A broken tire chain. Screwdriver.
Sickle-guard off the mower. The box'a shells. His deer
rifle. Finally he found the old rags he was lookin' for.
They was in a pile wedged up under the seat frame. He
pulled them out there was somethin' hard inside when he
opened them up the pint he'd been lookin' for the other
night fell out right there on the floorboards beside him.

He pushed the other stuff underneath got back up on
the seat. He opened the window threw out the pint wiped
hisself an' the truck off the best he could with the rags then
threw them out too.

He felt a little better now. Thinkin' a little clearer.
Seemed like just tryin' to clean hisself up a little helped
some.

Guess he might just as well start for home.

Sure why not? Hell, if he got started right away he might
even beat 'em home. Pull right down by the barn he was
in his barn clothes anyway clean out the calf stalls after
that she'd never be able to smell the puke on him that's
for sure.

Then just go in change clothes wash up go in for dinner
like nothin' had happened.

'Course her folks usually stopped over for Sunday dinner. Usually stopped in on their way back from church.

So what? So what'd he care about them two old farts?

Hell he'd faked it through plenty'a Sunday dinners with them before. Bullshitted the ole man a little about fishin' makin' sure he kept his eyes where the ole lady couldn't see 'em wolfin' his food down sayin' he had to get right back out in the barn there was somethin' pressin' he hadda find to do.

Shit yeah why not go home? He had to go sometime couldn't jus' sit here freezin' to death. Jus' walk in slip upstairs take a shower put on some Sunday dress clothes come down eat a little dinner shoot the shit with the ole man roughhouse with the kid a little till the game come on turn on the Packer-Bear game suck on a few beers to take the edge off pretty soon the beer an' the game would drive them home he'd be alone with just Cathy an' the kid the kid sittin' on one knee Cathy on the other his arm around each of 'em givin' 'em a little hug now'n again gettin' up when the game was over the Packers winnin' Donny Anderson havin' a big day pattin' Cathy on the rump givin' her a wink where the kid couldn't see it tellin' her he was goin' out to do chores she should get the kid to bed early tonight he had to get up early for school tomorrow besides he kinda felt like ʲgettin' to bed early hisself she'd know what he meant.

Then takin' her long'n slow'n easy like they used to. Doin' everything to each other. Knockin' each other out. Knockin' each other out so bad they could hardly get up off the bed when they finished. Her finally gettin' up goin' to the bathroom tellin' him just to lay there her comin' back with a warm washcloth a dry towel him just layin' there feelin' it while she cleaned his off.

Then come Monday mornin'. Come Monday mornin' he'd get up bright'n early his hangover almost over the shakiness leavin' his nerves hardly bitin' each other at all his stomach back where it was s'posed to be bein' able to look in their eyes again them lookin' back in his—yeah come Monday mornin' he'd hit it bright'n early get his chores done get in in time to have a nice breakfast with Cathy an' the kid before they left for school laughin' an' jokin' all the while like they used to soon as they left he'd get in his truck drive over to see the Jew writer from the city they say he'll buy any chunk'a land he can get his hands on don't even care too much what he pays make a good deal might even wrap it up fast enough so he can get over to the school before it closes take the janitor job surprise Cathy walk right in her classroom an' tell her see the happy look on her face—

Russ slapped the gearshift in reverse stepped down hard on the footfeed. Nothin' happened. Hell no wonder it wasn't even runnin'. Funny thing he hadn't even noticed it wasn't runnin' anymore no wonder it was so cold in there.

He turned the starter over. Nothin' happened. Sure it turned over but it didn't fire. He tried it again the same thing. Then he sneaked a look at the gas gauge he didn't wanna but he did he already knew what he was gonna see.

It was. Dry's a bone.

Shit!

Just when he was all set. Just when he had it all figgered. Hell he'd'a gone right home done just what he planned this sucker hadn't run outta gas!

Well he had to do somethin'. Even if it was wrong.

Couldn't jus' sit here'n freeze to death.

Could he?

He got out got down on his hands'n knees in the snow hunted around till he found the pint funny thing it was there just about where he pitched it he held it up brushed the snow off tipped it to one side the booze inside moved hell them babies don't ever freeze solid no way that ninety proof stuff's gonna freeze solid it don't ever get that cold.

He got back in the truck slammed the door broke the seal took a healthy slug.

That baby warmed 'im up.

What the hell'd he done so bad in the first place?! Hell it weren't no big deal crime for a man to go out'n hang one on once'n awhile. Man wasn't a man if he didn't. Hell if she'd'a wanted to marry one'a them four-eyed long-haired faggots she'd'a done it in the first place—like that Boyd creep she went to Lauderdale with.

Besides—she was a helluva one to look down her nose at him for goin' out hangin' one on once'n awhile maybe even playin' around a little. She was the one started it— it wasn't him went down to Florida laid up with a guy ten whole days! Him sittin' home half-crazy s'posed to believe she never let him put the blocks to 'er! What the hell kinda man was that?! Shit he'd guarantee her one thing ain't no broad'd spend ten days in the sack with Russ Simpson Jr. he wouldn't be in with both feet!

Shit he didn't ever remember breakin' no cherry.

Shit for all he knew maybe the kid wasn't even his!

He took another healthy slug. He'd had so much the last three days he couldn't even taste it no more he hadn't eaten or nothin' there weren't no other tastes left in his mouth to get in the way it went down like sugar-water.

But he could feel what it was doin' for him. He could feel it hit home spread out from the middle of his guts move out in bigger'n bigger waves all through his body thawin' out the froze solid part way down in his deep below makin' his head light puttin' the hinges back in his nerves warmin' him warmin' him makin' it so he could almost stand hisself again.

Startin' to unwind. Uncoil. The rattler startin' to uncoil one coil two coil one slug two slug keepin' on till the pint was damn near killed his body strung out straight the whisperin' outta his brain.

Only one more thing he needed now he'd be really straight. Funny thing about his body the only things that could get him real straight when he felt like this was booze an' that—the two of 'em together.

He killed the pint rolled down the window flung the dead soldier out in the snowbank rolled the window back up just sat there thinkin' about the other thing.

Gettin' hornier'n a three-peckered goat. Needin' to lay down with a woman. Not much carin' who. Lettin' his cock turn his head off. Doin' it then jus' layin' there.

Yeah man that's the cut-out valve.

He got out an' started walkin'. Carol's trailer was only 'bout a half a mile away. Right now it could just as well been Cathy only Carol was about six an' a half miles closer.

He looked back once just as he cleared the field started down Athletic Field Road his ole truck looked kinda funny sittin' there with a load'a corn'n oats a few bales of alfalfa for roughage kinda funny just sittin there in the middle'a the football field right about there in the same spot—'course now it was wintertime an' the spot was all covered with ice froze solid with ice.

Yeah she got knocked up all right. Knocked up higher'n a kite. Her belly swellin' up like a Holstein cow. First time he laid eyes on her again that day she come home from finals he could tell.

So could Mummie an' Daddy.

She hadn't been home twenty minutes he got the call down to the cement plant he'd gotten a job drivin' truck. Maybe twenty-five they wanted to call this Boyd creep first give him first crack but she wouldn't let 'em kept tellin' 'em it was his Russ Simpson Jr. was it.

He'd just pulled in empty with a Redi-mix truck. His

boss Tony Saleruso hung out the office door told him he was wanted on the phone.

"Hey, Russ, you're wanted on the phone."

"The phone . . . ?"

"Yeah, the phone."

"Ah . . . where?"

"The office. . . . Where the hell you think, the gravel pit?"

Funny thing he knew somethin' was up right off the bat. 'Course maybe it was because it was the first phone call he'd ever got since he'd been there.

"They . . . say who it was?"

"Nah. Just some girl."

Tony laughed slapped him on the shoulder as he went through the office door ahead'a him Tony was a pretty nice guy even if he did get drunk an' argue politics a little too much.

"Must be she couldn't wait for you to get through work —wants to meet you somewhere for a little nooner."

That was the only other thing Tony ever talked about. First week Russ was there he almost started believin' Tony knocked one off ever' noon for lunch in the cab'a one'a his trucks 'course maybe he did there was plenty'a girls workin' around the plant ninety percent of 'em with at least one eye on the boss.

Just then Russ remembered Cathy was due home from school any day now the warm feelin' jumped right through him then the scary feelin' came again funny she'd call him here at work hell he hadn't heard a word from her since that night.

"Nah, it's just . . . my girl—must be she just got home from college today, wants to . . . let me know."

Tony pointed at the phone layin' there off the hook just kept on walkin' back into his inner office he didn't shut the door all the way though.

Russ picked up the phone it felt a little hot in his hand.

"Hello . . . ?"

"Russ . . . ? Is that you, Russ?"

"Yeah, it's me . . . Cathy."

"It's . . . good to hear your voice, Russ."

"Yeah . . . same here."

"Ah . . . say, Russ, are you . . . are you pretty busy right now?'　'

"Well, I . . . I am kinda drivin' a cement truck—see this is a cement plant, ah, you know, trucks an' . . . ever'thin'."

"Yes, I know, I looked it up in the phone book. Daddy said he'd heard you were working there."

"Yeah. I am."

"Yes. That's what the man who answered the phone said."

She didn't say nothin' for a few seconds neither did Russ he couldn't think'a nothin' to say but somebody in the background on her end could he couldn't make it out but it sounded like her mother ole mean-mouth.　　. . . .

"Russ, could you come over, ah, some time today—?"

The voice in the background spoke again.

"Mother, please . . . ah, as soon as possible . . . ?"

Tony's secretary walked in came over to the desk Russ was talkin' from opened a drawer got out some forms fiddled around with some carbons. . . .

"Russ, are you still there . . . ?"

"Yeah . . . yeah, I'm still . . . here."

Now the secretary was lookin' for some paper clips to hold the papers together at least that's what Russ figgered she was huntin' for they was sittin' there right in plain sight on top of the desk so he picked up the box handed them to her funny thing seemed like more'a his mind was on what the secretary was doin' than what he was hearin' comin' over the phone.

"Well . . . ?"

"Yeah . . . yeah I s'pose I could."

"When?"

"Well, I dunno . . . after work, I guess."

The other end of the line went blank she was probably holdin' her hand over it when she came back on her voice had a little more edge to it she sounded tired maybe almost ready to cry.

"Russ, please, could you come over almost right away? Daddy wants to talk to you . . . it's quite . . . important."

"Well, I . . . I'll have to ask my boss. . . ."

Tony was already standin' in the doorway between the two offices leanin' against the side'a the doorway chewin' on a toothpick. He was tryin' to give up smokin'.

"Go ahead, Russ—take the rest'a the day off."

"Yeah, Cathy . . . yeah, I can . . . come."

"Thank you, Russ . . . thank you . . . very much."

It sounded like she was about to cry but the phone just clicked in his ear. He laid the phone back down on the desk where he found it Tony was still leanin' against the doorway chewin' his toothpick.

"Better put it back on the hook. It works better that way."

Russ mumbled sorry put it back on the hook.

"You look a little pale around the gills, boy. What happened, she swallow one'a them watermelon seeds?"

Funny thing Tony sayin' it right out like that made him feel a little better hell that's what he wanted wasn't it he even managed a little smile when he answered.

"Yeah, that's . . . about it, I guess."

"Happens to the best of us."

Just then his secretary ducked under his leanin' arm comin' back in the outer office with her bundle'a papers Tony dropped his arm slapped her on the butt.

"Don't it, Rande?"

The secretary tossed her head snapped a look at Tony over her shoulder.

"You said it, boss."

Russ turned started headin' for the outer door Tony yelled after him just as he was breakin' into the sunlight.

"Take the pick-up. Hell, you're lucky—you ain't got no cement plant she can get her hooks in."

Russ turned back he just remembered he hadn't never thanked Tony but him'n his secretary musta already gone back in his inner office so Russ turned around again walked over to the truck.

Just as he was pullin' out through the plant gates the noon whistle blew.

They was all sittin' in the livin' room waitin' when he got there. It all seemed pretty formal the few times he'd been in the house before she'd always taken him in through the kitchen this time she was waitin' by the front door they was all dressed up like they'd jus' come from church or maybe jus' goin'.

Cathy didn't say nothin' just opened the door stood there waitin' for him to come in not even lookin' at him just waited for him to come in follow her into the livin' room he peeked a fast look at her belly on the way in it was there all right.

She sat back down in the chair she'd been sittin' in Russ could tell it was hers there was one'a her brand fil- ter-tips Salems with lipstick on it burnin' in the ashtray beside it she had taken up smokin' this past year while she was away to school.

Russ sat down in the chair left for him. Nobody said nothin'.

By now he knew somethin' was up for sure. For one thing the ole man even had his recliner chair jacked all the way forward first time Russ had ever seen him sit straight up that way.

He finally spoke up 'course not before Meanmouth told him to.

"Walt. . . ."

The ole man opened his mouth but nothin' came out so he closed it again started over.

"Well . . . let's get going."

Didn't nobody make a move though. They all jus' sat there like before their eyes glued to the floor. Russ didn't mind he was in no hurry to get down to the sheriff's office whatever they had in mind.

"Where . . . we goin'?"

The ole lady jerked her head up musta been the sound 'a Russ's voice was the last straw for her she got so excited she almost looked at him.

"Havent' you anything better than that to put on?!"

At first Russ couldn't quite figger what she meant for a hairy second there he thought she was talkin' about the rubber he'd bit the end off but then it dawned on him she was talkin' about his clothes he looked down at his sweatshirt Levi's engineer boots they was pretty smeared up all right made him feel like the day he met Cathy in the book line ever'body else had on dress pants.

"I don't usually drive a cement truck in my suit, ma'am."

Now she looked at him the first time so far as Russ could remember those little red pig eyes jumped outta the little slits dug way back deep in the black holes man those eyes wanted to cut him ever' way but loose after that he didn't much care if she ever looked at him again.

"The least you could have done was take off those filthy boots—you've gotten mud all over my clean carpet!"

Cathy's head jerked up now the look she gave her mother just about matched the one the ole lady'd give Russ.

"Mother, it's a little late for that now."

Now it was Cathy's turn to look down the bore she looked the ole lady right square in the eye didn't flinch till Meanmouth gut-shot her with the words: "Yes, you've seen to that well enough."

Now the ole man finally lifted his head opened his eyes looked at all'a them closed them again there was a look on his face like he'd been hit behind the right ear with the dull end of a single-bladed ax.

"No need to get up in the air. That ain't gonna get us nowhere."

It made Russ feel a little better to hear him talk that way 'course from what he'd heard Walt Suring hadn't been nothin' but a common ever'day workin' man till he hit it fairly big turnin' out ball bearings durin' the war why shouldn't he talk that way?

Now the ole lady turned on him. Looked to Russ like she'd saved her best for Walt if looks could kill that poor ole fellow woulda never got up outta that recliner chair again.

"No, we mustn't get up in the air, must we, Walt? We're supposed to just sit here and let those two track mud all through our house and not say a word. Well, you . . . you sit there! Not me! I didn't work my ass to the bone all those years gettin' where we are to let those two dirty little pigs . . . !"

Russ had a feelin' she coulda said a lot more knew all the words Carl Swenson told him once he knew her when she was just one'a the Winter girls use'ta wait tables over to the Country Club 'course that was before they hit it fairly big turnin' out ball bearings during the war.

The ole man stood up. Russ was so surprised he stood up too. So did the two women.

"Yes. We . . . we might's well get started. Get it . . . over with."

The rest of 'em just followed him out the door.

They all got in Walt's big Lincoln Continental sittin' there in the garage beside the ole lady's Cadillac. Cathy got in the back Russ was about to climb in beside her but the ole lady brushed by him climbed in herself so Russ couldn't do nothin' but climb in up front beside Walt.

Just as they were turnin' out onto the road Russ heard a kinda chokin' sound from the backseat like maybe one'a the women back there was tryin' to hold back some cryin' it musta been the ole lady 'cause when Cathy spoke up her voice sounded pretty steady.

"You could have let us go by ourselves."

If it had been the ole lady she recovered in a hurry.

"And let him run out on us? Hmph, I know his type, they like to get a girl in trouble and take off for California. Oh no, I'm not letting either one of you out of my sight until it's legal—there won't be any Simpson bastards running around my house."

His name rang out there in the car like somebody sayin' shit who couldn't swear very well. At first it pissed him off he was about to turn on her but then the rest'a what she said started to sink through his mind they weren't takin' him to the sheriff or nothin' like that they was on their way to get married!

He didn't say nothin' then just sat there settled down deep in the big thick soft leather seats lookin' out the green-tinted windshield down the long black shiny hood at the silver Continental ornament on the front just sat there lookin' at it startin' to think about marryin' Cathy havin' that kid in her belly maybe even drivin' a car like this someday hell maybe ole Walt might even give 'em one for a weddin' present. . . .

Nobody else said nothin' either. They all just drove along real quiet-like till they got across the state line.

The first place they stopped was the clinic. The ole man parked the car they all got out trooped into the waitin' room the ole lady stepped up told the pretty young girl at the desk what they wanted she'd been watchin' them come in was already reachin' for the forms before the ole lady even opened her mouth.

They took Cathy first. A young guy dressed in doctor white came out motioned to her to follow him led her through the open double doors Russ watched them goin' down the long hall Cathy looked kinda scared he remembered from school she was always afraid'a needles he wasn't too hot for 'em hisself.

Then they came for him. Another young guy looked the same as the first but wasn't led him down the same hall as they was walkin' along the young doctor looked over at Russ looked at his cementy sweatshirt down at his cementy Levi's his engineer boots the mud dried on them now looked him over pretty good in that one fast sideways glance then looked up at Russ's face got his eye give 'im a nice friendly smile.

"Knocked her up, huh?"

Russ just smiled nodded his head.

It was the same comedian brought them out the results of the blood tests too they was all sittin' in the waitin' room waitin'.

"Well, you passed your tests—must have both stayed up all night studying for 'em."

He flashed his big smile at ole Walt an' Meanface but they weren't havin' any so he kinda cleared his throat made like he was lookin' down at the forms winked over at Russ an' Cathy then looked back up at ole Walt an' Meanface looked them straight in the eye real serious doctor-like.

"Yes, I see no reason whatsoever why this young couple shouldn't be able to conceive a normal healthy child . . . none whatsoever."

Then he handed the forms to Russ his face still real doctor serious but his eyes startin' to sparkle the smile startin' to pull at the corner'a his mouth Russ saw him glance over at ole Walt an' Meanface she looked like she'd just swallowed some Eagle lye then he turned real quick an' headed back down the hall looked like he was headin' fast for his office so he could get in there before he busted out laughin'.

Russ was startin' to feel pretty good too. Almost like laughin' hisself. He looked over at Cathy she was runnin' her fingers lightly over the little round piece'a tape they'd put over the spot on the inside'a her elbow where they'd drew the blood he looked down started doin' the same to his too she looked over at him gave him a little smile the first real one since this whole thing started he smiled back at her as big as he could even winked a little—

"That'll be twenty dollars, please."

By the time Russ got over to the receptionist's desk ole Walt already had his billfold out handin' her twenty Russ caught his arm pulled his arm back not tough just hard enough to let him know he meant it reached in his front pocket pulled out his small wad peeled off a twenty.

"Put your money away . . . Walt. I'm payin' for this."

Walt didn't say nothin' just kinda looked at Russ maybe a little different than he had before shrugged put his twenty back in his billfold with all the rest.

Russ handed the pretty young girl the twenty she took it smiled up at him quick then looked back down marked the receipt said it real low so nobody else but Russ could hear her.

"The courthouse is right across the street."

Russ looked her right straight in the eyes when she handed him the receipt she had real nice kind eyes he put as much as he could into his "Thank you, ma'am" funny thing how much better he felt since he got outta that car came in here to this clinic hell it was nothin' but a bare ole whitewashed clinic but them people in there sure made it seem mighty nice'n cozy.

He folded up the receipt put it in his pocket turned an' marched right over to Cathy took her hand led her out the door.

Wasn't nothin' ole Walt an' Meanface could do but follow.

They walked that way all the way across to the courthouse. Him walkin' fast her hangin' onto his hand ever' once'n awhile lookin' up at him an' smilin' the other two trailin' along behind walkin' that way right up the cement walk right up the cement steps past the statue of a man on a horse through the big double doors down the long hall right up to the opening in the counter where the sign said MARRIAGE LICENSES HERE.

"Say ma'am . . . I'd like to get me one'a them marriage licenses."

The woman turned her eyes were sparkly too hell this state hadda lotta mighty nice people.

"You would, eh?"

"You bet."

"What about her—you want to get one for her too?"

"That's right—one for her an' one for me."

That really broke Cathy up. She busted out laughin' hell they probably heard 'er all the way across the street to the clinic wasn't long before Russ an' the lady behind the counter were laughin' right along with her Cathy laughin' an' chokin' tryin' to stop poundin' Russ on the back.

"Russ . . . Simpson . . . you're . . . too much . . . too much . . . !"

Ole Meanface came rushin' down the hall Walt draggin' along behind she pushed right up to Cathy looked at her laughin' her arm around Russ's neck his face grinnin' too the lady's eyes sparklin' hell that ole woman had a look on her face like Hitler givin' one'a his speeches even sounded a little like him.

"What are you laughing about?! I said, what are you laughing about?"

"You wouldn't . . . understand, Mother . . . you . . . wouldn't understand—"

"Well! Well! This is hardly a time . . . !!!"

She was so mad she couldn't talk couldn't say another word her little red pig eyes about to come jumpin' outta them deep black hollows her mouth twisted up on her teeth like she wanted to rip away at Cathy her hands comin' up in fists for a minute there Russ thought she was goin' to start poundin' on her him too even the lady behind the counter anybody in sight—

Ole Walt musta thought so too he stepped up took ahold'a her arms that was the strongest Russ ever saw him act when he spoke up he meant it too.

"All right, Pearl . . . outside. Let's wait out there until . . . until the young folks . . . get their business taken care of."

Pearl went too. Her body let out one big shiver then she put her head down turned an' followed Walt looked to Russ like she kinda started to sniffle as she went down the hall musta too 'cause Walt put his arm around her helped her down the outside steps.

Cathy stood watchin' them go kinda said it to herself. "Yes, it is, Mother . . . yes, it is."

Things went along quite a bit better after that. Pearl seemed to settle down get used to the fact her daughter Cathy Ann Suring was goin' to get married to Russ Simpson Jr. particularly when she saw them standin' there at the altar.

Ole Walt was pretty good all along. Hell they even ended up standin' up for the weddin'. A church weddin' no less.

That was all Pearl's idea. After they left the courthouse they got back in the car just sat there for a minute nobody seemed to know just exactly what they was s'posed to do next finally it was Pearl who piped up.

"Well, I don't know about the rest of you, but I could use a drink."

Russ damn near fell outta the car particularly when ole Walt seconded the motion.

"So could I."

Cathy was all smiles.

"I'd love a martini."

Russ didn't see no reason he should stand in the way.

"B'lieve I could stand a couple myself."

They all got back outta the car trooped across the street to where the sign said THE INDIAN ROOM The Finest In Food and Cocktails Air Conditioned.

It was downright amazin' how that woman changed once she got a couple'a drinks in her. Hell she no more'n got one foot through the door she started lightin' up like one'a them aluminum Christmas trees smilin' this way'n that chatterin' back'n forth with one after the other around the table even turnin' her head toward Russ throwin' him a bone once'n while 'course she looked over his left shoulder when she did.

"I'll bet you're getting hungry by this time . . . ah Russ?"

"Yeah, I forgot my lunch in the Redi-mix truck."

"Goodness sakes, that's right—you've been working all morning—you're probably hungry as a tiger. . . ."

"Gettin' there. 'Course all this runnin' around . . . kinda made me forget about eatin'."

"Well, we'll take care of that in a hurry. Waitress . . . waitress! We would like a menu, please."

"The luncheon menu, ma'am?"

"Does it have the hungry truck-driver-size steaks on it?"

"No, that would be the dinner menu—"

"Then bring us the dinner menu—and another round of drinks."

"Yes, ma'am."

Ole Walt started to raise his hand at the waitress like he was back in first grade tryin' to catch the eye'a his teacher.

"You better skip me this round, miss—"

Ole Pearl reached over pushed his arm down.

"Have another one, Walt—forget about your stomach for one day."

Walt was shakin' his head.

"Well now, I dunno, she kicks back like a mule I have more'n one—"

"Bring him another Corby's and ginger, miss."

"Yes, ma'am."

Pearl dismissed the waitress with the closest thing to a smile Russ'd ever see her pull off turned back to his left shoulder.

"I imagine you get up pretty early in the morning?"

"Not too bad—five-thirty-quarter to six—don't have to be to the plant till seven. 'Course I like to get there a little ahead'a time, hose down my truck a little before I start rollin'."

Cathy smiled at him looked like it made her feel pretty good to see her mother'n him talkin' together like that.

"Do you like driving a truck, Russ?"

"It aint'—aren't . . . ah isn't too bad. I mean, I always kinda liked . . . drivin'."

Ole Walt took another slug'a his Corby's an' ginger he was startin' to set up pretty straight hisself.

"Ain't nothin' wrong with drivin'a truck. Started out drivin' myself, runnin' logs from Catskill down to the mill the other side'a Hudson, use'ta make ten-twelve runs a day with that big White. Hadda little game we use'ta play with the other 'skinners, see who could make the most runs a day, weren't no hydraulic booms in those days, had to unload them big white pines with nothin' but pulley an' tackle—"

Pearl cut him off with her almost smile it wasn't quite as friendly as the one she gave the waitress this one woulda frosted the balls off'a brass monkey ole Walt stopped too Russ kinda hated to see him do it he kinda wanted to hear about how they got them big white pines unloaded but ole Walt stopped the second she gave him the almost smile right there where he was hookin' up the pulley an' tackle his voice stoppin' dead he'd been goin' along kinda fast in that low dead voice'a his kinda fast like he knew he had to get it out in a hurry before he got the signal it was the most Russ ever did hear him say in one sittin'.

"I suggest we order. It's after three and we still haven't got the minister."

Cathy's head kinda jerked up on that one.

"Minister . . . ?"

"Of course. You can't get married without a minister."

"Well, I . . . I was kinda just thinking of going to a judge . . . or . . . whoever it is . . . does that kind of thing. Weren't you, Russ?"

"I . . . tell you the truth, I . . . ain't really thought about it . . . too much."

Pearl gave Cathy her biggest smile looked like she was really startin' to enjoy this whole thing Cathy didn't exactly smile back she had that look on her face like she'd go along if she had to but she didn't have to like it.

"Don't be silly, I wouldn't think of having you two married before some dirty old Justice of the Peace—why, it was so filthy dirty in the J.P.'s house we were married in I couldn't wait to get out of there—even his shirt was dirty, wasn't it, Walt?"

"Dont' seem to me I rec'lect—"

"Of course it was."

Well Pearl had her way. They finished eatin' Russ had the biggest steak he ever saw they drove out to the edge'a town stopped in front of a big Lutheran Church Pearl took her purse went into the parsonage alongside by the time she came out it was all arranged.

Once she got that done there was no stoppin' her. She got back in that car told ole Walt to drive downtown before they knew what hit 'em she had lined up a photographer ordered corsages hustled them around to pick out some rings took 'em a long time to find some Russ could afford finally found two plain gold bands $8.50 apiece he wasn't about to let ole Walt pay for them too.

They were married that evening at six o'clock.

The next night when he came from work to pick her up he had it all figgered out. He had borrowed the pickup from Tony he had his check it was $104.03 after takin' out he had called ole Mrs. Langdon she had an apartment they could get for fifty dollars a month that took care'a everything gas an' lights an' all he walked in that door his check in his hand he wasn't about to take no shit from nobody she was waitin' for him too all packed ready to go only thing she hadda check in her hand too only thing hers was for five thousand dollars.

It was s'posed to be for both'a them to go back to school. Cathy signed it over to him he used it to put down on the farm.

Russ turned in off the road started down the path to Carol's trailer. Funny thing he had it all to do over again he'd'a told Walt to stick that check up his ass Pearl doin' the shovin'.

Nobody answered when he first rapped on the door. All of a sudden that really pissed him off. Seemed like all of a sudden he'd had about all he could take. Seemed like all of a sudden the pint he'd killed back at the truck the whole weekend all the goddam thinkin' goin' on in his head the whole goddam works flared red he grabbed ahold'a that goddam door screamed out her name like to'a ripped it off the hinges would'a too if just then she hadn't unhooked it from the inside, it come open in his hands.

"Russ . . . !"

He just stood there squeezin' the door till he got things back in focus then he walked in sat down at the table.

Nobody said nothin'. Even he could see they was tryin' not to notice how he looked. Carol just stood there lookin' at him twistin' a dishrag in her hands. The boy musta been helpin' her he stood there by the sink with the dish towel in his hands.

Russ looked over at the boy. The boy looked back at him.

"How you doin,' boy?"

"Not bad."

"That's . . . good."

"Yeah."

The boy turned back to wipin' his dishes. Carol moved in closer to the table.

"You . . . want somethin' to eat, Russ? We just finished . . . just doin' up the dishes."

She laughed a little nervous laugh.

"Guess we got a pretty late start today—here it's almost one o'clock an' we're just finishin' up the breakfast dishes . . . 'course it's Sunday, we never get up till we feel like it on Sunday." She trailed off like she didn't know what more there was for her to say so she laughed the nervous laugh instead.

"Almost . . . one o'clock . . . ?'

"Just about. Joey, go see what time it is."

The boy dropped his dish towel an' went to see.

"Almost . . . time for the game."

"What . . . game . . . ?"

"The Packers . . . an' the Bears."

"Oh."

The boy came back.

"It's three minutes to one o'clock."

"Thank you, Joey."

"Game starts at one-thirty."

The boy said it to the tray'a dishes but Russ knew it was meant for him.

"You . . . like football, boy?"

"Yeah. I'm for the Packers. You wait'n see—the Pack will be Back."

"You better b'lieve it. Bet I know who your favorite player is . . . ? "

"Who?"

"Donny Anderson."

"Hey, how'd you know . . . ?"

"Just hadda feelin'."

The boy laid his dish towel down turned to look Russ straight in the eye.

"You wanna stay an' watch the game with me?"

Carol gave her little nervous laugh stepped in toward the boy.

"Joey, maybe Russ has other plans—'

"It's OK Carol . . . well now, I was kinda plannin' on goin' on over to Dobchek's to watch the game with the boys . . . but I've done that plenty'a times before."

Russ turned to look at Carol she just stood there waitin' for whatever he was goin' to say.

"I'd like to stay to watch the game with you, Joey . . . if it's all right with your momma. . . ."

Carol never batted an eye kept them locked right into Russ's.

"You can stay . . . as long as you want to, Russ."

Seemed like all of a sudden Russ kinda ran outta gas hisself. Seemed like all of a sudden he couldn't hold his head up another second his whole motor stopped runnin' all he wanted to do was lay his head down on that skimpy little trailer table lay his head down on that table go to sleep forget about the whole damned works Cathy kid farm bills mortgages money church Sunday dinners in-laws the whole fuckin' mess jus' lay his head down on that table.

When he came to they had him stretched out on the couch tryin' to take his clothes off. How the hell they ever got him over there he'd never know.

Carol saw his eyes open.

"Just lay here, Russ. We'll get your clothes off wash you up a little, then you can take a nice nap—"

Russ tried to sit up got halfway there.

"No. . . . I'll miss the game."

"Sleep for just a little while then—we'll wake you up when it comes on—"

The boy was pullin' off one'a his boots.

"I wont' let you miss the game, Russ, ain't no need to worry about that—' '

Russ got all the way sat up this time.

"Gimme a drink."

"Joey, go get that bottle under the sink."

"Which one?"

"You know which one."

Carol smiled at Russ kept unbuttonin' away on his shirt she already had his mackinaw off.

"Caught him samplin' it the other day."

Russ tried to push her fingers away.

"I can . . . undress myself."

"Sure you can—but I can do it faster."

She pulled off his shirt he leaned over his arms behind him to help her almost slid forward off the couch. Carol held up his shirt wrinkled her nose pitched it over by the washer alongside the mackinaw.

"You won't mind terribly if I wash them out a little, will you?"

"No."

He was sitting in his Levi's an' socks by now. The boy came back with the bottle. Russ uncorked it took a fairly healthy slug. The boy watched like he had just thrown one for forty an' goal so Russ took another even bigger that one went for the touchdown.

Carol was already stuffin' his other things in the washer.

"C'mon give me your pants."

"You mean ah . . . just take them off . . . ?"

Carol laughed it wasn't nervous no more.

"Yeah, unless you want me to stick you in the washer too."

She wrinkled up her nose again.

" 'Course that wouldn't be too bad an idea."

"Guess I do smell pretty bad."

"Just a combination of barn, brewery, an' you know what else."

"What else, ma?"

"Remember that day you tried smokin'?"

"Yeah . . . !"

Carol motioned at Russ again.

"How'sa about the pants . . . ?'

Russ stood up started unbuttonin' them the boy just stood there watchin'.

"You still get sick from smokin', Russ?"

"Naw, I got the . . . flu, or somethin'—"

"Russ, I'm tryin' to teach Joey something . . . tell him the truth."

Russ sat down again started pullin' his Levi's down over his knees.

"Yeah, I still get sick from smokin'—"

Carol put her hands on her hips gave Russ one of them looks.

"Drinkin' too. Neither one of 'em's . . . no good for you."

The boy looked away from Russ. "You do 'em."

Russ finished pullin' off his Levi's flung them over to Carol. "Yeah, but I ain't . . . too damn smart."

The boy was still standin' there his head hangin' Russ felt kinda foolish sittin' there in his shorts talkin' to him about things like this.

Carol didn't look at either one of 'em when she spoke just kept bent over the washer by now she was puttin' in the soap'n things.

"Russ . . . don't be too hard on yourself. See, Joey here is . . . he's quite a fan of yours, Russ. He . . . knows all about you."

Now the boy's head came up again he turned back to Russ.

"Yeah, I gotta scrapbook tells all about you—all fulla things you done, how you was the best football player Iola ever had—all kinds'a things . . . !"

"You . . . got a scrapbook . . . 'bout me?"

"Yeah, ma gave it to me. It's all fulla things—how you was the fastest runner, the best thrower, kicker—man, that Hudson game musta really been somethin'!"

Russ looked over at Carol she was still bent over the washer seemed like it was takin' her an awful long time gettin' that thing goin'.

"It was . . . Joey. Yeah, it was."

"Did you really score every single point in that game?"

"That's what the papers said, didn't they?"

"Sure did! You want me to show you? I got the scrapbook right under my bed."

"Nah, that's all right. I remember pretty good."

"Tell me about it—tell me how you was behind then you came back in again after you got hurt scored two touchdowns an' one field goal in the last quarter—tell me about it, Russ . . . !"

Russ laughed his wasn't nervous no more neither.

"Sounds to me like you got it pretty well down pat."

"Tell me about it anyway—was you really the best player Iola ever had, the best one ever 'round this whole part'a the country?"

"That what the scrapbook said?"

"That's what it said—I can show you."

"Then I guess it must be true."

"Think you was as good as Donny Anderson?"

"Oh, I dunno."

"Think so, Russ?"

"Maybe. If I'd a played as long as he did."

"I'll bet you woulda, Russ— I'll bet you woulda."

"Maybe."

Sunday afternoon didn't turn out to be half bad. By the time the game came on Russ got hisself shaved cleaned up they all gotta big laugh about the clothes he put on while his was gettin' washed'n dried one'a Carol's mother's slacks she'd forgot there one time that ole warhorse musta weighed in at 250 if she was a pound they wrapped 'em around his waist about twice pinned 'em with a safety pin for a top he had on the baggy sweatshirt Carol used for cleanin' house all'n all he musta looked a sight but Russ didn't care some of the power was back.

He even managed to get down a bowl'a soup an' keep it there. That took the edge off the burnin' in his guts helped fight down the sickenin' feelin'.

Russ didn't drink much all afternoon neither. Just enough

to stay ahead'a the mad. Keep ahead'a that gettin' lost ever'thin's lost goin' crazy snappin' feelin'. Just sippin' enough so he wouldn't feel like he'd gotten outta the world an' didn't see how he could ever get back in . . . scared that he didn't really wanna. Takin' another pull when his words started ringin' in his head when he started wonderin' why he was sayin' them. Savin' the healthy slugs for when his head talked so loud he could hear it through the game . . . talkin' clear . . . "it's no use . . . it's all no use. . . ."

But he stayed ahead of all of them. Stayed ahead eatin' sippin' talkin' laughin' watchin' the shadowy little men on the TV screen chasin' each other through the big game. The shadowy little men in green an' gold chasin' the ones in red an' blue till they got caught an' the ones in red an' blue chased the ones in green an' gold.

Stayed ahead with Carol an' Joey. Stayed ahead watchin' them when they wasn't watchin' him sometimes even when they was. Stayed ahead feelin' them feelin' him feelin' each other. Stayed ahead feelin' the feelin' inside that trailer.

It was cold outside. It even started to snow a little along about half time. But it was warm all afternoon in that trailer.

It was a good game. The Packers won the toss elected to receive. The Bears elected to defend the goal to the south that way they'd have the wind behind them in the fourth quarter.

The Bears kicked off. Travis Williams an' Donny Anderson were back Anderson the short man on the ten Williams deep on the two the kick went to Williams about two yards into the end zone he brought it out Anderson blocking in front'a him the rest'a the team wedgin' out from the middle tryin' to spring Williams right up the middle the wedge broke down the Bears come streamin' through

Anderson picked up the first man but there was too many they snowed Williams on the twenty-eight.

Joey was on the edge'a his chair.

"C'mon, Roadrunner!"

Then the Bears got to 'im.

"Shiiitt!"

"Joey!"

He turned to Russ. "I thought he was goin'!"

"Nah, the blockin' broke down—they couldn't set up no lane for 'im."

"See the one Anderson threw?"

"Yeah, he can block all right."

"Could you block as good as him?"

"Maybe . . . on a good day."

"Was you as fast as the Roadrunner?"

"Nah, ain't nobody as fast as Williams—least not many."

"Could you run as good?"

" 'Pends on what you mean by good. He's faster, maybe even a little shiftier . . . but I could run over 'em better."

"Papers say you could run over anybody once't you broke in the clear."

"Yeah, I guess I was pretty hard to stop once't I got rollin'."

Russ reached over an' rubbed up the top'a Joey's head he moved over a little closer to Russ they was sittin' together on the couch Carol on the chair where she could watch them.

Russ patted the couch beside hisself.

"C'mon over, Carol, join the experts."

"I can see good from here, Russ."

Russ winked at her.

"Bet you can see better from here."

She came over sat down on the other side'a Russ them couches in them trailers is small he could feel them against him on both sides to make'a little more room he lifted his arms put them on the back'a the couch behind them wasn't long before both of 'em was leanin' their heads back on his arms.

Funny thing it wasn't till then Russ remembered what he'd come here for in the first place. Funny thing it didn't seem important no more he wasn't even horny no more it felt better this way.

The Packers finally broke through in the second quarter. Anderson took a little pitchout from Starr on the halfback option started circlin' to his left like he was gonna run wide just waitin' for his blockin' to set up. The Bears committed themselves to the run the deep men started creepin' up Anderson stopped caught Carroll Dale sneakin' behind the deep safety for the touchdown.

Joey damn near pounded a hole in Russ's shoulder. When Dale snagged the perfect spiral over his shoulder Joey doubled up his fist caught Russ about ten good ones in the muscles. Russ barely felt it he was already startin' to jump to his feet when he saw the play start to form the minute the deep backs committed themselves Anderson cocked his arm he was up an' throwin' hisself he could feel the tinglin' he knew the play could go all the way all he had to do was lay it in there so he did.

Carol was the one caught the worst of it. Russ still had his arm around her neck when he came up to make the throw dragged her right up along with him like to throw her head right through the TV set to the waiting Dale.

They was all laughin' Carol rubbin' her neck. "First time I ever had my head used for a football."

"First pass I've completed in a long time, head or no head."

Joey just kept jumpin' up and down, "Hey, did you see that? Did you see that, Russ? Did you see the way Anderson laid it in there? Way to go, Donny, baby—way to go!"

Dale nonchalanted the ball to the referee none of that pounding it to the ground doing the phony dance shit he'd done it too many times before he just tossed it to the waiting ref as he passed by trotted up the field Anderson waiting for him they clasped hands the camera holding close on them as they trotted toward the bench Anderson pulling his helmet off as they trotted upfield the camera holding close on his golden head his golden head filling the screen the trailer Russ felt like reaching out and patting the screen funny thing he felt like crying again too.

That was the score at half time—seven to nothin'.

"Want a sandwich, Russ?"

"What'a'ya got?"

"How about a CW with L an' M on WW?"

The look on Russ's face she had to laugh the kid laughed too then snuggled over on the couch beside Russ whispered loud in his ear. Russ could feel his hot breath on his face feel his body pressing against his the whisper so loud everybody in the trailer could hear. "That's a chicken white with lettuce and mayo on whole wheat."

Russ didn't let on went along played the straight man.

"Yeah, I'll have a chicken white with lettuce and mayo on whole wheat."

Carol went along too.

"Well, Russ Simpson Jr., how in the world did you ever figure that out?"

The kid poked him in the ribs tried to look real innocent his face was as obvious as his whisper.

"Oh, I dunno—a guy hangs around old has-been waitresses as much as I do gotta catch on sooner or later."

Joey stayed right where he was pressed up against Russ all through the half-time ceremonies.

There was just that one time there he couldn't stay ahead'a the other feelin'. That was when the high school bands came marchin' out the TV cameras went up close on the baton twirler leadin' them out she looked so much like Cathy he couldn't breathe so he closed his eyes got his breath when he opened them again she was gone no not really gone just not close anymore just another little baton twirler with all the rest of 'em.

Then the game was on again. The way them big bad Bears come roarin' outta the chute after half time Russ knew they was in for one helluva thirty minutes of football. Maybe the kid felt it too Russ could feel his body tighten up he leaned forward sat on the edge of the couch the whole rest of the game. Even Carol quit cleanin' up the half-time mess sat down a tray of dirty dishes balanced on her knee. It was in the air. Russ sucked in his gut licked his lips. It started right with the kickoff lasted right to the final whistle.

This time it was the Bears' turn to receive. Gale Sayers took the kickoff started up the sidelines the whole Packer team sucked over to pinch him off he veered in toward the middle turned it on went by the two guys comin' at him so fast they couldn't even cross-body block 'im that's all she wrote now he was all alone. By the time they got turned around he was in the end zone.

7—7.

Joey let out a little whistle never moved. Carol got up an' carried the tray to the sink she didn't say anything she knew better than to talk at a time like this.

It stayed that way till late in the fourth quarter. The Packers were drivin' Starr mixin' up his plays peckin' away here forcin' it a little there sendin' Grabowski up the middle swingin' Anderson to the outside slantin' Williams off-tackle three yardin' them to death makin' the Bears' defense pinch in the linebackers play up close then poppin' one fast over their heads to the big tight-end Fleming pitchin' a short one into the flat to one'a the swingin' backs suckin' suckin' the whole defense up tighter than they wanted playin' the sucker game like only Starr could.

Then it come. The bomb. Starr sent Dale on a fly pattern for about the tenth time Bennie McRae stayed with him like he knew he had to but he was lookin' back up the field all the while the Packers' short game was goin' good probably another slant maybe even a draw to Grabowski no Starr was fadin' back farther not really fadin' more like suckin' it was a screen it was a screen to Williams—

"Screen! Screen!" Joey screamed.

But it wasn't. Just then Dale went into high gear Starr looked down the field the ball went by McRae Dale had two steps on him there was no way he could catch him he'd been suckered.

The throw was too long. Starr had been pressured he'd been forced to throw just a split second before he wanted he'd led Dale too much he wanted to make sure he didn't underthrow give McRae a chance to pick it off Dale gave it all he had runnin' flat out them long antelope legs'a his the long lean body his arms fingertips all reachin' for it reachin' . . . it glanced off his fingertips.

Joey had been reachin' out right along with Dale holdin' his breath his mouth ready to explode with the catch; now he let out a "shit," sank back down on the couch. Russ hadn't moved. Funny thing, he kinda knew it wasn't in the cards today.

Dale turned an' trotted back up field. McRae trotted alongside. The camera moved in close on them McRae glanced over at Dale shook his head he had a sheepish grin on his face he knew he'd lucked out. Dale just kept on trottin'.

That made it third. Third an' four. On the Bears' forty. The Packers set up the same way. Starr took the snap

Dale going deep Starr workin' back the Bear line slammin' in trying to get to hit the Packer line pass-blockin' high hand-fightin' givin' ground McRae stayin' step for step with Dale Starr an' the resta the Packers givin' ground the other ends an' back circlin' back to help out—

The screen! This time it was the screen. Dale started his kick but Starr didn't throw deep he didn't look downfield he just swung to his right flicked the ball over to Anderson waitin'.

The screen was set up. It was set up good. The deep Bears had gone into a semi-prevent defense after the bomb the linebackers had started playin' back to plug some'a the gap to shut off the short pass Dale had taken McRae an' Taylor deep on the double-coverage the Bears were spread out pretty good except for the lineman in on Starr he waited till the last minute just when they was about to snow him under after they was in so deep they didn't have a prayer against the screen Starr turned an' nonchalanted it to Anderson.

He should have made it. At least the four for the first down.

But one guy wasn't suckered. Butkus. He rolled off his block worked his way into the middle'a the Packer screen bounced off another block; on the way down he reached out one big ham-hand got ahold'a Anderson's ankle held on Anderson dragged him to the line'a scrimmage but that was as far as he got. It ain't too easy runnin' with 250 pounds strapped to a man's left ankle Russ knew that for sure.

Joey hadn't moved this time either maybe they both knew in their hearts Anderson wouldn't make it.

That was the game. Fourth and four on the forty. The Packers lined up in field goal formation Mercein came in his head down glanced up once at the flags whippin' in his face that ole wind was comin' at him about thirty knots just the way he walked on he didn't look none too confident.

He set up on the forty-seven, Starr crouchin' for the snap. It came Starr grabbed it spun the lacing outta the way set it. Mercein's foot hit it he tried to keep it low outta the jet stream it tailed off Sayers picked it off right under the crossbar ran it all the way back to the Packer forty-eight it took the last two Packers Starr an' Mercein to bring him down. Sayers didn't look none too happy about it even then kicked the dirt with his cleats when he got up probably been a long time since a quarterback an' a kicker brought him down when he was breakin' into the clear.

But he still looked happier than the Packers. Their defensive team walked on the field went into their huddle broke took their positions. Their offensive team an' the spare parts got up off the bench strung out along the sidelines cuppin' their hands hollerin' out somethin' to the defense yeah they all did what they was s'posed to but none of 'em looked real happy about it.

There wasn't too much noise in the trailer neither. Nobody was talkin' it up too much anymore there wasn't none'a that winnin' chatter.

All there was was that losin' quiet. It didn't take no genius to know that when they got the ball on your forty-eight a thirty-knot wind behind them a kicker like Percival lickin' his lips on the bench just enough time left to set up for even better field position you stand a pretty goddam good chance'a losin'.

That's exactly what the Packers did. They lost. Ten to seven. The Bears gave the ball to Sayers twice for field position he did even better than that he ran it down to the twenty-three right smack dab in front'a the crossbar. They called time out Percival strolled in smilin' all the way split the uprights the smile never left his face.

The game was over.

Yeah, Russ thought, the game is over. The game is over. But it can't be. There's gotta be more to it than that. But there isn't. There isn't an' wasn't an' never will be.

Funny how down'n out he felt now. So long as the game was goin' on he was all right maybe not all right but stayin' ahead holdin' hisself together but the minute the game was over there came that empty feelin' that nothin' feelin' that what the hell was there to do now that he had to face it feelin'.

Russ leaned forward an' switched off the TV. He couldn't just sit here waitin' there wouldn't be another game till next Sunday. Now there was a dead silence in the trailer. At first nobody moved just sat there starin' at the dying picture it was like they was all hooked into the TV set they couldn't move till the little spot in the middle died all the way out let them go.

"Shit!"

"Joey—"

"Well, he never makes the big ones . . . does he, Russ?"

"I wouldn't say . . . never."

Russ picked up the bottle drained it off. It didn't do a thing just laid there.

Joey got up put on his coat pulled his stockin' cap down over his long face went outside wasn't long before Russ could hear him whistlin' though.

Now they had their chance. A couple'a minutes later they really had it Joey stuck his head back inside the door. "Hey, Ma, I'm goin' over to Brian's to play Monopoly."

She couldn't keep from glancin' at Russ when she was sayin' it. "All right Joey—be back by ah . . . eight though."

The kid stuck his head in further where he could see Russ. "You still goin' to be here Russ—hey, maybe I'll bring Brian over to meet you, he knows all about you."

She didn't look at him this time, just talked fast. "Sure, Russ will still be here—but don't bring Brian over this time, there'll be plenty other chances for Brian to meet him."

Joey's face still hung in the door the question on his face all of a sudden Russ could feel the chill comin' through the open door startin' to fill the trailer.

"You . . . you goin' to be around some now, Russ?"

"Yeah, sure . . . yeah, I'm gonna be around some."

"Well . . . see you later, Russ."

"Yeah, kid, see you later."

Joey slammed the door shut it sounded awful loud in the small trailer the sound seemed to hang in the air an awful long time ringing in Russ's head.

Carol sneaked a look at Russ it was ready there on her face.

Funny thing he didn't even want it. He couldn't even think about it of all the things he could'a thought about all he could think about was his goddam manure spreader sittin' there froze fulla shit in that goddam snowdrift.

That was the goddamnedest thing. The minute the game was over that awful feelin' come creepin' his head went right to that manure spreader sittin' there in the snow went right back to where the whole thing started Friday afternoon zeroed right in on that spreader the snowdrift tryin' to jerk her through the tractor breakin' sounded like the reduction gear left rear wheel—

"You got any more to drink?"

"No."

"Not even any beer?"

"You drank it all with lunch. I could . . . go out an' get you some. . . ."

Her voice was lower now when they was alone it was startin' to take on that whispery sound.

"Nah."

He was on his feet before she knew it.

"Gimme my clothes."

She didn't move.

"Where . . . you goin', Russ . . . ?"

She said it kinda funny-like. Like maybe she thought he didn't have someplace to go to.

"Just . . . gimme my clothes."

All of a sudden he couldn't wait to get outta that trailer get it over with the plan comin' back in his head again.

"I got things to do."

Carol turned went over got his clothes from where she'd folded them on top of the dryer came back held them out to him her voice was real whispery now.

"You can stay here with us, Russ."

"I got . . . somethin' to do."

She stood watchin' him put on his clothes never said nothin' till he was almost finished settin' down pullin' on his boots.

"Why do you do it, Russ?"

He looked up kept pullin' on his boot.

"Do what?"

"Get drunk. Come to me."

He finished pullin' on the boot reached for the other one. He meant to tell her about the way things built up how he could feel them comin' on all week the pain over his heart the tightness in his throat cookin' the stew her bringin' home the check gettin' the spreader stuck smashin' the tractor—

"That kid I got ain't mine. She went down to Lauderdale got herself knocked up. The guy Boyd wouldn't marry her took off for California. Her parents an' her rigged it up for me to take the rap. Paid me off five thou. Five big ones. Put down on the farm with it."

He finished pullin' on the other boot. Stood up. Looked

at Carol. She was standin' there with her hand over her mouth like she was afraid she'd say somethin' she shouldn't'a.

Her breath came out with a whooze.

"Russ . . . honest . . . ?!"

"Would I lie . . . 'bout somethin' like that?"

He put on his mackinaw started for the door.

"Russ, you can stay here with us. We . . . both like you . . . a lot. You can see how Joey likes you. He thinks you're the greatest thing ever. Russ, he knows all about you, I've told him all about you, Russ . . . Russ . . ."

He pushed by her went out the door. It was pretty dark already the wind pickin' up pushin' the powder snow that had fallen that afternoon ahead of it.

Carol was still talkin' after him. Still standin' in the door'a her little trailer talkin' after him while he was walkin' through the dark an' wind an' driftin' snow away.

Russ couldn't even tell just exactly for sure what she was sayin'.

"Russ, can't you see how much he looks like you? Russ, can't you see?"

It didn't seem to take near as long to get back to the truck as it had comin' from it. That was one'a the things he always had noticed it never seemed to take as long goin' back as gettin' there.

The moon was up pretty good by the time he got there though. Hangin' right there over the goalposts it made him think'a some corny old song use'ta be big when he was back in high school somethin' about moonlight nights an' tearin' the goalposts down yeah *We Will Have These Moments to Remember.*

The truck was sittin' there where he left it not that he expected it to go nowhere. Sittin' there right in the mid-dle'a the football field covered with a fine powderin'a snow

looked kinda pretty just standin' there the moon glancin'
off it the cold diamonds sparklin' just sittin' there all
alone.

Be a shame to smash it up.

Russ reached in the corner'a the box right behind the
cab where he always kept it pulled out the red five gallon
can'a gas he always kept there just in case somethin' like
this happened ain't no good farmer ever takes his truck
out without a five gallon can'a gas behind.

He brushed all the snow away from the gas snout took
the cap off poured the five gallons in almost all of it at
the last moment there he thought of somethin' saved
about a gallon took it in the cab with him.

He turned the switch on pumped the footfeed pulled
the choke all the way out. If she didn't start he'd have to
go back to Carol an' Joey's.

She started. Damn near right off. He ground her a few
times she fired he pushed the choke halfway in she caught
an' held.

When he pulled up outta the field onto Athletic Field
Road he looked back gave the goalposts a little wave.

They didn't wave back.

The first place he stopped was the County Farm. It
wasn't as though he planned it that way he was just goin'
by an' the truck kinda stopped.

He didn't go all the way in. Just sat there in the truck
lookin' at it right about there where the driveway meets
the road right about there were Carol picked him an' Ox
up that time.

He wondered why he stopped. There wasn't much to
see just the buildin's sittin' there in the moonlight the
lights on in the house the same thing he'd seen a thousand
times before.

He felt awful sad though. They couldn't'a wanted him

very bad just to drop him off like that never come back to pick him up again.

Even after they said they was gonna.

No they couldn't'a wanted him very bad.

The next place he stopped was Dobchek's. He didn't go in there neither just stopped in the parking lot across the highway sat there in the truck lookin' at it.

Lookin' at the sign.

DOBCHEK'S
STOP! GIVE YOURSELF A BREAK

Lookin' at the big plate glass windows. Watchin' the people eatin' behind. Watchin' them drink. Watchin' the lawyers lift their martinis with the onions their little fingers stickin' out beside. Watchin' the lawyer's wives the fat ones with the Grasshoppers the skinny ones with the Pussy Cafes what the hell they call 'em. Watchin' the doctors sawin' into their T-bones their wives suckin' up the lobster. Watchin' the rich-bitch students their long hair almost hangin' in their plates never did an honest day's work in their lives. Watchin' their dates the rich-bitch college cunts leanin' across the table toward them smilin' their fuckin' smile up in the longhair's face—

Russ shivered. All of a sudden it was cold there in the truck freezin' to the bone cold he'd been sittin' there watchin' a lot longer then he knew seemed like he'd been sittin' there forever.

He started up the truck. Let it warm up. Turned the heater on. Felt the heat workin' through the cab.

He could still just go home. They'd be in bed by now maybe even sleepin' maybe he could just slip in lay down beside her. . . .

There'd still be tomorrow mornin'. Come Monday mornin' he'd have to get up an' face it all.

No, jus' goin' home wasn't goin' to pay up his bills. Buy red'n white bikes an' fur-trimmed coats.

'Course jus' sittin' here in the parkin' lot wasn't goin' to get him much neither.

But he still didn't go. He turned his head back away from the road looked at the sign once more. Looked at the blue fire dancin' away from the neon jumpin' out over the snowbanks at him on sparkly diamond legs. Lookin' at the sign a long time like he'd never seen it before.

Then back to the windows. Back to the big plate glass windows scratchin' a peephole on his frosted-over side window so he could see better starin' across the road at those big plate glass windows an' the people behind them like a whipped starvin' dog been shut outside the door.

Starin' at them eatin' an' drinkin' an' laughin' an' smilin' their fuckin' smiles into each other's face.

Now the mad came. Real hard. First it drained his body dry he could even feel it suckin' on the roots of his hair pullin' at his fingernails then it come swooshin' back crickling his skin workin' in deeper deeper explodin' in his guts the big red ball explodin' the waves'a fire poundin' through him fryin' his brain clenchin' his fists—

He slammed the truck in low stomped down on the footfeed. At first he thought he was goin' to zoom it right across the highway put it right through them big plate glass windows take a few'a them pigs with 'im but his brain unlocked in time. That wouldn't work they'd never pay off on that so his hands spun the wheel headed the truck outta the parkin' lot away from the highway away from Dobchek's up the small side road curled around up behind the hill.

When he got up there he stopped the truck. Pulled it off to the side'a the narrow road as much as he could the right side up against the snowbank leavin' enough room for a car to get through if one should happen by.

'Course he didn't have to worry about that much. Nobody come through this side road in the dead'a winter 'less they had to.

He reached under the seat pushed the other stuff aside pulled out his deer rifle. When he had that out he reached back under felt around until he found the shells.

He laid the rifle across his knees fed the magazine full pumped one up in the chamber stuffed in the one more dumped the rest'a the shells in the pocket of his mackinaw.

He got outta the truck. Climbed across the bank his feet sinkin' in after he got past the frozen bank sinkin' in to his waist goin' up the hill fallin' down holdin' the rifle over his head to keep it from gettin' wet sinkin' in stumblin' fightin' his way up the hill hardly knowin' he was goin' up that hill barely knowin' what he was doin'.

When he got up there there was Dobchek's down below.

He laid down in the snow. He slipped the safety off put 'er on semi-automatic he couldn't make out the sights so he just sighted along the barrel.

He jus' kept pullin' the trigger pumped the whole load into the sign. When the last casing jumped out all that was left burnin' was the word BREAK.

For a minute there he thought about reloadin' pumpin' another load through them plate glass windows but he didn't.

Russ Simpson Jr. was no killer neither.

He just picked up the empty rifle went back down the hill to the truck.

He stayed on the side road took the back road home. Funny thing he felt a little better now but not enough to quit.

No he wasn't goin' to quit this time.

He hadn't really planned on goin' home first. The side road came out on 9H just when he was comin' up on the curve by the bridge he decided he might just as well go home first take a look around see if ever'thing was OK.

He went in the barn first. It was warm inside from the cows' bodies. He could smell silage. She'n Phil musta fed them all right. Good ole Phil he'd be back again tomorrow to help her out every other tomorrow as long as he had to there'd be no need to worry about that. Later on she could sell them if she wanted to should be eight-ten thousand more with them an' the machinery an' the feed'n all.

All of a sudden the shaking came. Even though it was warm in here he felt cold an' the shaking came an' wouldn't stop so he huddled up against Crooked Horn's side.

She was nice'n warm. He could feel her body warm through his clothes. He put his hands between her belly and her leg like he used to do when he was a kid on the County Farm it was real warm up inside there pretty soon the shaking stopped.

The moonlight was comin' through the frost-covered windows throwin' funny shadows. He walked through the whole barn checkin' all the cattle. They were layin' down chewin' their cuds they'd been fed plenty all right there was still hay left in their mangers some of it pushed out on the floor in front when Russ walked through some of 'em started comin' to their feet some of 'em bellerin' a little slammin' against their stanchions like maybe they knew somethin' was wrong.

But ever'thin' was all right here. He left the barn an' latched the door behind him.

Walked a few feet away then turned back jus' stood there lookin' at his barn.

It was a pretty good old barn.

Then he turned back toward his truck. Pretty ole truck standin' there in the moonlight waitin' patiently.

Still he didn't get back in the truck. Jus' stood there in

his moonlit yard lookin' around at the buildin's thinkin' about the coat'a paint he'd planned on puttin' on maybe next year if things went good how he should'a fixed that leak in the house roof before the spring rains came even walked back around behind the barn stood there lookin' at his spreader feelin' of the manure yeah it was froze solid all right should'a threw the tarp over it Friday wonderin' if the freezin' would bow out the sides or bottom tear up the conveyor apron any—

He turned walked stiff-legged away.

But he still didn't get in the truck. The moonlight was bright as day the wind had died down still as death icy cold Jack Frost on the windowpanes sparkling all around him sparkling sparkling all across the yard along the electric line wires down the yard-light pole out over the fields before he knew it he was walkin' across the fields his fields their fields walkin' careful puttin' each foot down just so walkin' on top the frozen crust still feelin' the ground under his feet Christ he'd worked his balls off here in these fields worked his balls off that's one thing nobody could say he didn't try didn't work his balls off thinkin' things like that an' others how in the ole days a man could make a good livin' off this place have eight-ten kids send them to college the old man he'd bought it off told him so he was no liar neither he'd done it.

Thinkin' other things. Here he had oats last year. Good oats. Forty bushel to the acre oats. Over there corn. Good corn froze a little early before it got dented all the way but it was keepin' fairly good. On the back forty alfalfa mixed with brome grass. Good catch if it didn't winterkill.

Winterkill. If it didn't winterkill some day the snow would melt the water would run off make a pond over there in the low spot he could smell the thawin' earth feel it under his shoes see the little alfalfa sprouts pushin' up through the dry brown of last year see the field greenin' over there'd be'a good crop again . . . if it didn't winterkill.

But the mortage'd still be there—both of 'em. The bills pilin' up faster'n he could pay them. Cathy'd still be workin' out. An' he'd still be gettin' drunk an' blowin' it come Las' Friday.

This way she'd clear eight-ten thousand sellin' out another twenty big ones on the mortgage-life insurance.

He started runnin' back across the field. Runnin' runnin' his feet breakin' through the crust bringin' him to his knees lungin' back up runnin' runnin' tuckin' his arm carryin' the ball again runnin' runnin' breakin' through breakin' through that fuckin' line runnin' runnin' slammin' over the linebacker runnin' runnin' give 'im the hip straight-arm the silly sonuvabitch runnin' runnin' there she is there she is the fuckin'. . . .

Goal line? End zone? Where were the cheers?

No, just his truck. There were no cheers. Maybe there never really was. Just him standin' there alone suckin' for breath pukin' his guts out against the side'a his ole red '57 Ford.

That's the way it always was. Always would be.

But he still didn't get in the truck. He wiped his mouth rubbed the puke off his hands in the snow went in the house.

He didn't make no particular try at bein' quiet jus' walked in up the stairs like he always did.

But they didn't hear him. They was sleepin' together huggin' each other like they always did when he was gone.

They didn't wake neither when he walked in the room sat down in the chair beside their bed.

They didn't wake up all that night. He sat there watchin' them sleep God all them hours the moonlight comin' through the window showin' them up real plain he could see them real plain their arms huggin' around each other him sittin' there watchin' them all the while but God they never did wake up.

An' now it was time for him to go.

God he was beat. He could'a so easy jus' laid his head down there beside 'em went to sleep. . . .

But he didn't. He stood up leaned over them kissed them each one on the cheek God they still didn't wake up.

So he had to go. The moon was goin' down. It was gettin' darker that phony time jus' before the sun comes up—it had come Monday mornin'.

He turned an' walked outta the room. Down the kitchen steps. Into the kitchen. He put on the light. Took the pad'n pencil hung by the telephone. Ripped off a sheet wrote on it.

Dear Cathy,
Burn this as soon as you read it so Duane don't try to take the insurance money away from you. I done it for you an little Russell. So you can get that fur-trimmed coat you always wanted for Xmas him that red an white bike with banana seat. Cathy you're still my best girl. The only one I ever had. I lied about Carol. I love you now jus like I did from that first time I seen you in the book line back in school. This is the best way I can show you.
                    Forever an ever,
                    Russ Simpson Jr.
P.S.
Cathy do me a favor will you. Kinda watch out a little for Carol Gore an Joey I guess hes my kid too.

Her purse was sittin' there on the cupboard by the door so he stuck it in there. It'd be the first thing she'd grab when they come to tell her.

He walked out the door of his house.

Walked across his porch down his steps along the flat rocks he'd put down for a walk walked straight along to his truck.

This time he got in.

Monday Morning

YEAH HE got in the truck.
She kicked right off too sometimes she didn't that was a
sign too he almost gave the horn a little toot like he usually
did when he pulled by the house but he stopped his hand
in time that warm-sad feelin' fillin' the cab nothin' in there
now but that warm-sad feelin' an' what was left of him—
him Russ Simpson Junior it almost made him wanna laugh
Junior for Christ's sake Junior!

Pullin' out the driveway. Pullin' out the driveway now
lookin' left'n right first like he always did what difference
did it make now might even be better that way look even
more like an accident but somebody might get hurt ha!

Acceleratin' now. Acceleratin' now shiftin' up the ole
motor complainin' pistons slappin' good thing he took the

truck acceleratin' acceleratin' slammin' her into second the corner comin' up runnin' runnin' no better get 'er in high might look funny this far down the highway they check the gearbox find 'er still in second runnin' runnin' swingin' high on the curve would she think he was good enough now runnin' runnin' the bridge comin' up fast they'd be in better hands with Allstate runnin' runnin' the rail big in the windshield America Love It Or Leave It runnin' runnin' now zeroed in on the rail give Russ Simpson Jr. that ball one last time runnin' runnin' one last time breakin' through that fuckin' line runnin' runnin' slammin' over the linebacker runnin' runnin' give 'em the hip runnin' runnin' straight-arm the silly sunsabitches runnin' runnin' there she is there she is the fuckin'. . . .

Goal line. End zone. Where were the cheers?